"The newscaster said you were convicted of killing a man,"

Elizabeth said. *"Did* you kill him?"

"I was convicted, wasn't I?"

"I know that. But were you guilty?"

"Would you believe me if I told you that I'm innocent?"

"Yes, I'd believe you."

Running his hands through his thick, wavy hair, Reece snorted. "Lady, are you that naive? Would you take the word of a stranger, someone you don't know the first thing about?"

But I do know things about you, Reece. Less than I want to, but more than you could ever realize.

Dear Reader,

Talk about starting the new year off with a bang! Look at the Intimate Moments lineup we have for you this month.

First up is Rachel Lee's newest entry in her top-selling Conard County miniseries, *A Question of Justice*. This tale of two hearts that seem too badly broken ever to mend (but of course are about to heal each other) will stay in your mind—and your heart—long after you've turned the last page.

Follow it up with Beverly Barton's *The Outcast*, a Romantic Traditions title featuring a bad-boy hero—and who doesn't love a hero who's so bad, he's just got to be good? This one comes personally recommended by #1-selling author Linda Howard, so don't miss it! In *Sam's World*, Ann Williams takes us forward into a future where love is unknown—until the heroine makes her appearance. Kathleen Creighton is a multiple winner of the Romance Writers of America's RITA Award. If you've never read her work before, start this month with *Eyewitness* and you'll know right away why she's so highly regarded by her peers—and by readers around the world. Many of you have been reading Maura Seger's Belle Haven Saga in Harlequin Historicals. Now read *The Surrender of Nora* to see what Belle Haven—and the lovers who live there—is like today. Finally there's Leann Harris's *Angel at Risk*, a story about small-town secrets and the lengths to which people will go to protect them. It's a fittingly emotional—and suspenseful—close to a month of nonstop fabulous reading.

Enjoy!

Leslie Wainger
Senior Editor and Editorial Coordinator

THE OUTCAST

BEVERLY BARTON

Silhouette®

INTIMATE™MOMENTS®

Published by Silhouette Books

America's Publisher of Contemporary Romance

SILHOUETTE BOOKS

ISBN 0-373-07614-2

THE OUTCAST

Copyright © 1995 by Beverly Beaver

Books by Beverly Barton

Silhouette Intimate Moments

This Side of Heaven #453
Paladin's Woman #515
Lover and Deceiver #557
The Outcast #614

Silhouette Desire

Yankee Lover #580
Lucky in Love #628
Out of Danger #662
Sugar Hill #687
Talk of the Town #711
The Wanderer #766
Cameron #796
The Mother of My Child #831
Nothing But Trouble #881

BEVERLY BARTON

has been in love with romance since her grandfather gave her an illustrated book of *Beauty and the Beast*. An avid reader since childhood, she began writing at the age of nine and wrote short stories, poetry, plays and novels throughout high school and college. After marriage to her own "hero" and the births of her daughter and son, she chose to be a full-time homemaker, a.k.a. wife, mother, friend and volunteer.

Six years ago, she began substitute teaching and returned to writing as a hobby. In 1987, she joined the Romance Writers of America and soon afterward helped found the Heart of Dixie chapter in Alabama. Her hobby became an obsession as she devoted more and more time to improving her skills as a writer. Now, her lifelong dream of being published has come true.

To some special friends who have added so much joy to my life in some of the silliest, nuttiest, wildest and craziest ways, The Wednesday C.C.B. Brunch Bunch: Marilyn Elrod, Joyce Farley, Linda Howington and Cheri Vaughn, and in the past, Laurie Hester and Debbie Moore, and on certain occasions, Brenda Hall and Edna Waits.

Chapter 1

He was out there somewhere. Alone. Angry. Injured. And afraid he wouldn't live long enough to prove his innocence and make the guilty pay.

Elizabeth Mallory shuddered, as much from the premonition as from the chill of the February wind whipping across the front porch of her mountain cabin home. With a cup of strong black coffee in her right hand, she stood in the open doorway, gazing out over the freshly fallen snow. The first faint hint of morning painted the eastern horizon with various shades of red, from palest pink to deepest crimson. Clouds swirled, dark and foreboding in the gray sky, warning of more sleet and snow.

Elizabeth had sensed a winter storm brewing for days. She was never wrong about her weather forecasts. And she was never wrong in her premonitions. That's what bothered her. The stranger had invaded her thoughts months ago, and no matter how hard she tried to shake him, she couldn't. The first time he had come to her in a night dream. She had awakened from a deep sleep, trembling from the intensity of the vision. She had seen his hands. Big, strong hands—covered with blood. And then she'd seen his stunned face. Those fierce masculine features. Those amber eyes. She had tried to connect with his feelings, but without success. Who was this man? she'd wondered. Where was he? And why was she dreaming of him?

There was only one man in her life, if you didn't count O'Grady, a friend of her aunt Margaret's who did odd jobs around the greenhouses and kept her supplied in firewood for the long winter months high in the Georgia mountains. Sam Dundee had been her stepfather's younger brother, and when her parents had died in an automobile accident while she'd been a child, Sam had become her legal guardian. As much as she loved Sam and he her, the love they shared was platonic, the deep care and concern of family.

So there had been no one. Not in her bed. Not in her heart. Not until the past few months when she had been unable to control the visions of a tormented man pacing back and forth inside a cage. She had wanted to comfort him, but she couldn't. She could not reach him, no matter how hard she tried. Her telepathic abilities had always been somewhat untutored, not nearly as finely honed as her clairvoyant and precognitive powers, but there was more to it than that. This man, this tortured stranger, shielded his emotions, keeping everyone out, including Elizabeth.

Since childhood she'd known she was different. Her mother and stepfather had brought her to Sequana Falls, deep in the north Georgia mountains, home to her great-aunt, who also possessed psychic abilities and was the only one who'd ever been able to understand the soul-felt pain Elizabeth endured because of her powers.

Except for a brief sojourn from her mountain retreat to attend college, Elizabeth secluded herself from the world. Her abilities to predict the future, to foresee forthcoming events and read minds created problems for her from which not even Sam Dundee, with all his macho strength and loving concern, could protect her.

Cloistering herself away from the world had helped her live a somewhat normal life. She had sworn, after the terrors of living away from Sequana Falls for three years to acquire a college degree while still a teenager, that nothing and no one could ever persuade her to leave her sanctuary again.

Elizabeth allowed the hot coffee to warm her mouth before traveling downward, creating a soft heat within her body. She breathed in the fresh, crisp air—unpolluted mountain air, air closer to the heavens, as if it mingled with God's breath.

She tried to keep her eyes open, tried to focus on the snow-laden trees in the forest surrounding her. But the images formed in her mind, forcing her to see them, whether she wanted to or not. Darkness enveloped her. Night. Tonight! The stranger was running. Running in the freezing sleet, his feet weighted down by the heaviness of the packed, frozen snow beneath him. He slipped, righted himself, ran more slowly. Then he slipped again, lost his balance and fell into a snowdrift.

The cup in Elizabeth's hand trembled, sloshing warm coffee over the rim and onto her fingers. Shaking her head, she tried to dislodge the vision, to force the images to stop. She groaned deeply, softly. The pain of seeing the stranger's predicament and being powerless to help him frustrated Elizabeth.

Suddenly she felt MacDatho's cool, damp nose nuzzle the hand she held clutched at her hip. Her thoughts cleared. Nothing but dark clouds and white snow appeared in her line of vision. Turning her head slightly, she looked down at her companion. He gazed up at her with those serene amber eyes of his, as if he, too, had seen exactly what she had seen, as if he knew that a stranger was about to enter their lives.

Running her fingers through his thick winter fur, Elizabeth crooned to the big black animal, reassuring him that she was all right. She had raised MacDatho from a pup, his mother Elspeth, her German shepherd pet of many years, his father a wolf from out of the forest.

"You know, don't you, my fine lad?" Elizabeth said. "He's coming to us. Tonight."

MacDatho made a sound—not a bark, not a growl, just a rumbling sound. An affirmation of his mistress's words. He leaned his head against her leg, allowing her to pet him.

"I don't know what sort of man he is." Elizabeth nudged MacDatho, leading him back inside the cabin. She closed the heavy wooden door, shutting out the cold morning.

A fire blazed brightly in the enormous rock fireplace in the living room. MacDatho followed Elizabeth to the large, sturdy plaid sofa. When she sat, he lay at her feet.

"He's in trouble and he needs me, but that's all I can sense." Elizabeth placed her mug on the rustic table beside the sofa. "I can't read him, Mac. Odd, isn't it? I can read everyone, even Sam some of the time, but I can't get past the barrier this man has put up." Elizabeth was puzzled that she could pick up no more than a tiny fraction of the stranger's thoughts or emotions. Nothing solid. Nothing complete.

Elizabeth curled up on the sofa, bending her knees so she could tuck her feet behind her. For the first time in her life Elizabeth Mallory was afraid of another human being without knowing why. Out there somewhere was a man she didn't know, a man in some sort of trouble, a man making his way to her cabin—to her. For months she had been tormented by images of this man's life. Bits and pieces of loneliness and pain. Fragments of anger and fear. If only he would allow her to see inside, to share what he was feeling. But it was obvious to Elizabeth that he shielded himself from emotions so completely that he never permitted anything or anyone past his protective barriers. Although Elizabeth knew him, would recognize him the moment she saw him, he didn't know her. When they met tonight—and they would meet tonight—he would have no idea that he was more than an invading presence in her life, that he had held a special place in her thoughts for many months, that he had become important to her even though they didn't know each other.

As much as she feared this unknown man, Elizabeth longed for him to enter her life. Anxiety and uncertainty warred with desperate need. Fear battled desire. Dread fought with longing. Elizabeth closed her eyes. The moment she envisioned his hard, lean lips forming a strangled cry and heard him pray for help, she knew she was this man's only hope—this lonely and unloved outcast.

* * *

Slouched over in the seat, his shoulders slumped, eyes downcast, Reece Landry screamed silently at the injustice that had brought him to this point in his life. He'd been screaming for months, but no one had heard him.

He had never pretended to be a saint, never considered himself a good man, and he was guilty of many sins and a few crimes. But he was innocent of the murder that had placed him in this sheriff's car, on this Georgia highway in the middle of a once-in-a-decade winter storm, being taken to Habersham County, to Alto, Georgia, to be locked away inside Arrendale Correctional Institute for the rest of his life.

No one had believed him, except perhaps his lawyer. But he wasn't even sure about Gary Elkins. His half sister, Christina had hired the man. And despite the fact that Chris professed she believed he was innocent, she couldn't disguise the doubt in her eyes. No matter how much he wanted to trust Chris, she was, after all, a Stanton, and he knew better than to trust a Stanton.

Gary had told him not to lose heart, that he would appeal the case, that sooner or later they would find the real murderer. Reece wasn't so sure. In the five months since B. K. Stanton's death, the police hadn't sought another suspect. Just about the whole town of Newell believed Reece Landry was guilty.

With his head still bent, pretending sleep, Reece glanced around inside the car. The doors were locked, opening only from the outside. A Plexiglas partition separated him from the two deputies in the front of the car. He'd known Jimmy Don Lewis most of his life, and the two had never liked one another. Jimmy Don had always been a cocky little SOB. Harold Jamison wasn't much more than a kid, red haired, freckled, with a warm, friendly country-boy grin.

Reece sat perfectly still, but in his mind he tugged on the chains binding his hands and feet, broke free and overpowered the deputies.

Hearing a chinking sound, Reece checked outside. Sleet mixed with snow peppered the windows.

In about an hour they would be in Alto. Reece could almost hear the gate closing behind him, could feel the walls shrinking to encompass him in a cage from which he would never escape.

Guilty. Guilty of murder in the first degree. He would never forget listening to the verdict being read or seeing the faces of the twelve jurors as they watched him during the trial. Not once had any of them looked at him with pity or uncertainty. He'd known, in his gut, that they would never set him free. B. K. Stanton had been the wealthiest and most powerful man in Newell, and Reece Landry had been the only suspect in his murder.

What the hell had he expected? The deck had been stacked against him since the day he was born. No one who lived on Lilac Road had a chance of gaining respectability, least of all the bastard son of a dirt farmer's daughter who had given her heart and her body to a married man.

He had grown up in Newell, in that tar-paper shack on Lilac Road, across the street from the local whorehouse and a half mile away from the best bootlegger in the county. He'd grown up hard and tough and just a little mean. Being born a bastard, raised in poverty, with a son of a bitch for a stepfather did that to a boy.

He had learned young that it didn't pay to care about anyone or anything except himself. The only person he'd ever loved, the only person who'd ever loved him had been Blanche, his beautiful, badly used and abused mother. But when he was twelve she'd died and left him with her sadistic husband.

He'd wondered why Blanche had ever married Harry Gunn. She had told him once that they were lucky to have Harry, someone to keep a roof over their heads and food in their stomachs, that not just any man would be willing to take another man's leavings.

And that's what he and his mother had been—B. K. Stanton's leavings.

The screech of tires coincided with the sudden jolt that sent Reece forward in his seat, only the safety belt stopping his headlong dive through the Plexiglas partition. The car somersaulted off the road, rolling over and over, landing right side up again as it skidded straight into the side of the mountain. A loud blast, the shattering of glass and screams of the startled deputies blended with the cry of the violent winter wind and the clink of frozen rain hitting the vehicle. The car's tumultuous movement tossed Reece about inside the back seat, despite the restraint of the safety belt. He grabbed in thin air for something to help him keep his balance as the car scraped along the side of the mountain, caving in the side of the car where Reece sat, then coming to a crashing halt as it ran head-on into an immovable object.

The pain in his head blinded Reece momentarily, a purple blackness swirling in front of his eyes. Running his hand over his face, he felt the wet warmth of his own blood. Another pain shot through his leg, the one caught between the seat and the crushed side of the car. He snapped the safety belt open, struggling to move. Tugging fiercely, he freed his trapped leg. Pain shot through his leg, and a sharpness caught his breath, sending an intolerable ache through his chest.

With his vision lost, Reece's other senses took over, intensifying the pain of his injuries, creating a sour taste in his mouth and alerting him to the sweet, sickening smell of his own blood.

What the hell had happened?

Reece's vision cleared to a blurred fuzziness. Pale light, then streaks of colors floated in front of him. He heard the deep moan of another man and wondered who else was hurt.

When he tried to move, every inch of his body protested as intense pain warned him to stay still. Slowly, with the fuzziness fading and forms taking shape, Reece's vision cleared. Trying not to jar his body or move his head, he scanned the inside of the car. The Plexiglas partition was still intact, but the front seat was now shoved several inches into the back. The side of the car where Reece had been sitting was dented, caved in enough so that the glass had shattered, but a huge limb blocked escape by that route.

Forcing himself to endure the pain, Reece turned his head, knowing his only hope was to kick out the right window. Did he have the strength? Would it matter if he did?

He had no idea what condition Jimmy Don and Harold were in, whether they were dead or alive.

Reece tried to move again. Excruciating pain took his breath away. He tried again, lying down in the seat and positioning his feet. He kicked at the window. Once. Twice. Nothing. Then, garnering all his strength, Reece gave the kick all he had, crashing the window.

He eased his big body through the opening, the howling wind eating through his coveralls, the torrent of wet snow sticking to his hair and face like drops of chilled glue.

Landing flat on his face, Reece struggled to stand, but his legs wouldn't cooperate. He had to get up. He had to check on Jimmy Don and Harold. With his ankles shackled together, he found walking on the frozen ground difficult.

Reece couldn't remember a time in his life when he'd ached so badly, when every muscle in his body had cried out for relief. He wondered if he'd cracked a couple of ribs. Just how the hell was he going to escape when it was all he could do to breathe?

Knowing he couldn't leave without checking on the deputies, Reece crawled on his knees to the front side of the car. Fighting his pain and struggling against the wet, freezing sleet mixed with snow that hammered his unprotected head and face, Reece grasped the door handle and pulled himself to his feet. His leg ached like hell.

The sheriff's car had ended its wild ride with its left side butted up against the mountain, the hood crushed, like a squeezed accordion, into an enormous old tree. Snow blew into the car through the shattered windshield, covering both deputies. Reece tried to open the door, but it wouldn't budge. He called out to the men inside, knowing he couldn't leave them to die. Reece rammed his shackled fists through the window.

Peering inside he saw that Harold Jamison had been crushed by the steering wheel. He lay slumped over, his bloody face turned to one side, his sightless eyes staring off into space. Harold had been crushed to death, his body trapped.

Jimmy Don moaned, but didn't open his eyes. Reece laid his hand on the man's shoulder. "I'll get you some help. Just hang on."

Reece scanned his surroundings, seeing only the sleet and snow that obscured his vision and limited his ability to navigate. The highway couldn't be more than a few yards away, could it? Maybe he could flag down a passing car or truck. But who in their right mind would be traveling in this weather? And if he flagged down a car for help, how would he explain not staying around until assistance arrived?

Then he remembered the radio in the car. Maybe the communication device was still operational. It was worth a try. Reece reached over Jimmy Don, checked the radio and sighed with relief when he found it still working. He radioed for help, giving the dispatch as much information as his limited knowledge permitted. When he was asked to identify himself, he cut the conversation short. He had to get away before it was too late. He'd done what he could to help Jimmy Don. It was probably more than the deputy would have done for him, under similar circumstances.

Reece winced, as much from the cynicism of his thoughts as from the constant pain in his head and body. He squeezed Jimmy Don's shoulder.

"I've radioed for help. Just hang in there."

Jimmy Don opened his eyes, his mouth trembling. He struggled to speak, but only a groan passed his lips. His body shook, then jerked. His head fell back against the seat.

"Jimmy Don!" Reece sought a pulse, but found none.

He knew what he had to do in order to survive, but he couldn't help feeling a certain amount of disrespect rifling Jimmy Don's corpse. He did it just the same, finding the keys that would free his hands and feet. Free! Free to run? Free to be hunted down and killed? No! Somehow, some way, he'd get away, he'd go back to Newell and find the person who'd killed B.K. Fate had intervened, giving him a chance to prove his innocence.

If he'd thought having the key would solve his problems easily, he'd been dead wrong. After several tries, he decided it was damned near impossible to insert the key and unlock the handcuffs. Cursing under his breath when he dropped the key to the ground, Reece lowered himself to his knees and retrieved it. He had to get out of these damned cuffs and chains or he'd never be able to escape.

Placing the key in his mouth, Reece lifted his hands and lowered his head. Damn but this was going to be tricky. He tried and failed, then tried again. Help should be arriving before too long. He didn't have all the time in the world to get away, but it looked like it just might take him half a day to free himself. On the fourth try, he inserted the key and said a silent thank-you to whatever higher power there might be. Clamping down on the key with his teeth, holding it as securely as he could, he turned his head, twisting the key in the lock. Reece believed the sweetest sound he'd ever heard was the lock on his handcuffs releasing.

He snapped the cuffs apart, flung them out into the snow and rubbed his wrists. Bending, he unlocked the shackles around his ankles and kicked them away.

The deputy wouldn't need his coat, but Reece would if he was to survive in this weather. He eased Jimmy Don's heavy winter jacket off his lifeless body and lifted his 9 mm automatic from its holster. Then he pulled the deputy's wallet from his pocket and removed the money inside, shoving the bills into the jacket.

Tramping through the packed snow, hearing the thin layer of forming ice crunching beneath his chilled feet, he struggled around the car, praying he could find his way to freedom.

A warm stickiness dripped down his cheek. Reaching up, he wiped away the moisture, then looked down at his hand to see a mixture of melting snow and fresh blood. God, how his head hurt!

With slow, painful steps, Reece made his way to the roadside. He had no idea where he was or in which direction he was headed. All he knew was that he couldn't stick around and get captured, get taken to Arrendale and locked away for the rest of his life. He hadn't killed B.K., but the only way he could prove it was to return to Newell and find the real murderer.

Damn, it was cold. Even in the sheepskin-lined jacket he'd stolen from Jimmy Don's dead body and the heavyweight navy blue winter coveralls issued to him at the county jail, the frigid wind cut through his clothing like a rapier slicing through soft butter.

He stumbled along the shoulder of the highway, finding it less slick than the icy road. Taking one slow, agonizing step at a time, Reece longed to run, but he did well just to continue walking.

He didn't know how long he'd been traveling away from the wrecked car when he saw the headlights of an oncoming vehicle. God, what he'd give for the warmth and shelter inside a car. If only he could sit down a few minutes and thaw out his frozen hands and feet. Trudging out into the road, Reece waved his hands about, hoping the driver would see him, and praying he wouldn't run him over.

The vehicle, an older model Bronco, slowed, then stopped, the motor running and the lights cutting through the heavy cloud of falling snow.

"What's the matter, are you crazy?" A middle-aged man, wearing what appeared to be camouflage hunting gear, got out of the Bronco.

"My car skidded off the road a ways back," Reece lied. "It's a total wreck. I need a ride to the nearest town."

"You hurt?" the gruff-spoken, ruddy-faced man asked.

"Banged my head pretty bad, bruised my leg and I could have a couple of ribs broken."

"Get in. I'm heading for Dover's Mill. Planning on getting me a bite to eat and a warm bed for the night. We can see if they've got a doctor who'll take a look at you."

"Thanks." Reece eased into the Bronco, slamming the door behind him. The warmth inside surrounded him. The comfort of sitting down spread an incredible ease through his aching body.

"I'm Ted Packard." The Bronco's driver held out his hand to Reece.

Reece hesitated momentarily, then offered the man his cold, bloodstained hand. "I appreciate the ride, Mr. Packard."

Ted eyed Reece with skepticism as he shifted gears, putting the vehicle in Drive. "What's your name, boy?"

"Landers. Rick Landers."

"Well, Rick, normally it wouldn't take us fifteen minutes to get to Dover's Mill, but with this damned storm, it could take us an hour."

Thankfully, Ted Packard wasn't a big talker or overly inquisitive. He'd seemed to accept Reece on face value, believing his story of having wrecked his car. The warmth and quiet inside the Bronco relaxed Reece, lulling him to sleep. When Ted tapped him on the shoulder to awaken him, Reece couldn't believe he'd actually dozed off.

"This here's Dorajean's," Ted said. "Best food in Dover's Mill. We'll ask inside about a doctor for you."

"Thanks." Reece opened the door, but found stepping out into the frigid afternoon air far more painful than he would have expected. He kept his moans and groans in check. "I don't think I need a doctor. At least, not right away. But I sure could use a hot cup of coffee and a bite to eat."

"Suit yourself," Ted said, exiting the four-wheel-drive vehicle. "You can call a local garage about your car, but I doubt there's much they can do until this storm lifts. If your car's totaled, it won't matter anyway, will it?"

"Right." Although his steps faltered a few times, Reece followed Ted into Dorajean's.

The restaurant buzzed with activity, obviously filled with stranded motorists. Every booth and table was occupied, leaving only a couple of counter stools free. Sitting beside Ted, Reece ordered coffee and the day's special—meat loaf, creamed potatoes and green peas.

The waitress, a heavyset, fiftyish redhead, flirted outrageously with Ted, the two apparently old acquaintances. Reece gulped his first cup of coffee, relishing the strong, dark brew as it warmed his insides. A TV attached to the wall possessed a snowy image of a newscaster. The sound had been turned down, but Reece could hear the static drowning out the broadcaster's voice. A nervous tremor shot through Reece's body. How long would it be before the sheriff's car was found and the authorities discovered that convicted murderer Reece Landry was missing? A few hours? By nightfall? Early morning?

Reece sipped his second cup of coffee, enjoying it even more than the first. He glanced around the restaurant, noting the homey atmosphere, the red gingham curtains and tablecloths, the old-fashioned booths still sporting the outdated jukebox selectors. He wondered if the contraptions still worked.

The place was cram-packed with people of various ages, sexes and races. Water from the melting snow that had stuck to customers' feet dotted the black-and-white tile floor. Reece glanced out the windows, the heavy falling snow so thick he couldn't even see Ted's car in the parking lot.

The front door swung open. Reece's heart stopped. A local deputy walked into Dorajean's. Damn! He warned himself to stay calm, but his gut instincts told him to run. Hell, he was wearing county-issued coveralls, another deputy's winter coat and carrying a gun registered to the sheriff's department. What should he do? Did he dare risk staying long enough to eat? Surely the deputy wouldn't spot one man in the middle of so many people.

The deputy walked over and sat on the empty stool next to Ted Packard. Reece clutched his hands into fists at his sides to keep them from trembling. He wasn't going to get caught. He couldn't bear the thought of going to prison. He had to stay free long enough to find out who had killed B.K.

"Here you go, sugar. Dorajean's special for today." The redhead set the plate of piping-hot food in front of Reece.

"Thanks." He was hungry. He hadn't been able to eat more than a few bites of his breakfast this morning.

"You look like you've been in a fight, good-looking," the waitress said. "You got bruises all over your face and some dried blood on your forehead."

"Wrecked his car a ways back," Ted said. "I gave him a lift into Dover's Mill."

Why didn't they just shut up? Reece wondered. The more they discussed him, the more likely the deputy would take notice.

Reece shoved a spoonful of meat loaf into his mouth, following it with huge bites of potatoes and peas. Then he felt someone watching him. Not turning his head, but glancing past Ted, he saw the deputy glaring at him.

Reece stood. He had to get away. "Where's your rest room?"

"Round the corner, to the right," the waitress told him.

"Thanks."

Reece scanned the restaurant, looking for another entrance. There wasn't one. He headed in the direction of the rest room, then made a quick turn and walked into the kitchen, hugging the wall, hoping the cook wouldn't notice him. Easing slowly toward the back door, he breathed a sigh of relief when he stepped outside. The thick veil of snow created limited visibility, so Reece wasn't surprised when he stumbled over a low stack of wood and fell headlong into a row of metal garbage cans. Dammit, what a racket they made.

A sharp pain sliced through his side, and another zipped up his injured leg. Blood oozed down the bridge of his nose. He wiped it away. Every inch of his body ached, every bone, every muscle, every centimeter of flesh.

He headed into the wooded area behind the restaurant, not daring to go back into the parking lot. Sooner or later, when he didn't come back to the counter, Ted and the waitress would wonder what had happened to him. It couldn't be helped. He had to find someplace to stay until he'd mended enough to travel home to Newell.

When Reece tried to run, the pain hit him full force. He walked as fast as the snow-laden ground would allow, then as the cold seeped into his body and he became one with the pain, he increased his speed, finally breaking into a run.

Incoherent thoughts raced through his mind. Panic seized him, forcing him onward when common sense would have cautioned him to stop. Bleeding, out of breath and disoriented, Reece felt himself falling, falling, falling. When his body hit the ground, cushioned by a good seven inches of snow, he wanted nothing more than to lie there and go to sleep. Can't do that! Got to get up. Keep moving.

Come to me. I'm waiting. I can help you.

Reece heard the voice as clearly as if someone was standing beside him, speaking. Dear God, I'm losing my mind, he thought. I'm hearing voices.

With an endurance born of a lifetime of struggle and determination, Reece rose to his knees and then to his feet. He walked. He ran slowly. He fell. He picked himself up and walked again. He sloshed through a partially frozen stream, the water rushing around chunks of ice. His foot caught on a limb and he fell, his hip breaking through the ice. Cold water seeped into his coveralls. Righting himself, he stood and tramped down and out of the stream.

Minutes ran together, warping his sense of time, until Reece had no idea how long he had trudged through the woods. The sky had turned from gray to black. Not a star glimmered in the heavens. Swollen snow clouds blocked the moon, allowing only the faintest light to filter through the darkness. Reece couldn't see a damned thing, not even his own hand in front of his face. And he was so numbed from the cold and the constant pain that he barely felt the chilling wind or the freezing dampness.

It had to be night. That meant it had been hours since he'd left the restaurant back in Dover's Mill. Why hadn't he found shelter? Surely someone had a cabin or a shack out in these woods.

Reece felt his legs give way. He stumbled to his knees. Knowing that if he lay down in the snow he would never get up, Reece struggled to stay awake, to keep moving. He began crawling. One slow, painful inch at a time.

Beckoned by an unseen force, by a comforting voice inside his head, Reece refused to surrender to the pain and hopelessness. Then suddenly a sense of excitement encompassed him. That's when he saw it—an enormous wood-and-rock cabin standing on a snow-covered hill. Lights shone in every window as if welcoming him home. Dear God in heaven, was he hallucinating? Was the cabin real?

With what little strength he had left he forced himself to his feet, then checked in his pocket for the automatic. He was going to find out if that cabin was real. If it was real, then someone lived there and that person wouldn't take kindly to an escaped convict spending the night.

Lifting his feet, forcing himself to trek up the hill, Reece felt weighted down with numbness. The cabin hadn't disappeared. Still there. A warm, inviting sight. Only a few yards away. Huge steps, wide and high, awaited him. Pausing briefly, he stared up at the front porch. He'd have to break in, maybe through a window. But first he'd try the door, test its sturdiness, check out the lock.

One step. Two. Three. Four. He swayed, almost losing his balance. Can't pass out. Not now. So close. He lifted his foot up off the last step and onto the porch. The front door was so close, but somehow it seemed a mile away. If he couldn't figure out a way to pick the lock on the door, did he have the strength to smash in a window? Whoever lived inside was bound to hear the noise. He ran his hand over the bulge the 9 mm made in the coat pocket. Would he use the gun? Could he? Whoever lived inside would be an innocent victim.

Reaching out, his hand trembling, he grabbed the door handle. With shocking ease the door opened. Reece couldn't believe his good fortune. The door hadn't been locked. Who in their right mind would leave a door unlocked?

He eased the door back an inch at a time, hesitant, wondering what he would face inside the cabin. When he had opened the door completely he stared into the softly lit interior, the warmth of the house enveloping his frozen body, creating razor-sharp pricks of pain as the protective numbness began to thaw.

The smell of chicken stew permeated the air. And coffee. And something rich and spicy. Cinnamon. Maybe an apple pie.

He heard a noise, a low animal groan, then a deep growl. That's when he saw the animal. Thick black fur. Eyes like amber glass ovals. Sharp white teeth—bared. Hackles raised. What the hell was it? It looked like a damn wolf.

"Easy, Mac." The voice was gentle, soothing and captivatingly feminine. "It's him."

Reece gazed into the eyes of the most incredibly beautiful woman he'd ever seen. She stood just inside the enormous great room of the cabin, the wolf at her side. Her hourglass figure was covered with a pair of faded jeans and a red turtleneck sweater, overlaid with a plaid jacket. Reece couldn't stop staring at her, gazing deeply into her pure blue eyes.

"Shut the door behind you." Her voice held a melodious quality. "You're letting out all the heat."

Reece slammed the door, then closed his eyes for a split second. Shaking his head to dislodge the cobwebs of confusion was a mistake. Pain so intense that he nearly doubled over shot through his head.

"You're injured." She took a tentative step toward him, the wolf following. "Let me help you."

Reece touched the 9 mm in his pocket, then glared at the woman, hoping she wouldn't do anything foolish. What could he say to her? How could he explain being here inside her cabin? Unless she was a total fool, she'd soon realize he was wearing county jail coveralls and a deputy's stolen coat. Under the best of circumstances Reece wasn't much of a sweet-talker, and now sure as hell wasn't the time to learn how to become one.

"I need food and shelter for the night." He watched her face for a reaction. "I'll leave in the morning." She only stared at him. "I'm not going to hurt you. You don't need to be afraid of me."

The wolf took several steps ahead of his mistress, stopping only when she called his name and ordered him to sit.

"You don't need to be afraid of me, either," she said. "I only want to help you. Please trust me."

Reece grunted, then laughed, deep in his chest. "Yeah, sure. Trust you. Trust a stranger. Lady, I don't trust anybody." Reece couldn't figure her out. Why wasn't she

screaming her head off? Why wasn't she deathly afraid of
him? Any sensible woman would have been. "I'm hungry.
I need some food. A cup of coffee to start."

"All right. Please come in and sit down. I'll get you some
coffee." She turned, but the wolf continued watching Reece.

"No, you don't. Stop!" She could be going to call the
law, to turn him in. Reece covered the distance separating
them in seconds, his head spinning, darkness closing in on
him. Grabbing her by the arm, he whirled her around to face
him. "I don't want you out of my sight. Understand?"

He wished the room would stop moving, wished his
stomach didn't feel like emptying itself, wished the pain in
his body would stop tormenting him.

"I'm not your enemy," she told him.

He heard her voice, but could no longer see her face.
Darkness overcame him. His knees gave way. His hand
slipped out of his pocket. He swayed sideways, then, like a
mighty timber whose trunk had just been severed, Reece
Landry dropped to the floor.

Opening his eyes, ...

Chapter 2

Elizabeth knelt beside the stranger who had invaded the
sanctuary of her home as surely as he had invaded her heart
and mind repeatedly over the past few months. MacDatho
sniffed the man's feet and legs, then lifted his head to stare
at his mistress, their eyes connecting as they shared a common thought. This man, although weak, sick and at the
moment disabled, could be dangerous. Her mind warned
her to be wary of him; her heart told her to help him.

Touching his cheek, Elizabeth sensed the tension within
his big body, despite the fact that he appeared to be unconscious. A day's growth of dark brown stubble covered his
face, adding to his strong, masculine aura.

"He's cold, Mac. Almost frozen." Elizabeth began unbuttoning his heavy jacket. "We've got to get him out of
these wet clothes and warm him up."

The man groaned. His eyes flickered open, then shut
again. Elizabeth's hand stilled on his chest. She felt the
hard, heavy pounding of his heartbeat and sensed the great
strength and endurance he possessed.

Working quickly, she finished unbuttoning the sheepskin
jacket, pushed it apart across the stranger's broad chest and

tried to lift his left shoulder so she could ease his arm out of the garment.

Opening his eyes, Reece stared up at the woman leaning over him fiercely tugging on his jacket sleeve. What the hell was she trying to do, undress him? Was it possible that she was actually trying to help him? Well, he didn't want her help; he didn't want anybody's help. He'd learned long ago not to trust people, especially those who pretended they wanted to help you.

Reece grabbed the woman by the neck, shoving aside the thick, long braid of dark hair that hung down her back. Gasping, she stared at him, her big blue eyes filled with surprise. Then he heard the animal at her side growl as it lowered its head and bared its fangs, its hackles bristling in warning.

"Let go of me." Elizabeth kept her voice soft, even and as unemotional as possible.

"And if I don't?" Lying on his side, Reece pulled her face down next to his. There was a smell of woman about her, sweet and clean but slightly musky. He could sense that she was just a little bit afraid of him and trying her damnedest not to show it.

"MacDatho could rip out your throat if I gave him the order." She was so close to this man, only a breath away, their mouths and noses almost touching. Warmth spread through her body, a result of fear, uncertainty and sexual awareness. Some deep-seated yearning within her urged her to taste his lips, to warm their cool surface with the heat of her mouth.

Reece reached up with his other hand, encompassing her neck completely with both hands. "And I could snap your soft, silky neck like a twig." Glancing at the woman's huge dog, he wondered if the animal would attack with or without his mistress's command.

Reece felt the woman's pulse beating rapidly in her neck. No doubt about it, she was afraid of him. Good. He needed her scared so she wouldn't do anything stupid. If he could control her, he could control her animal. But the moment he glanced from the dog back to her face, he almost regretted having threatened her. There was a wounded look in her eyes.

MacDatho growled deeply, raising his tail, his teeth still bared.

"No, Mac. I'm all right." Trying to convince herself as much as MacDatho, Elizabeth sent a message to Mac that this stranger was their friend, a friend in need of their help.

MacDatho eyed the stranger, then lowered his tail, but his hackles remained raised and his teeth partially bared in a snarl.

"You've got that animal trained pretty good, haven't you?" Keeping a tight hold on the woman, Reece raised himself up off the floor. Every bone, every muscle, every fiber of his being ached. The warmth inside the cabin sent pinpricks of pain through his body, the frigid numbness slowly replaced by nearly unbearable feeling.

"We're going to get up off the floor," Reece said, shoving himself against the soft solidity of the woman's body.

Elizabeth followed his orders, struggling to stand when he forced himself to his feet. He kept a stranglehold on her neck with one hand, the other hand biting into her shoulder. Once on his feet, he swayed. Elizabeth slipped her arm around his waist, instinctively trying to help him. He jerked away from her touch, momentarily releasing his hold on her.

She had never known anyone so afraid of human contact, so distrustful of another person's offer of help. "You need to get out of those wet clothes. You need to get warm."

Reece grabbed her by the arm. MacDatho growled again. Elizabeth sent Mac a silent message to stay calm, but she could sense his intention to attack Reece—and soon.

Elizabeth had only one choice. When she was on her feet again, she bowed her head, concentrating completely on stopping Mac from acting on his animal instincts to protect her.

"I don't want to hurt you," Reece heard himself saying and wondered why he felt such a strong need to reassure this woman. He pulled her close to his side, forcing her to walk beside him to the enormous rock fireplace.

Shivers racked his body. His hands trembled, and for a moment he wasn't sure he would be able to continue stand-

ing. When he shoved Elizabeth away from him, she almost
lost her balance, but she caught hold of the wooden rocker
near the wood stack on the wide hearth. MacDatho approached Reece with slow, deliberate strides.

You mustn't attack him, Elizabeth warned. Closing her
eyes, she cautioned MacDatho that this stranger was an
alpha male, a pack leader, the dominant animal.

Mac stopped dead still, eyeing Elizabeth as if questioning her, then he looked at Reece, dropped his tail, cringed
low on his hind legs and began making licking movements
with his tongue.

"What the hell's wrong with him?" The damned dog
acted as if he'd suddenly become deathly afraid of Reece,
and his actions didn't make any sense.

"It's Mac's way of accepting you, of letting you know he
wants to be your friend." No need to explain to this stranger
that she had convinced MacDatho that another male animal was the dominant one. He probably wouldn't understand, anyway.

"I don't want his friendship, or yours, either." The pain
in Reece's head intensified, the tormenting aches in his body
blazing to life as the numbness faded. "I'm hungry. I need
some food. And some aspirin."

"If you'll come into the kitchen, I'll fix you something.
Or if you want to rest in here, I'll bring out something on a
tray."

"You're not going anywhere without me." Reece glanced
around, looking for all the exits from the huge room. No
matter what she said or how sweetly she acted, he couldn't
trust this woman. He didn't dare.

He wouldn't hurt her. Hell, he wouldn't even hurt her
damn, crazy dog. But he couldn't let her know that she had
nothing to fear from him or she might destroy his only
chance of escaping a prison sentence and proving himself an
innocent man.

"Come into the kitchen. I have some leftover chicken
stew from supper."

Elizabeth glanced back at the stranger as he followed her
toward the kitchen. He walked on unsteady legs, his move-

ments slow paced and lethargic. If he made it to the kitchen it would be a miracle. The man was dead on his feet.

Reece felt the dark, sinking nausea hit him. His knees buckled. He grabbed at thin air, trying to steady himself. *Don't you dare pass out again! If you do, you'll wake up in prison!* He heard the woman say something to him, but the loud, buzzing roar in his head obliterated her words.

"Please, let me help you. You need to lie down." Elizabeth reached out to him, trying to touch him.

Irrational panic seized Reece. The woman was lying to him, trying to catch him off guard. She didn't know him. Why would she want to help him? He couldn't trust her.

"Stay away from me!" Clutching the gun in his right hand, he pulled it out of his coat pocket, then shoved her away, pointing the weapon directly at her.

He swayed toward the wall, his shoulder hitting the wooden surface with a resounding thud. Blackness encompassed him.

Elizabeth watched, feeling totally helpless as the stranger slid down the wall, falling onto his side. Rushing to him, she knelt beside him and realized two things. He was still alive. And he held the gun in his hand with a death grip.

"Come on, Mac. We've got to take care of him. He's probably suffering from hypothermia and Lord knows what else." Elizabeth wished her abilities extended to healing. Unfortunately, she didn't have the magic touch, only a basic knowledge of herbs and the power of the mind to restore one's health.

"I don't know how we'll ever move him. He's such a big man." After prizing the gun from his tenacious grasp, Elizabeth proceeded to remove the stranger's coat, then his shoes and socks. When she saw the county jail identification stamped on the dark blue coveralls he wore, she realized that this man, this stranger who had invaded her mind and her heart months ago, was an escaped convict.

Her trembling hands hovered over his body. Her mind raced through the thoughts and images that had been bombarding her for months. She tried to sort through her feelings, to separate her emotions from logic. This man posed a threat to her. That was a certainty. But not physically. She sensed he would never harm her, that he did not have the soul of a killer.

But he was dangerous.

"If only he'd regain consciousness." Elizabeth spoke more to herself than MacDatho, although the wolf-dog listened intently. "He's too heavy for us to move, and he needs to be in a warm bed. He could have a concussion. Look at the dried blood on his forehead and the swelling right here." Her fingers grazed the knot on his head, encountering the crusted blood that marked a line between his eyebrows and down his straight, patrician nose. She lifted a lock of brown hair, matted with blood.

Elizabeth would never have been able to explain to anyone else how she felt at this precise moment, for indeed, she could not explain her feelings to herself. All she knew was that she must help this man, that she and she alone could save him from not only the immediate physical pain he endured, but from the agony of being trapped like a caged animal, doomed to suffer for wrongs he had not committed.

With utmost haste Elizabeth divested the stranger of every article of clothing except the white boxer shorts that were plastered to his body. Where earlier the stranger had felt cold, nearly frozen to the touch, he now felt somewhat warmer.

Elizabeth rubbed his face. "Please come to, just a little. I don't think Mac and I can get you to a bed without your cooperation."

Why couldn't he have stayed unconscious when he'd first passed out in the living room? At least it was toasty warm in there, the roaring fire close. She could have made him a pallet on the floor until he'd regained consciousness. But no, he had to pass out in the cool, dimly lit hallway leading to the kitchen.

Elizabeth slapped his face gently at first, then a bit more forcefully. "Come on. Wake up."

Reece moaned. Elizabeth smiled.

"That's it, come on. All I need is partial consciousness. Just enough to get you moving."

Reece moaned again. His eyelids flickered. He heard a feminine voice issuing orders. She was demanding that he awaken, that he get on his feet. Why didn't she leave him alone? He didn't want to open his eyes. He didn't want to stand. He didn't want to move. But she, whoever the hell she was, kept prodding him, kept insisting that he help her. Help her do what?

Elizabeth said a prayer of thanks when she had roused the stranger enough to get him to sit up. His head kept leaning sideways, resting against his shoulder. He couldn't seem to keep his eyes open. Finally, summoning every ounce of strength she possessed, she helped him to his feet. He slumped against her, his heavy weight almost sending her to her knees. She struggled against her body's insistent urging to release the burden far too enormous for her to carry.

"Come on. Help me, dammit! I can't carry you." Elizabeth encouraged him, both physically by squeezing her arm around him, and mentally by concentrating on discovering his name.

For months she had been, unwillingly, a part of this man's life. She had witnessed his suffering, his anger and his degradation at being caged, but she had never been able to delve deeply inside him. She had sensed fragments of his emotions, caught quick glimpses of his past, present and future. But nothing concrete. Not even his name.

He leaned more and more heavily against her as she tried to force him to take a step. Finally she shoved him up against the wall, bracing her body against his, trying to keep him standing. If only she could get through to him. If only he wasn't shielding his mind.

She ran her fingers over his face, gently, caressingly. Lowering her voice she spoke to him, pleadingly, with great concern. She felt the breach, the slightest opening in his mind.

"I want to help you. You need me so much. Don't fight me."

Reece! His name was Reece. He had given her that much. If he hadn't been so weak, so helpless, she doubted he would have let down his protective barrier long enough for her to have gained even that small piece of information.

"We need to get you in a warm, soft bed, Reece. You're sick, and I need your cooperation so I can help you get well."

The voice spoke to him again. So soft and sweet. The woman cared about him. She wanted to help him. Was she his mother? His mother had been the only person who'd ever given a damn about him. No. It couldn't be Blanche. Blanche was dead. She'd died years ago.

"Reece, please, take just a few steps. My bedroom is right through that door."

Her bedroom? Was she one of Miss Flossie's girls? Was she trying to seduce him? No. That couldn't be it. Miss Flossie had gone out of business ten years ago, and it had been longer than that since a woman's tempting body had been able to seduce him into doing something foolish. He chose the time, the place, the circumstances and the woman. Reece Landry was always the one in control.

"Take one step. Just one." If she could persuade him to take a step, then he'd realize he could still manage to walk, and she might have a chance of getting him to bed.

MacDatho sniffed around the discarded clothing that lay on the floor, pawing at the coveralls, his sharp claws ripping the material.

"Reece, listen to me. You're safe here with me. No one's going to put you back in a cage. Can you hear me?"

"No cage." He slurred his words, but Elizabeth understood.

"Let's walk away from the cage."

"Away from the cage," he said.

If she couldn't get him to walk soon, she'd just have to lay him back down on the floor and do the best she could for him.

Reece took a tentative step, his big body leaning on Elizabeth for support.

"That's it, Reece. Walk away from the cage."

She guided his faltering steps out of the hallway, through the doorway leading to her room and straight to her bed. He dragged his feet, barely lifting them from the floor, but he cooperated enough with Elizabeth that they finally reached her antique wooden bed, the covers already folded back in readiness. Trying to ease him down onto the soft, crochet-lace-edged sheet proved impossible. Elizabeth simply released her hold around his waist, allowing him to fall across the handmade Cathedral Window quilt she used as a coverlet.

MacDatho stood in the open doorway, guarding his mistress. Pushing and shoving, tugging and turning, Elizabeth managed to place Reece's head on one of her fat, feather pillows. His boxer shorts were as damp as his other clothing, but she hesitated removing them. Feeling like a voyeur, Elizabeth tugged the wet shorts down his hips, over the bulge of his manhood, down and off his legs. With a speed born of her discomfort at seeing him naked when he was unable to protest, and the need to warm his shivering body, Elizabeth rolled Reece over until she was able to ease the covers away from his heavy bulk. Quickly she jerked the top sheet, blanket and quilt up over his hairy legs, sheltering him from the cold. Then she reached down to the foot of the bed where a wooden quilt rack stood, retrieved the heavy tartan plaid blanket hanging alongside a Crow's Foot quilt and spread it on top of the other cover.

Sitting beside Reece, she laid her hand on his warm forehead. As long as he'd been exposed to the frigid weather there was every possibility that his injuries had created serious health problems.

He looked so totally male lying there in her very feminine bed, his brown hair dark against the whiteness of her pillowcase. Even in sleep, his face was set into a frown, his eyes squinched as if he'd been staring into the sun. His face was long and lean, his mouth wide, the corners slightly drooped, the bottom lip fuller than the top. His stubble-covered chin boasted a hint of a cleft.

Mentally, Elizabeth began sorting through her knowledge of herbal medicine, taught to her by her great-aunt Margaret, a quarter Cherokee. If only Aunt Margaret was here now, but she wasn't. The old woman was past seventy and stayed close to home during the winter months. Besides, with the roads in such deplorable condition, Elizabeth doubted she could get into Dover's Mill and back, even in her Jeep.

Reece had so many problems with which she would have to deal. His ears and nose and hands had begun to regain some of their color but still remained unnaturally pale. The best remedy to reverse the hypothermia and possible frostbite would be to keep him warm.

Reaching under the weight of the covers, Elizabeth lifted Reece's hands and laid them on top of his stomach, elevating them slightly. Then she slipped a small pillow from a nearby wing-back chair beneath the cover and under his feet.

Glancing across the room to the well-worn fireplace surrounded by a simple wooden mantel, Elizabeth realized the fire needed more wood. It would be essential to Reece's recovery to keep her bedroom warm. Just as she rose from the bed the lights flickered, then dimmed, returned to normal and suddenly flickered again, this time dying quickly. The warm glow from the fireplace turned the room into golden darkness, shadows dancing on the walls and across the wide wooden floor.

"Damn!" She'd been expecting this, knowing how unreliable the electricity was here in the mountains during a storm. She'd light the kerosene lamps and keep the fires burning in all the fireplaces and in her wood-burning kitchen stove. The generator that protected the precious environment of her greenhouses had probably already kicked on. She would check to make sure the generator was working before she gathered all the ingredients for Reece's treatment.

An antiseptic to clean his head wound would be needed, birch perhaps, along with some powdered comfrey to promote the healing. Mullein would do nicely to help with the frostbite.

Having made her mental list of necessary herbs, Elizabeth double-checked to make sure Reece was covered completely before adding another log to the fire.

"Stay and keep watch, Mac. If he needs me before I return, come for me."

The antique grandfather clock in the living room struck the midnight hour. Resting in a brown leather wing-back chair by the bed, Elizabeth tucked the colorful striped afghan about her hips, letting it drape her legs. She had done all she could do for Reece, cleaning his cuts and bruises, then applying powdered comfrey. The mullein had served several purposes in its various forms of healing aids—as an oil to treat the frostbite, as a bactericidal precaution and as a decoction to calm Reece's restlessness. While he'd been partially awake she had persuaded him to drink the warm mullein brew.

MacDatho lay asleep to the right of the fireplace, in a nook between the wood box and the wall. Elizabeth dozed on and off, mostly staying awake to keep vigil, unable to refrain from staring at the big, naked man resting uneasily in her bed. This man was a stranger, an escaped convict, guilty of some horrible crime. In her mind's eye she kept seeing his large, well-formed fingers dripping with blood. Had he killed someone? Was she harboring a murderer? Obviously her visions of his being caged came from the fact that he'd been imprisoned, locked away securely behind bars.

She had been trying unsuccessfully to break through the mental shield he kept securely in place, even while he slept fitfully. Occasionally Elizabeth caught a glimpse, a glimmer, a sliver of emotion. She simply could not believe Reece was a murderer.

Perhaps she didn't want to believe him capable of murder. After all, the instincts within her feminine heart pleaded with the logical side of her brain to protect him, to heal not only his body but his soul. How could she argue with her unerring instincts? But this was the first time she'd ever been unable to read a person, at least partially. Even Sam Dundee, obstinate, rigid, controlled, self-sufficient Sam, hadn't been able to hide his thoughts and feelings from her all the time. Perhaps it was because Sam trusted her.

Reece was different. He didn't know her, had no reason to give her his trust, to open up his thoughts and feelings to her. Most people had little or no control over her ability to sense things about them, a curse for her far more than a blessing. But Reece seemed to possess a shield that kept her out. Odd that the only man she had ever allowed in her bed was the one man who refused her admittance into his private thoughts and feelings.

Elizabeth dozed in the chair the rest of the night, waking at dawn when she heard Reece groaning. He had tossed the covers off and was thrashing wildly about on the bed. Jumping up from the chair, she placed her knees on the bed, lowered herself enough to grab his flying arms and found herself tossed flat on her back, lying beneath a naked Reece.

She stared at his face, next to hers on the pillow. His eyes were still closed. Where she had held his arms in her strong grip, trying to calm him, he now held her arms over her head, the weight of his body trapping her partially beneath him, her hip resting against his arousal.

His breathing slowed, his raging movements ceased and he lay quietly, his body unnaturally warm. Elizabeth tugged on her trapped arms. Reece tightened his hold momentarily, then when she tugged again, he released her, flopping one big, hairy arm across her stomach. Elizabeth sucked in a deep breath.

How had this happened? She was alone in her bed with a naked man—a big, strong naked man. Reece. The stranger who had invaded her heart five months ago. The stranger who was an escaped convict.

Of all the men she'd known in her twenty-six years, none of them had made her feel the way Reece did. She wanted to console him, to soothe him, to whisper words of comfort. She also wanted to be held in his arms, to be kissed by his firm lips, to be covered with his hard body, to be...

Elizabeth squirmed, trying to free herself. Reece didn't budge, the weight of his body keeping her trapped. What was she going to do? She couldn't just lie there until he rolled over. Stay calm. Don't panic. Think. Once again Elizabeth concentrated on forming a mental link with Reece. Once again his mind denied her access.

Reece covered her breast with his hand. Elizabeth gasped, totally shocked by the intimacy of his action. Although she still wore her clothes, her jeans, sweater and jacket, she suddenly felt undressed. She seldom wore a bra, wasn't wearing one now, and the pressure of Reece's hand cupping her breast made her feel naked. When his finger and thumb pinched at her nipple, it responded with immediate erectness, jutting against her sweater, answering the call of Reece's command.

No man had ever touched her the way Reece was doing now. The few young men she had dated in college had seen her as a freak once they'd found out she possessed psychic abilities, some even ridiculing her as a fraud. Despite her desire to know the pleasures of love and marriage and motherhood, Elizabeth had accepted her self-imposed solitude here in her mountain retreat—here in her grandmother's home where she was safe from the outside world.

But the outside world had invaded her privacy, had indeed burst into her life in the form of one big, angry man...a man now fondling her intimately.

She covered his caressing hand with her slender fingers, gripping his hand, lifting it from her breast. Only partially conscious, Reece moaned and curled up against her, nuzzling her neck with his nose. Shivers of apprehension raced up her spine. Spirals of inner warmth spread through her body.

"Reece?" She had to get away from him, from the power of his touch, the strength of his masculinity. She tried again to move away from him. He pulled her closer.

"Reece, please let me go. I can't stay here with you like this."

She saw his eyelids flicker, open briefly and close. He ran one hand up and down her shoulder, then caressed her waist, her hip, the side of her leg. Tremors racked Elizabeth's body, heat curling inside her, moisture collecting in preparation. This had to stop! It had to stop now! She wasn't prepared for such intense emotions, for feelings beyond any she had ever experienced.

"Reece!"

He opened his eyes, smoky amber eyes, eyes that looked right at her without seeing. She gave him a gentle shove. He turned over onto his back, closing his eyes and groaning softly. Elizabeth eased away from him. Once on her feet she pulled the covers up over his body, but not before she'd taken a good look at the man who had created such wanton desire within her.

She guessed his height at well over six feet, probably two or three inches over. He was muscular but lean, his hands and feet large and well shaped. Curly, dark brown hair covered his arms and legs, a thick mat on his chest tapering down to a narrow line across his stomach and then spreading out to surround his manhood.

Elizabeth swallowed hard, mesmerized by his masculine body, by the perfection, the sculptured beauty. Her fingers itched to reach out and touch him, to caress the very maleness of him. Hastily she pulled the sheet, quilt and blanket over him, covering him up to his neck.

His breathing seemed even, his sleep natural. She thought it would be safe to leave him alone for a while, long enough to fix herself a bite of breakfast, take a quick shower and renew her strength through a few moments of meditation. She'd have MacDatho stand guard. He would be able to sense any change in Reece and alert her.

Elizabeth leaned over, placing her hand on Reece's forehead. He was warm, perhaps a little too warm, even feverish.

She'd just have to rush through breakfast and a bath. Reece didn't need to be left alone for too long. Cradling his rough, lean cheek in her hand, Elizabeth gazed down at the sleeping man. Tiny, almost indiscernible flutters spread through her stomach. So this was what sexual attraction felt like. When she'd been a teenager she'd been so sure she was in love with Sam. He'd known better. Now she did, too. Sam had been comforting, reassuring, safe. Reece was none of those things, and yet . . .

She left him then, left him to rest, left him in order to free herself from the magnetism he possessed, a magnetism that drew her to him as she had never been drawn to another man.

After a shower and change of clothes, she allowed herself five minutes of meditation before she devoured a bowl of oatmeal and a cup of coffee. Then she bundled up to go outside and check on her greenhouses. During college when she had decided that she could never live in the outside world, she had sought a profession suitable to her personality and life-style and had chosen horticulture. She not only loved flowers and herbs, trees and shrubs, but she had a deep reverence for nature, a respect for all living things. She'd borrowed the money from Sam to install a small greenhouse behind the cabin. Her nursery business had grown by leaps and bounds, so that now she had two large greenhouses and a mail-order business that kept her knee-deep in work. Aunt Margaret and O'Grady helped out occasionally, and in the rush seasons of fall and spring planting, she often hired part-time help from Dover's Mill.

Returning from her outside trek, Elizabeth laid peppermint leaves and elder flowers on the counter. If Reece's fever rose any higher, she would prepare a tea made from equal amounts of the two ingredients. Drinking the tea would cause profuse sweating and hopefully break the fever.

Although early-morning light should have illuminated the house through the many windows, the dreary gray sky obscured the faraway sun, keeping the house in shadows, the only light coming from the fires burning in the fireplaces and the glow from the kerosene lamps. Even though the phones should be working soon, it could be days before electrical power was restored. Thank God the generator worked perfectly, protecting her greenhouses. She supposed she should have opted to hook the house up to a generator, too, but she simply couldn't justify the expense. Despite Sam's efforts to give her money, Elizabeth prided herself upon her financial independence. Her business would sink or swim on her merits as a businesswoman. She wasn't a child any longer; she wasn't Sam's responsibility.

After pouring herself a second cup of coffee, Elizabeth turned on the portable radio nestled between pieces of her prized blue graniteware collection sitting atop the oak sideboard. Picking up the radio, she ventured out of the kitchen and down the hallway. The radio music was country-western, a current Vince Gill hit. Just as she walked into her bedroom the news came on, the announcer alerting people in the Dover's Mill area of an escaped convict, armed and dangerous.

"Reece Landry, convicted murderer, escaped from a county vehicle taking him to Arrendale Correctional Insti-

tute in Alto after the car skidded off the highway and hit a
tree during yesterday's severe storm. Both deputies were
killed in the accident. Landry, convicted of murdering
Newell industrialist B. K. Stanton, was being taken to Arrendale to serve a life sentence. Landry is six foot three, a
hundred and ninety-five pounds, with medium-length
brown hair and brown eyes. He is armed with a 9 mm automatic taken from Deputy Jimmy Don Lewis. Our local
county sheriff is joining forces with the sheriff's department in two other counties to help in the search for Landry.
The search has been hampered by the severe weather. If
anyone has any information, please contact the sheriff's
department immediately. Do not approach this man. He is
armed and dangerous. We repeat, Reece Landry is armed
and dangerous.''

Elizabeth turned off the radio, placing it and her coffee
cup on a corner desk. She walked over to the bed where
Reece lay sleeping. He'd thrown off the quilt and blanket,
leaving only the sheet covering him from the waist down.

''Did you kill B. K. Stanton?'' Elizabeth whispered, not
expecting an answer but hoping she could sense Reece's innocence or guilt. She sensed nothing.

Sitting in the wing-back chair beside the bed, she reached
out to touch Reece's forehead. Hot. Burning hot. The fever
had risen, but he wasn't sweating. His skin was dry. She
went into the bathroom, drew a pan of cool water, took a
washcloth from the stack in the wicker basket where she
stored them and returned to Reece's bedside. Placing the
pan on the nightstand, she dipped the washcloth in the water, wrung it out and began giving Reece a rubdown. If the
rubdown didn't cool his fever, she would prepare the me-
dicinal tea.

The moment the damp cloth touched his body Reece
moaned, then flung his arm out, batting at the air. He hit
the side of Elizabeth's shoulder. Grabbing his arm, she
lowered it to his side and continued her ministrations. Time
and again she dipped the cloth into the water, wrung it
lightly and massaged Reece's face, neck, shoulders and
chest.

Realizing her rubdown had done nothing to lower his fever, she went to the kitchen, prepared the peppermint-and-elder tea and brought the brewed medication and an earthenware mug to her bedroom. After pouring the concoction, she sat on the bed by Reece and lifted his head. As she'd done the night before, she placed the cup to his lips, shifting it just enough for the liquid to dribble. When the tea ran down his chin, Elizabeth inserted her finger between his closed lips, prizing his mouth open. She repeated the process. Reece accepted the tea. She kept her arm securely behind his head, holding him inclined just enough so he could swallow the medicine without choking. When he downed the last drop in the mug, Elizabeth sighed. Now all she could do was wait and pray.

Lowering his head to the pillow, Elizabeth turned so that her back rested against the headboard of the huge old bed her great-great-grandfather, a carpenter, had made as a first-anniversary gift for his wife. Their seven children, four of whom had grown to adulthood, had been born in this bed.

Time passed slowly as Elizabeth sat beside Reece, her hand idly brushing his shoulder, her fingers soothing the thick, springy hair on his chest. Moisture coated her fingertips when she touched his forehead. He was sweating. The fever had broken!

By noon Elizabeth had pushed and tugged Reece enough to change the bed linen after he'd stained them with perspiration. He lay sleeping peacefully, warm but not feverish, the flesh on his ears, nose and hands that she had feared frostbitten now a healthy pink. Perhaps he would awaken soon. When he did, he would be hungry. He'd probably want breakfast.

Glancing down at the man the radio announcer had called armed and dangerous, Elizabeth breathed deeply, wondering if she was a fool to trust him not to harm her. Fool or not, she could not deny the way she felt about him, the deep emotions he stirred within her. For five months this stranger had been a part of her. Without even knowing him, she had allowed him into her heart.

Elizabeth leaned over and kissed Reece on the cheek. He didn't stir. She ran her fingertips across his full lower lip.

Suddenly she sensed a desperate need, a soul-felt cry for help. Laying her fingertips across his mouth, Elizabeth concentrated on zeroing in on Reece's emotions. Anger. Pain. Hatred. Fear.

"God sent you to me, Reece Landry. Somehow I'm going to find a way to help you," Elizabeth vowed.

Chapter 3

Warmth. Blessed warmth. Reece lay in the soft warmth, savoring the comfort, his mind halfway between sleep and consciousness. He stretched his legs, which were covered by a downy, heated weight. His muscles ached; his head felt fuzzy. Was he dead? Had he frozen to death in the snow? Was this delicious warmth coming from hell's brimstone fire? Couldn't be, he thought. This wasn't punishment; this was heaven.

Slowly and with some difficulty, Reece forced his eyelids open. He wasn't quite sure where he was, but one thing was for certain—he hadn't died and gone to hell. He gazed up at a split-log-and-plank ceiling, the wood a mellow gold. Looking around the room, he noticed the massive stacked logs of the outer walls and the rustic rock fireplace where a cheerful fire glowed brightly. Across the wooden mantel lay an arrangement of dried flowers intermingled with large pine cones and wide plaid ribbons. Several dried-flower wreaths decorated the walls, along with a few framed charcoal nature drawings of trees, flowers and even one of a wolf.

Wolf! Last night he'd broken into this cabin. No, he hadn't really broken in. Some fool had left the door unlocked. Reece shook his head. It didn't hurt! Reaching up to touch his injured forehead, he immediately realized that the dried blood had been washed away and the swelling had diminished considerably.

Had he imagined that damned black wolf, snarling, growling, threatening, warning Reece not to harm his mistress? The woman! Had he imagined her, too? Big blue eyes. Thick dark hair lying across her back in a long braid. Full, tempting breasts. Strong arms. Comforting voice.

He could hear that voice calling his name. *Reece. I want to help you. You're safe here with me. No one is going to put you back in a cage.*

How the hell did she know his name? And why would she help him? Why had she taken care of him? Tiny pieces of his memory returned, fever-induced dreams of tender, caring hands bathing his body, stroking his face, doctoring his wounds, pouring some sort of hot, mint-flavored tea down his throat.

Reece sat up in bed with a start, the full implications of his fragmented memories hitting him. He had forced his way into the woman's home, unlocked door or not. And he had threatened her life before he'd passed out. But what had happened after that? Who had put him to bed?

The sudden realization that he was completely naked took him by surprise. Someone had carried him to this bed and undressed him. The woman couldn't have carried him. No way. Did that mean she had a husband? A father? A brother? He didn't remember anyone except the woman and her enormous animal protector.

Had the woman called the sheriff? Were deputies on their way here right now to take him to prison?

You're safe with me. No one is going to put you back in a cage.

Her words had been a promise, but Reece didn't trust promises. He'd found in his vast experience with the human race that most people lied whenever it suited them.

Reece tossed back the covers, slid his legs out of the bed and touched his feet to the floor. Although his body ached with a bearable soreness, neither his head nor his side hurt. Undoubtedly, none of his ribs had been broken in the accident—either that, or the woman who had tended his wounds had miraculously healed him.

He had to find the woman, had to ask her where he was and figure out exactly what his chances of escaping were. But he was buck naked and didn't see anything in the room that vaguely resembled his county-issued coveralls. However, he did notice a stack of folded clothes on the cedar chest at the foot of the bed.

Slowly, tentatively, Reece stood. Swaying slightly, his head spinning, he grabbed the bedpost. The faint vertigo passed as quickly as it had come. Righting himself, he walked around the bed, lifted the stack of clothing off the cedar chest and smiled when he realized he held a pair of men's briefs, a thermal top, a flannel shirt and a pair of well-worn jeans. There had to be a man in this woman's life, probably here in her home. Where else would she have gotten men's clothes? And from the look of them, the items belonged to a fairly large man, someone about Reece's own size.

But why couldn't he remember a man?

Taking his time, Reece put on the clothes, then looked around, wondering if the lady of the house had thought of footwear. Sure enough, resting on the wide rock hearth was a pair of thick socks and leather work boots.

Reece sat on the raised hearth, breathing in the aroma of aged wood burning slowly, and slipped on the socks and boots. Whoever owned these boots had a foot about a half size larger than Reece's, but the minuscule difference was of little importance. The jeans were a perfect fit, the flannel shirt and thermal top only a fraction large. The owner undoubtedly had the shoulders and chest of a linebacker.

Running his hand over his face, Reece noted the beginnings of a beard. He needed a shave, and he could do with a hot shower, even though he felt relatively clean. Memories of his ministering angel bathing him flashed through his mind. A shower and shave could wait. He needed to find his hostess. Reece laughed aloud. His hostess? For all he knew, the county sheriff could be waiting for him just beyond the half-closed door.

Reece inched the door open, peered out into the dim hallway, saw no one, but heard a man singing an old-fashioned tune, something from the forties or fifties. Following the music, Reece made his way down the hallway, noting the huge living room in the opposite direction and a massive wooden staircase leading to the second level of the cabin.

The kitchen door stood open. Bright sunshine poured in through the lace-curtained windows. Harry Connick, Jr.'s mellow voice singing "I'll Dream of You Again" drifted through the cabin from the radio-cassette player on the counter. Reece's vision took in three things in quick succession. A blue-granite wood-burning stove placed in front of a corner brick chimney, a round wooden table set for a meal, and a smiling woman holding a pan of biscuits. The smell of coffee, frying bacon and sweet spices made Reece's mouth water. He hadn't realized how hungry he was.

Then he heard a low growl and saw the big black wolf-dog he'd encountered the night before. That damned animal didn't like him. And why should he? Reece reminded himself that he had invaded the dog's home and threatened his mistress. Threatened her with his gun. His gun! Where was his gun? He'd been holding it when he'd passed out.

"Well, good morning." Elizabeth thought Reece looked rather handsome with a two-day growth of beard and wearing Sam's old clothes. "I'd about decided you were going to sleep away another day."

Reece stopped dead still in the doorway. "Lady, who the hell are you?"

The practical realist in him warned that this woman was a stranger and not to be trusted, but his male libido reacted differently, appreciating the woman's earthy beauty, the ripe fullness of her sturdy body, the basic sensuality that surrounded her like a visible aura.

Elizabeth set the pan of biscuits on a hotpad atop the counter, turned to Reece, took several steps in his direction and held out her hand. "I'm Elizabeth Sequana Mallory. You're in my home, on my mountain, in Sequana Falls."

Reece didn't make a move to enter the kitchen or to take Elizabeth's hand. Why the hell was she being so friendly? She acted as if he were a welcome guest. Was the woman crazy?

"Breakfast is just about ready. Come on in and sit down." Elizabeth turned, busying herself with preparing two plates. "How do you like your coffee?"

"Black." Reece walked into the kitchen, stopping abruptly at the table, grabbing the top of the wooden chair.

"I see the clothes and boots fit you all right." Elizabeth placed two plates of eggs, bacon and hash browns on the two blue place mats.

"Your husband's?"

"No." Elizabeth poured coffee into two Blue Willow cups.

"What did you do with my gun?" Reece clutched the back of the chair.

"It's in a safe place." Elizabeth set the cups on the table, pulled out a chair and sat down. "Aren't you hungry?"

Reece glared at her. What did she think this was, a damned picnic? Although they were total strangers, this woman was treating him like a long-lost friend.

"Don't worry, Mr. Landry, when you leave I'll return your gun to you." Elizabeth lifted the cup to her lips.

Reece watched her sip the hot coffee. Her lips were full, soft and a natural rosy pink. He remembered that those lips had touched his cheek. She had kissed him! Her small hand held the cup securely as she continued leisurely sipping the coffee. Reece noted the delicate size of her hands, but remembered their strength, remembered those slender fingers caressing his face, touching him lightly.

Dragging his eyes away from her lips and hands, Reece suddenly realized she'd called him Mr. Landry. She knew who he was. He hadn't been imagining things when he thought he'd heard her calling him Reece.

"How do you know my name?"

"Sit down, Reece. Your breakfast is getting cold."

What the hell was wrong with this woman? Didn't she have the good sense to be scared? After all, she obviously knew he was an escaped convict, a murderer on his way to a life term in the state penitentiary.

Releasing his death grip on the chair, Reece reached out, grabbing Elizabeth by the shoulders, turning her in her seat. She stared up at him with surprised blue eyes. The expression on her face was a mixture of fear, doubt, hope and supplication. This woman—Elizabeth—wanted something from him. But what?

"What's going on with you?" he asked. "If you know who I am, why haven't you called the sheriff?"

"I know who you are, Reece Landry." You're the stranger in my heart, the man who has invaded my thoughts for five months. "I heard a news bulletin on the radio yesterday morning telling about a sheriff's car that wrecked and the escape of a convicted murderer who was being transported to Arrendale."

"You heard a bulletin on the radio yesterday morning?" How was that possible? He hadn't escaped until yesterday afternoon. "What day is this? How long have I been here?"

"You came here the night before last. You were exhausted, injured and suffering from minor frostbite and exposure. Then you ran a high fever for a while."

"Son of a bitch!" Reece loosened his hold on Elizabeth's shoulders, noticing for the first time that her wolf-dog had moved to her side. "Have you notified the sheriff's department?"

"I can't. The phone's out." Elizabeth hated herself for lying to Reece, but she felt it was a necessary fabrication. The phone had been working since early this morning, but she had unplugged it, preventing anyone from calling her.

Elizabeth laid her hand atop Reece's where it rested on her shoulder. As if he'd been burned by her touch, he jerked his hand away.

"So you're stuck with me for the time being, huh?" Just because she hadn't been able to notify the authorities of his whereabouts didn't mean he was safe. From the looks of the sunshine and blue sky he saw outside the windows, the winter storm had passed. Even if she couldn't telephone for help, that didn't mean a search party wouldn't show up on her doorstep any time now.

"Why don't you sit down and eat. You've got to be hungry. You haven't eaten a bite in a couple of days." Elizabeth didn't think she'd ever seen anyone as wary, as suspicious as Reece. Didn't the man trust anybody?

Reece pulled out the chair, sat down, picked up the Blue Willow cup and tasted the coffee. The brew was warm, rich, full-bodied, with a hint of flavor he couldn't quite make out. He swallowed, then frowned, wondering exactly what the unique taste could be.

"Vanilla almond," Elizabeth said, as if she'd read his mind. "I grind my own coffee beans." She nodded at the counter where an antique coffee grinder perched on a wooden shelf alongside several other antique utensils.

Nodding in acknowledgment of her statement, Reece picked up his fork, lifted a hefty portion of scrambled eggs and put them in his mouth. Suddenly he had the oddest sensation that he'd somehow stepped into the twilight zone, that he had escaped from the sheriff's car and found his way to never-never land. Nothing about this place, this isolated cabin in the woods, or this woman—sultry, earthy and incredibly beautiful—seemed real.

Any woman, alone the way Elizabeth Mallory was, would be afraid of an escaped convict, but Reece sensed more curiosity than fear emanating from the woman sitting across the table from him.

While he continued eating, devouring the tasty breakfast, he watched Elizabeth as she broke open a biscuit, buttered it and fed small pieces to her wolf-dog. The animal ate heartily, consuming three biscuits in quick succession. Elizabeth laughed, the sound piercingly sweet to Reece's ears. There was no pretension, no coy feminine silliness to her laugh. The sound came from her heart—warm, loving and completely genuine. Any fool could see the mutual love that existed between dog and woman.

"Where'd you get him?" Reece nodded toward Elizabeth's pet.

"Mac here?" She patted the animal's back, then scratched behind his ears.

"Mac?"

"Short for MacDatho." Elizabeth sensed a minute loosening of the tension in Reece, barely discernible but evident nevertheless. "My German shepherd, Elspeth, was Mac's mother. His father was a wolf."

"I'd guessed as much. Are there many wolves in these hills?"

"Some."

"Why'd you take care of me?" Reece asked. "You should have tied me up once I passed out on you. Instead, you put me to bed and nursed me. Now you're feeding me. Woman, haven't you got any sense at all?"

Elizabeth smiled. Dear God in heaven, he wished she hadn't smiled at him like that. He wanted to capture that smile, hold on to it, keep it from vanishing.

"The newscaster said you'd been convicted of killing a man," Elizabeth said. "Did you kill him?"

"I was convicted, wasn't I?"

"I know that. But were you guilty?"

Reece finished off the last bite of bacon, downed the remains of his coffee and shoved back his chair. Standing, he stared down at Elizabeth's upturned face. "Would you believe me if I told you that I'm innocent, that I didn't kill B. K. Stanton?"

"Yes, I'd believe you."

Running his hands through his thick, wavy hair, Reece snorted. "Lady, are you that naive? Would you take the word of a stranger, someone you don't know the first thing about?"

But I do know things about you, Reece. Less than I want to know, but more than you could ever realize. "You don't have the soul of a killer."

"What makes you think I don't?"

"I can sense it. I'm very good at sensing things." Did she dare try to explain her special gifts, her God-given psychic powers? Would he believe her if she did?

"You live up here in these hills all by yourself?"

Standing, Elizabeth began clearing away the table, stacking the dishes in the sink. "Just Mac and me. My great-aunt, Margaret McPhearson, spends a lot of time up here with me in warm weather. She lives in Dover's Mill."

"How do you support yourself? Do you have a job in Dover's Mill?" Reece couldn't imagine anyone with no income being able to afford such a luxurious two-story cabin.

"I operate a nursery. I have a degree in horticulture." Elizabeth turned on the water faucet and squirted dish-washing detergent into the sink.

"What sort of nursery? Flowers?"

MacDatho followed Reece to the back door, watching him intently when he opened the door and stepped out onto the porch. The dry, frigid air cut through Reece's clothing, but the sun warmed his face when he stared up at the sky.

Walking out onto the porch, Elizabeth waited for Mac to run outside before she closed the door. She turned to Reece, instinctively reaching out to touch his arm, but she suddenly remembered his aversion to being touched and withdrew her hand.

"Look over to the right and you'll see my greenhouses. I grow roses and a fairly large variety of flowers as well as herbs and spices and a few specialty shrubs. I sell in nearby towns to both florists and gardeners, and two years ago I started a mail-order business, which has grown by leaps and bounds."

"So, you're a successful businesswoman, huh?"

"I guess you could say that."

"How are you keeping the temperatures in your green-houses regulated without electricity? A generator?"

"Yes. The generator kicks in automatically when the electrical power fails, which is fairly often when we get a winter storm."

Reece glanced at her. The sun streaked reddish highlights in her dark brown hair and gave a golden glow to her olive skin. With the log cabin, the blue sky, the snow-covered forest as a background for her beauty, Elizabeth seemed as much a part of nature's perfection as her surroundings. Her calf-length, rust-colored corduroy skirt swayed in the cool February wind, revealing a pair of flat, plain, tan ankle boots. Her breasts swelled invitingly, not quite straining the buttons on her hunter-green-and-rust-striped blouse. Her baggy green sweater hung down past her generous hips.

Reece forced himself to look away, unable to deny his body's sexual urges. He wanted this woman. She was beautiful and sexy and caring. But who was he kidding? The last thing on Elizabeth Mallory's mind was sex—and it should

be the last thing on his mind. All he should be thinking
about was getting the hell away from here before the authorities showed up looking for him. He had to find a way
to get back to Newell, to hide out until he could discover
who had really taken his .38 revolver and blown B. K. Stanton to hell.

MacDatho ran down the steps and into the backyard, the
snow coming up to his belly.

"I wouldn't hurt you." Reece spoke the words in a low,
deep voice, not much more than a whisper on the wind.

Elizabeth heard him; her heart heard him. "I know."

He saw her shiver, and realized she must be cold. "Why
don't you go back inside? I didn't realize how cold it still
was. The sun had me fooled."

"Are you staying out here?"

"For a few more minutes." Reece leaned over the porch
railing, curling his fingers about the top wooden round.

Elizabeth laid her hand over his where he gripped the
railing. When he flinched, she squeezed his hand gently.
"Do you want to tell me about the murder? About what really happened?"

"What really happened was I had a motive for killing
Stanton and a lifelong reputation as a town bad boy. Once
they arrested me, they stopped looking for any other suspects. That's about it."

For a split second Elizabeth picked up the intense rage
burning inside Reece, then suddenly he shielded his emotions, almost as if he had felt her probing.

"There's a lot more to it than that, isn't there?" Elizabeth asked. "I want you to know that I'm here for you,
willing to listen when you're ready to talk, willing to do
whatever I can to help you. I know you can't bear the
thought of being caged again."

He stared at her as if he'd never seen her before, as if
she'd appeared out of nowhere, a blithe spirit sent to taunt
him. "Caged? Yeah, caged. That's exactly what it's like in
jail, what it would be like at Arrendale. I nearly went nuts
being locked up so many months."

"You couldn't post bail?"

"The district attorney persuaded the judge that I was a poor risk. The Stantons were generous supporters during the D.A.'s reelection bid. He owed the family a favor."

Elizabeth clutched Reece's hand. She longed to put her arms around him and comfort him. Something told her that it had been a long time since anyone had comforted Reece Landry. When she glanced at him, he was staring off into the distance.

"You won't be caged again, Reece." Tears sprang into Elizabeth's eyes. "I promise I'll do whatever I can to help you find the real murderer."

"Lady, why the hell would you do anything to help me? How can you believe that I'm innocent when you don't even know me?"

"I feel as if I know you, as if I've known you for months."

Reece turned sharply, staring at Elizabeth again. Her eyes were filled with tears. Was she crying for him? No one had ever cried for him. No one except his mother. Hesitantly, almost fearfully, Reece touched his fingertip to the corner of her eye, brushing away the tears.

"Elizabeth?" A tight knot formed in his throat.

"I'm all right."

"You're crying for me, aren't you?" He gripped her chin in his big hand, tilting her face upward. "Why?"

She gazed at him with such undisguised concern, such genuine human compassion. "Because you can't cry for yourself."

He kissed her then. He hadn't thought about it, certainly hadn't planned it. But nothing on earth could have kept him from tasting those sweet, rosy lips. Nothing short of being struck down dead would have prevented him from pulling her into his arms and devouring her with the heat of his passion. He had never wanted anything as much as he wanted to lift this woman into his arms and carry her back inside the house and to her bed. His body ached with the need for release, for the ease he knew he could find in Elizabeth's loving warmth. There was a passion inside her equal to his own. He felt it when she returned his kiss with enthusiasm, opening her mouth for his invasion, as surely as she had unlocked her door for him the other night.

He ended the kiss when the realization hit him that she had, indeed, left her door unlocked for him. How he could be so certain he didn't know, but certain he was. He grabbed Elizabeth by the shoulders, pushing her away from him and at the same time holding on to her.

"You left your door unlocked the night I came here."

"Yes."

"Do you usually leave your door unlocked?"

"No."

"Why did you leave it unlocked that night?"

Would he believe the truth or would he prefer a lie? she asked herself. "I left it unlocked because I was expecting you."

Reece glared at her, confused by her admission, wondering how the hell she could have known he was headed in her direction and why she would have left her door unlocked for an escaped convict.

"I don't understand you, lady. How could you have been expecting me?"

"Reece . . ." When she reached out to touch his face, he dropped his hands from her shoulders and backed away from her.

"What the hell are you, some sort of hillbilly witch?"

"Some people would call me a psychic. I was born with special abilities."

Reece looked her over from head to toe, his perusal stopping when he reached her face. "What sort of abilities?"

"I can sense things, see things. Sometimes I know things before they happen. I'm clairvoyant and precognitive. However, my telepathic abilities are limited."

"Are you kidding me?"

"I'm trying to explain why I knew you would be coming to me, and why you need me to help you."

"This is a bunch of bull, lady. If you think for one minute that I'll buy into this crap, then you've got another thought coming."

"Five months ago I began having dreams about you, then brief visions. I could see your face, sense your pain and anger and bitterness. I knew you were caged, that you were being punished for something you hadn't done. These dreams, these visions continued up until you arrived on my doorstep the night before last.''

Reece stood rigid and silent, staring at Elizabeth, astonishment in his amber eyes. "Are you trying to tell me that you've been messing around inside my head?''

"I'm telling you that I can help you, that I want to help you." When he didn't respond, she went on. "Don't you see that you were sent to me because—''

"Cut the crap, lady. I told you I don't believe you." Reece held up a hand in restraint as if warning her off.

"Stay out here as long as you need to,'' Elizabeth told him. "I have things to do inside, then I'll have to make a trip out to the greenhouses. Make yourself at home.''

Reece watched her disappear back inside the house. The frigid air began to chill him through his thermal top and flannel shirt.

He heard the back door open, then close again and realized MacDatho had followed his mistress inside. There was something damned strange about Elizabeth and her MacDatho. They didn't seem to belong in this century. Were they real or were they ghosts from some bygone era? Reece wondered if he was hallucinating. Could it be that he was actually lying out in the snow on the mountainside, dying slowly, freezing to death, and he had imagined the beautiful woman and her wolf-dog? Was Elizabeth a figment of his imagination? Had he dreamed her, as she claimed she had dreamed him?

If she and the wolf-dog and this cabin were real, then maybe she was a little bit crazy, living up here in the woods all alone. That would explain why she didn't lock her doors and why she didn't seem afraid of an escaped convict. Whatever the truth might be, Reece knew one thing for sure and certain—he had to find a way to get off this damned mountain and back to Newell. He wasn't going to get caught. He wasn't going to prison. Whatever he had to do to stay free, he'd do it. And if that meant using Elizabeth Mallory, if she even existed, then so be it.

*   *   *

Elizabeth had successfully avoided Reece Landry for most of the day, keeping busy with light housekeeping chores and necessary work in the greenhouses. His attitude toward her psychic abilities was nothing new. People who didn't know her tended to be skeptical; then once they accepted her unusual powers, people often treated her like a freak. She could never adjust in the world outside Sequana Falls. She'd learned that when she'd gone away to college.

She knew Reece had searched the house for the 9 mm belonging to the deceased deputy. He'd never find it. After sealing the gun in a plastic bag, she'd taken it with her when she'd gone to the greenhouses, finding a perfect spot for it between her two compost bins.

When Reece left, she would return the gun to him. She didn't like the idea of his using it, but knew it would offer him a small sense of security. If only he would accept her help, would open up to her and allow her to discover any possible knowledge of which he might not be aware.

Elizabeth removed the homemade beef pot pie from the oven, placing it atop the hotpad on the counter. Spooning generous helpings of the pie onto two Blue Willow plates, she laid the plates on a large tray already set with silverware and cloth napkins, piping hot coffee, small green salads and slices of made-from-scratch pound cake. Aunt Margaret had baked the pound cake before Christmas, and Elizabeth had frozen it for future use.

Picking up MacDatho's bowl from the floor, Elizabeth filled it with the remainder of the pot pie, then set it back down on the floor.

"I spoil you shamefully, you know that, don't you?"

MacDatho gazed up at her, his look telling her that he was worthy of being spoiled, then he wolfed down the warm meal.

Using her hip to shove open doors, Elizabeth carried the tray from the kitchen to the living room. Reece sat on the overstuffed plaid chair to the right of the fireplace. The sight of him sitting there, looking so at home, sent a fission of awareness through Elizabeth. A premonition? Or wishful thinking? Did she want her home to become Reece's home?

The radio-tape player, which Reece had apparently brought into the living room, rested on the floor beside his chair. The music playing was an old tape Elizabeth dearly loved, a mixed bag of cool jazz tunes. The soft, bluesy tones of saxophone and horn blended with piano, giving the listener a sensually romantic rendition of "Who Would Care?"

Reece looked up from the magazine he held in his hand, a recent copy of *Archaeology.* "I hope you don't mind, I borrowed your cassette player. Music helps me think. When I was a kid I used to sit out on my porch and listen to Willie Paul playing the piano over at Flossie's. He knew all the great jazz tunes."

Elizabeth set the tray atop the six-foot-long coffee table in front of the sofa. "Who was Willie Paul? And who was Flossie?"

Reece tossed *Archaeology* atop the pile of magazines in the big wicker basket beneath a nearby table. "Willie Paul was a black man who doubled as piano player and bouncer at Flossie's, a local night spot that also served the men of Newell as a brothel."

"Oh, I see." Elizabeth sat on the sofa, patting the cushion beside her. "I thought supper would be nice in here."

"You've been avoiding me all day, haven't you?" Reece got up, walked over to the sofa, but didn't sit down. "I guess I acted pretty ungrateful to you this morning. I've had time to think about things, and I realize that without your help, I might have died."

"Sit down and eat your supper." Elizabeth didn't look up at him, sensing the sexual arousal in Reece, knowing she wasn't ready to deal with the unnerving emotions he had created in her this morning, with nothing more than a kiss.

Reece laughed. "You sound like someone's mother. Are you always so maternal?" Sitting beside her, he lifted the coffee cup to his lips.

"You really grew up across the street from a . . . a house of—"

"A cathouse?" Reece tasted the coffee, then set it down on the tray, picking up a plate and fork. He wondered what she'd think if he told her that his first sexual experience had been with one of Flossie's girls. Misty, a very experienced redhead only five years older than he'd been at fifteen. "Yeah. Lilac Road was the most notorious street in Newell."

Picking up the folded white linen napkin from the tray, Elizabeth spread it across her lap. "I grew up here in Sequana Falls. My mother and stepfather brought me here when I was six, and we lived here together in my grandparents' home until my parents were killed in an automobile accident when I was twelve."

"You didn't live here on your own after they died, did you?"

"No, I lived with Aunt Margaret, my grandmother's sister. We divided our time between Sequana Falls and Dover's Mill." And Aunt Margaret taught me to accept my special abilities, not to fight them, and never to abuse the power.

Reece ate heartily, savoring every bite, and Elizabeth ate just as ravenously. Neither of them had eaten lunch. The hardwood logs burned in the fireplace. The cool jazz music filled the room, creating a mellow mood. Empty dishes lay stacked on the large tray. MacDatho snored softly on the braided rug before the hearth. Turning toward Reece, Elizabeth crossed one leg beneath the other, her entwined fingers cupping her knee. Reece rested his arm on the back of the sofa, then turned slightly, crossing his legs, his hand on his thigh.

"I'll have to leave in the morning." His words sounded loud in the peaceful stillness of the room.

Elizabeth shook her head. "You won't be able to leave."

"I'm all right. No permanent effects from the wreck or from my long trek in the snow. Just a few fading bruises and a little soreness." Reece leaned toward her, wondering why she wouldn't look at him. She had deliberately avoided any eye contact with him since their altercation on the back porch this morning. Had he hurt her feelings by not believing her claim to be psychic?

"It won't be safe for you to leave the mountain tomorrow."

"It won't be safe for me if I stay," he said. "I've been listening to radio newscasts all day. They're mounting a pretty big search for me. Since the weather seems to have cleared up, they'll be combing Dover's Mill and Sequana Falls."

"They won't be able to do anything for another day or so. There's another big snow coming. It's already started. It's snowing again right now."

"How do you know?" When she didn't reply, he realized she didn't want to tell him that her powers extended to predicting the weather because she was afraid of his ridicule. "Okay, so it's snowing now. Being snowed-in here won't keep me safe, and it isn't getting me any closer to proving my innocence."

"Be patient, Reece." Elizabeth looked at him then, her eyes pleading. "Your body and mind need rest, and you need time to think, to plan a strategy for when you return to Newell."

"All I need is a means of transportation. I guess I'll have to try my hand at hitchhiking or stealing a car. Somehow I'll have to elude the manhunt and steer clear of any roadblocks."

Elizabeth reached out, her hand hovering over his where it rested on the back of the sofa. Lowering her hand, she covered his, squeezing tenderly. "I have a Jeep you can borrow. I don't keep much cash on hand, but I have a couple of hundred I can give you."

"You'll loan me your Jeep and some money?" Reece stared at her, wondering if he'd ever be able to figure her out. "Why would you do that?"

"Because I believe you're innocent. Because someone has to help you." Holding his hand firmly, she smiled at him. "Because five months ago you came to me in my dreams because you needed someone. You needed me."

Gazing directly into her pure blue eyes, Reece realized she truly believed what she was saying—there was no doubt in her mind that he had been appearing in her dreams, that she had seen visions of his captivity.

"You don't believe me, do you?"

"Elizabeth, I . . . Hell, I'm a realist. I don't believe in anything I can't experience with my five senses."

"It's all right. I understand. It's not necessary that you believe me in order for me to help you."

Reece lifted her hand, turning it palm up. "You're a very unusual woman, Elizabeth Mallory. And if you're willing to help me, I'm not fool enough to refuse. Maybe God has finally decided to give me a break. Maybe he did send me to you. Maybe he gave you to me as a guardian angel."

Lowering his head, Reece brought Elizabeth's hand to his mouth, kissing the center of her palm. "If your predictions about the weather come true and we are trapped up here in this cabin together for a couple more days, then you may be in real danger from me."

She gave him a startled look, her eyes widening in surprise. "What sort of danger?"

"Man-woman sort of danger."

"You want me? Want to make love to me?" The very thought warmed Elizabeth's insides, tightening her nipples and moistening her femininity. What would it be like to make love with Reece Landry, to lie in his arms and know his complete possession? Elizabeth shivered.

He'd never known a woman so brutally frank. Most females he knew were experts at playing games, saying one thing and meaning another, lying when it served their purpose.

Grinning, Reece pulled her hand to his chest, laying it across his heart. "Yeah, I want to make love to you. You're a beautiful, desirable woman, and I haven't been with anybody in nearly a year."

"We're not ready to make love. Not yet." Removing her hand from his chest, she stood and walked across the room, halting in front of the wide expanse of floor-to-ceiling windows spanning the south wall of the living room.

Reece followed her, slipping his arms around her waist, drawing her back against his chest, positioning her buttocks into his arousal.

"Oh, I'm ready. I'm more than ready." He nuzzled the side of her neck with his nose.

Elizabeth loved the feel of him. His big, strong arms draped around her body, his face buried in her neck, his lips spreading kisses up the side of her jaw, his throbbing arousal pulsating against her, beckoning her to succumb to temptation. She wanted Reece. She'd never wanted a man before. Desire was a new emotion to her, one that she realized had been growing steadily within her since her first dream of a tormented, caged man in desperate need of her help.

"You're ready to have sex, Reece." Elizabeth knew she should withdraw from his embrace, should free herself from the chains of their mutual passion, but she couldn't bear the thought of ending such sweet pleasure. "You aren't ready to make love."

He chuckled, lowering his hands to cover her stomach, then the tops of her thighs, running his palms up and down, in and out, closer and closer to the apex between her legs. "Is there a difference?"

She covered his hands where they cupped her femininity. "Yes, there's a difference between love and sex. A big difference for me. I won't have sex without the loving. When we're both ready, I'll know."

Huffing loudly, Reece released Elizabeth and walked away from her. "Another one of your psychic talents, knowing when a man is ready to make love instead of just screw?"

Elizabeth swallowed the knot in her throat, emotion creating a physical ache inside her. He was angry. Not with her, not really. Reece Landry was angry with life. If only he would let her, she would teach him to release his anger, to free himself of its destructive hold. She had another day, perhaps two, to persuade him that she could do more to help him than lend him a Jeep and some money. Maybe a day or two would be enough time.

"It's snowing," she said as she looked out the window. "It will snow all night."

"Thanks for the weather report." Reece wanted to hit something, anything that would smash into a thousand pieces and release some of the tension inside him. Sex would have worked just fine, but his hostess wasn't a woman who had sex. She *made love*. Sex and making love meant the same thing to him, and he believed any fool stupid enough to think there was a difference was deluding himself—or herself. He'd had sex with his share of women over the years, and there had never been much difference in the experiences, regardless of who his partner had been.

"There is a difference, Reece. Someday you'll understand."

He didn't respond, not even with a nod or a grunt. Elizabeth watched him walk away, entering the hallway; then he stopped, but didn't turn around. "Where do I sleep tonight? I assume I've been sleeping in your bed the last couple of nights."

"Take the stairs. I built a fire in the fireplace in the first bedroom."

"Fine." He headed for the stairs, took several steps upward, then said, "Thanks."

"You're welcome."

Elizabeth hugged her arms around her body, the chill of Reece's anger and frustration issuing her a warning. She didn't know this man, despite his invasion of her mind, her home and her heart. She had hoped that once they came together she would be able to get past the shield protecting his thoughts and emotions. But she caught only fragmented glimpses inside his mind. Not enough to trust her body to him. Her heart was another matter. She feared it was already lost.

Chapter 4

Reece guided the razor down his cheek. Sam Dundee's razor. For two days he'd been wearing another man's clothes, a man whose shoes he didn't quite fill, and now he was shaving with that man's razor. He'd even slept in the man's bed last night.

Elizabeth had told him that Sam was her stepfather's brother and had acted as her legal guardian when her parents had been killed in an automobile accident when she was twelve. Reece didn't like this Dundee guy, and he wasn't quite sure why. He didn't even know him, but Elizabeth knew him. Elizabeth loved him!

Hell! He had to get off this mountain. Away from Elizabeth Mallory, away from her unnatural concern about his welfare, away from her all-too-knowing blue eyes and away from the way she made him feel every time he looked at her. It had been hell keeping his hands off her. He couldn't remember a time in his life when he'd wanted a woman so badly. He'd told himself this gut-wrenching hunger eating away at him was due to the fact he hadn't been with a woman in over a year, but he wasn't so sure.

He'd been alone with Elizabeth for three nights, two of them in a semiconscious stupor, but even on those two nights he could remember her gentle touch, her soft voice, her kindness and concern. He liked Elizabeth far too much, and he didn't want to like her. Caring about her would be dangerous for both of them. He'd only wind up hurting her if he allowed her to become involved in his problems. Besides, he didn't quite trust her. He'd never completely trusted another person—not even his own mother. Blanche had betrayed him from the moment she'd conceived him, bringing him into the world a bastard, a social outcast, giving him a stepfather like Harry Gunn, then dying on him before he was old enough to defend himself. No, he'd learned early that it didn't pay to trust anyone, not even the people who professed to love you.

The snowstorm had died sometime during the early morning hours. He'd awakened to the sound of silence, to the eerie quiet left once the wind had ceased its savage moaning. The search for escaped convict Reece Landry would be on again. It was only a matter of time before someone came snooping around Elizabeth's cabin. The electricity had been restored around nine o'clock. Things were beginning to return to normal. He couldn't risk staying much longer. He'd have to leave soon. He had no other choice if he wanted to stay free.

The jarring ring of a telephone echoed through the house like a sonic boom. The razor in Reece's hand stilled on his throat. If the phone was working again, then Elizabeth could call out. She could call for help. She could turn him in to the sheriff.

Dropping the razor into the sink, Reece picked up a hand towel, wiped the streaks of shaving-cream residue off his face and ran out into the hallway. When he reached the top of the stairs he heard Elizabeth's voice, but couldn't make out what she was saying.

He took the steps two at a time, halting just before reaching the living room entrance, bracing himself against the wall. His heartbeat accelerated; the pulse in his head throbbed.

"You didn't have to worry about me, Aunt Margaret. I'm fine. Really," Elizabeth said. "Mac and I weathered the storm without any problems."

Reece glanced around the corner, watching Elizabeth while she talked. Something was bothering her. Reece noted the way her hand clutched the phone, the way she stood, her feet shifting nervously as if she couldn't stand still.

"No, don't do that!" Elizabeth's voice sounded shrill. "I mean, don't send poor old O'Grady out in this weather. I don't need anything."

Reece eased around the corner, walking silently toward Elizabeth. When he was within two feet of her, she jerked around, her eyes widening, her mouth forming an oval of surprise. She draped the palm of her hand over the bottom half of the telephone.

"Who are you talking to?" Reece asked.

"My aunt Margaret."

"Who's this O'Grady you're talking about?"

"He's—" Elizabeth removed her hand from the telephone. "Oh, Aunt Margaret, you shouldn't have done that. You're wrong. There is no one here with me. I'm not in any danger."

Reece grabbed the telephone out of Elizabeth's hand, slamming it down onto its cradle. She glared at him.

"Just what do you think you're doing?"

"What made her think you weren't alone?" Reece grabbed Elizabeth by the shoulders. "What did you tell her?"

"I didn't tell her anything." Elizabeth struggled to free herself from Reece's biting fingers.

He tightened his hold. She cried out in pain. Releasing her shoulders, Reece grasped her around the waist, jerking her into his arms. "If you didn't tell her about me, then how does she know you're not alone? Why does she think you're in danger?"

"Dammit, Reece, you're the most distrusting man I've ever known." When he pulled her closer, his face only a breath away from hers, she squirmed in his arms. "Let me go."

"I have reason not to trust people, believe me." He pulled her so tightly against him she could barely breathe.

She looked up into his eyes, those searing amber eyes so like MacDatho's. He was as much a lone wolf, as much a wild animal as Mac. But with her, Mac was a gentle beast, confident and secure in her love. Reece didn't trust her enough to be tamed. A man as hard and tortured as Reece would have to trust a woman completely, would have to love her with his very soul before he would give her the power to tame him.

"Aunt Margaret has psychic abilities. That's the reason I'm here in Sequana Falls. My mother and stepfather brought me here so that she could be my guide, my teacher."

"Are you telling me that your whole family is a bunch of gypsy fortune-tellers?"

"Believe what you will. I'm telling you that Aunt Margaret sensed I wasn't alone, that there was danger lurking about." Elizabeth wasn't sure she could make Reece understand; in the three days he'd been with her, she hadn't been able to convince him of her psychic abilities. There was no point in explaining that she had felt Aunt Margaret's worry and concern, and had plugged in the telephone so her aunt could get in touch with her without the elderly woman delving into Elizabeth's mind and discovering Reece's presence.

"What's your aunt done to upset you?" Reece asked.

"She's sending O'Grady up here just as soon as the roads clear a bit."

"O'Grady?"

"He's Aunt Margaret's gentleman friend. He works for me. Helps me around the greenhouses. He drives my nursery van and makes deliveries into Dover's Mill and surrounding towns."

"When will the roads be clear enough for him to get up the mountain?"

Elizabeth hesitated momentarily, then told Reece the truth. "By morning if he drove the van. The weather's changing pretty quickly. A warm front is headed our way. O'Grady won't try to come in the van. He'll either borrow his grandson's Explorer or he'll get the boy to drive him up here today."

"If O'Grady can make it up the mountain today, then the sheriff's deputies can make it up here." Reece shoved Elizabeth away from him. She staggered slightly, then regained her balance.

"Now that the storm is over, they'll start checking Dover's Mill and the area around Hunter's Lake again. They're setting up roadblocks at all the major intersections and will be going to all the towns close to Dover's Mill, doing door-to-door checks. O'Grady will come up the mountain today because Aunt Margaret sent him. The local authorities won't start combing this side of the mountain until late tomorrow. They'll be looking for your frozen body."

"They think I'm dead?"

"They know that if you stayed in the mountains your chances for survival were slim. Once they've checked the few places you could have found shelter, they'll be convinced you froze to death."

"Are all these great revelations coming from shrewd female intuition or from your hocus-pocus abilities?"

"Would you believe me if I told you the truth?"

"Which is?" he asked.

"That I'm clairvoyant, precognitive and have limited telepathic powers."

Reece's gut tightened into a knot. Damn, but she talked a good game. She had him half-convinced she was a witch. After all, she had left her door unlocked for him, and she seemed to believe in him, in his innocence, with no proof whatsoever. She had nursed him back to health with astonishing speed and without the aid of modern medicine.

"Well, if you know all and see all, then you're aware that I'm planning on getting the hell off this mountain today. Before your aunt Margaret's boyfriend comes calling or before the deputies get within ten miles of this place."

"There's no need for you to leave yet." She knew he would be safe with her for another day. If only she could persuade him to stay until she'd had a chance to call Sam. In his business, Sam had contacts all over the world. It shouldn't be any big deal for him to run a check on Reece and get all the details about the murder, the trial and the possibility of other suspects.

"If you think you can persuade me to stay, then your soothsaying abilities just went haywire. No way am I hanging around here long enough to get caught. I'm not going to prison."

While they'd been talking, Reece had unconsciously backed himself against the wall. He balled his hands into fists, his whole body tightening into a rigid statue of fear and anger.

Elizabeth took slow, even steps, moving toward Reece with the unwavering certainty that she had to get through to him, she had to reach his mind, convince him that she wanted to help him, that he could trust her.

Reece glared at her. She came closer and closer. He wanted to warn her to stay away from him, but he didn't say a word. He simply watched as she stood in front of him, reached out and placed her warm hands on each side of his face. She shut her eyes.

Reece swallowed. A sensation of tender concern seeped into his mind. What the hell? She held his face, tracing his bones with her fingertips. He didn't know what she was trying to do, but he wanted her to stop.

When he wrenched his face out of her grasp, turning his head to the side, Elizabeth opened her eyes and smiled.

"I can't read your mind, Reece. You won't let me."

"Good for me!"

"But I can sense things. Just little things."

"Like what?"

"I can sense your loneliness. You're completely alone. Or at least, you think you are." Reece's inner turmoil stirred within Elizabeth, the great sense of bitterness almost overwhelming her. "You resent others. Your mother. Your father. Everyone who has touched your life in any meaningful way. You won't let anyone close to you for fear of being hurt."

"Shut up, dammit!" Reece turned his back on her and walked away, out into the hallway.

Elizabeth followed him, placing her hand on his back when he braced his open palms on the wall and leaned his forehead against the wooden surface.

He tensed at her touch, but she did not withdraw her hand. "You've been locked away for five months. All I could sense was a cage. But now I know it was a jail cell. The first time I saw you, I saw the shock and pain on your face. I saw the blood on your hands."

Reece whirled around, grabbing her by the shoulders, his eyes wild with the realization that Elizabeth knew things she couldn't possibly know.

"How the hell did you know I had blood on my hands? That was never in the newspapers, never on television or radio. How did you know?" He shook her soundly.

"Reece, stop it!"

He stared into her pure blue eyes, and the truth came to him as surely as if he'd been struck by a bolt of lightning and survived the ordeal. "I didn't kill him. I heard the gunshots. I ran into the library and found him. I tried to stop the bleeding, but it was too late. He died. Damn him, he died and his blood was all over my hands."

"It's all right, Reece. I believe you. I understand."

"How the hell could you understand? I'd hated him all my life, prayed for his death, but when the moment came, I didn't want him to die. I tried... I tried...."

Elizabeth felt the tears inside Reece, choking him, constricting his breathing, squeezing his heart. But his eyes remained dry, his face set in tense agony. She reached into his mind, but he shut her out. He wouldn't allow her entrance, refusing to accept her mental comfort.

Elizabeth slipped her arms around his waist. He was rock solid, his body rigid with control. "You're right, I don't understand. But I could, if you would tell me about him. About B. K. Stanton."

Reece felt her strong, supportive arms around him. Elizabeth Mallory was as sturdy and solid as the rock-and-log cabin in which she lived, as hardy and vigorous as the mountain she called home. He'd grown up mothered by a weak woman. Reliability and responsibility hadn't been Blanche's strong points. She'd been a fragile, needy woman who hadn't been able to take care of herself, let alone a child.

In his mind's eye he could see Blanche. Small, frail, her gray eyes looking to him for help, the only color in her pale face were the bruises left by Harry Gunn's big fists. Even though he'd been a scrawny kid, she'd expected him to help her. And God knew he'd tried. But in the end he hadn't been able to help her. All he'd gotten for his efforts were bruises and broken bones of his own.

He'd had no one to depend on, no one to defend him, and he'd learned not to care, to never expect anything from anyone. He'd lived his whole life alone, shielding himself from emotions, priding himself on the fact that he needed no one.

Elizabeth's embrace seemed to surround more than just his body. He felt cocooned in safety. Without thinking about what he was doing, without second-guessing his motives, without giving his doubts and uncertainties time to take control, Reece pulled Elizabeth into his arms, holding her against him, absorbing the power of her generous heart.

He'd been alone all his life, long before his mother had died. He had taught himself not to need anyone, not to depend on anyone. And here was this woman, this beautiful, unique woman offering him her comfort and her trust. Would he be a fool to accept what she offered, or would he be a fool to refuse?

Elizabeth tightened her hold around Reece, easing her hands up his back, stroking him, caressing his tight muscles. He lowered his hands from her waist to her hips, cupping her buttocks, dragging her into his arousal, telling her without words what she was doing to him.

She looked up at him with those trusting blue eyes, eyes that smiled at him, eyes that offered so much.

"You shouldn't look at a man like that. You're liable to give him ideas."

She opened her mouth on a sigh, her lips parting. Her face bloomed with color. Her fingers bit into his neck as she lifted her arms around his shoulders. "I want you to know that I care, that I can help you."

She could not, would not admit that she wanted him as a woman wants a man. The feeling was new to her, far too new for her to accept the desire and allow herself to act upon it. If making love with Reece was meant to be, and in her heart of hearts she believed that it was, then she and Reece would become lovers. But not now. Not yet. He wasn't offering anything except sex; she wanted nothing less than love. When he was prepared to make love to her, she would know. Her heart and her instincts would tell her.

Reece could not resist the temptation Elizabeth Mallory represented. She was comfort and safety and pleasure. He wanted all three. Lowering his head, he brushed his cheek against hers. She smelled like flowers—sweet, so very, very sweet.

"You smell good, sweet Lizzie. Like roses." He nuzzled her neck with his nose, breathing in that flower-garden scent.

"My perfume." She breathed deeply, succumbing to the heady intoxication of his touch. Turning her face upward, she offered him her lips. "I make my own perfume from roses."

Never having been a romantic man, Reece was stunned at his own thoughts. Her mouth looked like a rose, opening its pink petals just for him. And her eyes, half-closed now, were as deep and dark a blue as sparkling sapphires.

His lips touched hers, tentatively at first, and then as she responded, he took her mouth with total possession, savoring the feel of her body molded securely to his. She fit him; he fit her. Their bodies had been formed to entwine perfectly. Her full breasts pressed against his chest, her feminine softness centered on his male strength, her arms claiming him as surely as his did her, and their lips mating with the fierceness of lovers preparing to join in a more intimate fashion.

Reece ran his hand down her hip, lifting up her leg, pressing her to him. Elizabeth moaned into his mouth, clinging to him, squirming against him.

"If you want to help me, Lizzie, then be my woman. Now. For today." He kissed her again, taking both their breaths away.

She held on to him, but broke the kiss, laying her head on his chest. She heard and felt his wild heartbeat. "I can't have sex with you, Reece."

The instant tension in his body notified Elizabeth that he had understood only too well what she was telling him. He released her abruptly, turned and walked into the living room.

Elizabeth waited a few minutes, willing her raging senses to calm. It would have been so easy to give in to his needs and the needs of her own body. For the first time in her life she wanted to be with a man, to offer herself to him. But there was too much standing in the way, keeping them from the union of hearts and souls as well as of bodies.

She found him sitting on the sofa, bent over, his clasped hands resting between his knees. He didn't look up when she walked over and stood in front of him.

"Talk to me, Reece. Tell me about B. K. Stanton."

"You're damned and determined to hear the whole sordid story, aren't you?"

MacDatho, who'd been asleep in front of the fireplace, reared his head, focusing his amber gaze on Reece and Elizabeth. He stretched, then lowered his head, keeping his eyes open.

Elizabeth knelt in front of Reece, taking his hands into hers. "My knowledge of your life is limited. I really can't read your mind, and I can't help you if I don't know what we're dealing with."

"I don't see how you can help me, anyway, but if you want to hear my version of Reece Landry's life story, then I'll tell you. Once you've heard the truth, you may not be so eager to help me, after all."

Lifting Reece's right hand, Elizabeth sat on the sofa beside him, entwining their fingers, giving his hand a tight squeeze. "I want to know whatever you want to tell me."

Leaning back on the sofa, Reece closed his eyes. He didn't want to rehash all this old misery, but his gut instincts prompted him to share his past with Elizabeth.

"My mother, Blanche, was a beautiful woman. Blond and china-doll pretty. She worked at Stanton Industries years ago. A minimum-wage job. Anyway, to make a long story short, she had an affair with B. K. Stanton himself, who was a married man with children. When my mother discovered she was pregnant, good old B.K. offered to pay for her abortion."

Elizabeth sensed his anger. She tightened her hold on his hand. "But she didn't get an abortion."

"No, she decided to have me. I don't know why. All of us would have been better off if she'd just gotten rid of me."

"Don't say that, Reece. It isn't true."

Opening his eyes, he glanced at her and saw the tears caught in her thick, dark lashes. Sucking in a deep breath, he pulled his hand out of her grasp. "My mother didn't have anyone to take care of me, so she had to quit work. Stanton gave her a little money so he could keep on sleeping with her. But when his wife found out about Blanche and me, she made a lot of threats. I was six years old. That was the last time my father came around. Then about a year later my mother married Harry Gunn."

Silence hung in the room like a threatening black cloud promising a killer storm. Elizabeth shut her eyes, absorbing Reece's pain, a child's pain. In her mind she saw clearly a man's big, broad hand striking a little boy's face. The child fell to the floor, his amber eyes filled with hate.

As suddenly as the vision had appeared, it faded away. Elizabeth knew Reece had closed his mind to the memory. She tried to prize her thoughts back into his mind. She couldn't. He had, once again, safely shielded himself from his emotions.

"Your stepfather was abusive." She made the statement as unemotionally as she could, but she could not conceal the tears escaping from her eyes.

"Yeah, he was a real son of a bitch. Knocked me and Blanche around whenever the mood struck him." Reece placed his knotted fists atop his thighs.

"What a horrible life for the two of you."

"Blanche died when I was twelve, and things got worse. I was fifteen before I grew big enough to defend myself properly. The beatings stopped. I found trouble everywhere I looked, and I was always looking for trouble. I've had problems with the law since I was a kid."

No wonder Reece was such a hard man, such a loner. Elizabeth wanted to know more, wanted him to share all of his past with her. Her instincts told her that he had never told anyone else the things he was telling her.

"All those years, you knew B. K. Stanton was your father?" Elizabeth asked.

"Yeah, I knew the richest and most powerful man in town was my father. And I knew he didn't give a damn whether I lived or died." Reece closed his eyes, shook his head and groaned. "Damn, I wish I'd left that town—his town—before he decided to take an interest in me."

"When was that?"

"When I was sixteen he stopped me on the street one day. Just like that—" Reece snapped his fingers "—B.K. grabbed my arm and asked me if I was Blanche Landry's boy." Reece's stomach churned. A sour taste coated his tongue. Hot, bitter anger rose in his throat. "He offered me a part-time job. I had quit school, and he said if I'd go back to school he'd give me a job after school and full-time in the summer. We made a deal, my old man and me. Then when I graduated high school, I joined the marines, did my time and came out determined to make something of myself. My only mistake was going back to Newell."

"Why did you go back?"

"Damned if I know, unless..." Reece slammed his fist into the sofa arm.

MacDatho rose from the floor, watching Reece intently.

"I'm not going to hurt her, Mac," Reece told the wolf-dog. "You should know that by now."

"He knows." Elizabeth placed her hand on Reece's arm. "You went back to Newell because you had something to prove, didn't you?"

"I guess. I suppose I wanted B. K. Stanton to know I was going to college, that no matter what I'd come from, I was going to be somebody."

"You had a lot of mixed emotions about your father, didn't you?"

"I hated him. Plain and simple." Reece stood, stretching, exercising his muscles.

"Did you hate him enough to kill him?"

Reece turned sharply, glaring at Elizabeth. "I thought you believed me, believed that I didn't murder him?"

"I do believe you."

"Then why ask me if I hated him enough to kill him?" Reece walked to the windows, staring out at the sunshine spreading over the snow, glistening on the velvety white surface as if it were scattering crushed diamond particles everywhere it touched.

"What happened when you returned to Newell after the marines?" She should have known he'd been in the marines. Sam had been a marine. Reece Landry and Sam Dundee shared some common traits.

"I went to college, worked at Stanton Industries in my old job as a machine operator to help supplement Uncle Sam's financial aid. When I got my B.S. degree the old man offered me an office job. That's when I got to know the rest of the family."

"Your father's other children?"

"Yeah, my big brother, Kenny, the heir apparent, and my sister, Christina. Kenny and I hated each other on sight. I liked Christina, and she liked me. She's the one who hired a lawyer for me when I was arrested for the old man's murder."

Elizabeth longed to put her arms around Reece, to offer him the care and support he'd never known. But she knew he wouldn't accept her comfort right now.

"Your sister believed you were innocent?" Elizabeth asked.

"She wanted to believe I didn't kill our father, but she had her doubts. I could tell every time she looked at me, she was wondering if I'd done it."

"Why did the sheriff arrest you? What evidence did they have against you?"

He glanced at Elizabeth and suddenly realized how much he wanted her to believe him. "The gun was mine. I'd reported the .38 stolen a couple of days before somebody used it to kill the old man. They didn't find any fingerprints. Whoever used it had wiped the gun clean. And the usual paraffin test for powder residue was inconclusive because my hands had been covered with dried blood."

"Motive and weapon. You hated your father and the gun that killed him was yours."

"That's right, only there's more. B.K.'s wife, Alice, and the family lawyer found me leaning over my father's body with blood all over my hands and the gun at my side."

"Oh, Reece." She touched him then, unable to prevent herself. He tensed at her touch, but when she hugged up against him, he relaxed and slipped his arm around her waist.

"B.K. had called and asked me to come to his home. He said he had something important to tell me. When I arrived, the front door was standing wide open, so I walked in. I called out. B.K. told me to come on back to the study. Then I heard my father arguing with someone, but I couldn't make out the other voice. Couldn't even tell if it was male or female. B.K. was shouting, saying he could do whatever he damned well pleased, that nobody could tell him what he could and couldn't do.

"Before I reached the study I heard gunshots. I rushed inside and someone hit me from behind. They didn't knock me unconscious, but everything went black for a few minutes and I was pretty shaken up. I didn't see who had hit me. When my vision cleared, I staggered over to where B.K. lay on the floor. He was bleeding like a stuck hog. I knelt down, covering his stomach wound with my hands. He called my name. And then he died."

Elizabeth held Reece in her arms, trying to absorb some of his pain, longing for him to accept what she offered, knowing he had never shared as much of himself with another human being.

"Motive, weapon, opportunity." Elizabeth sighed. "They didn't believe you, of course, about the person who hit you over the head. And the authorities never looked for another suspect."

"Brother Kenny and his mother had their lawyer, Willard Moran, use all the influence the Stanton family had in Newell, and believe me, it was plenty. I spent five months in that damned little jail cell, feeling like a trapped animal, knowing I was doomed."

Elizabeth held him. He hugged her fiercely.

"During the trial my lawyer pointed out that if I'd shot B.K., I'd have hardly had time to wipe the gun clean before Alice and Willard found me. And there was no proof that I'd actually fired the gun. I was convicted on circumstantial evidence."

"The Stantons must be very powerful to possess that much control over the sheriff's department and the district attorney."

"The Stantons own Newell, and if the Stantons say I killed B.K., then the town has no choice but to agree."

"You were framed," Elizabeth said.

"You do believe me, don't you?"

"Yes, of course I do. Did you think I wouldn't?"

He buried his face in her shoulder, breathing her sweet rose scent, accepting her loving warmth as she held him.

Abruptly she pushed him away. The sense of loss overwhelmed him.

"O'Grady! My God, Reece, go upstairs and wait. O'Grady will be here in a few minutes."

"How the hell do you know..." Reece grinned. "I've got to get used to this sixth sense of yours."

"When O'Grady leaves, I want to talk to you about our calling Sam to help us," Elizabeth said.

"No way. This guy may be your stepuncle, your family and friend, but I don't know him from Adam."

"Sam will help us."

"I said no." Grabbing her by the shoulders, he gazed into her eyes. "Understand me, Lizzie. I don't want you calling Sam Dundee."

"You can trust him."

"I don't trust anybody, lady, you should know that by now."

"Even me, Reece?"

He hesitated momentarily. "I'm not sure, Elizabeth. I want to trust you, but—"

The sound of a horn alerted Elizabeth to the fact that O'Grady had arrived. "Go upstairs and stay there until I come and get you."

Reece followed her instructions, and Elizabeth opened the front door, stepping out into the frosty wind, waving at O'Grady as he exited the passenger side of his grandson's Ford Explorer. An eighteen-year-old Rod O'Grady waved at Elizabeth but made no move to leave the warmth of his vehicle. The deafening *boom boom boom* of the boy's stereo system threatened to bring the icicles down from the roof overhang.

Elizabeth gave O'Grady a big hug, then rushed him inside to the warmth of her cabin. "I told Aunt Margaret that there was no need for you to come all the way up here with the roads so bad."

Elizabeth motioned MacDatho out of the open doorway, then closed the front door.

"You know Margaret. She got one of her notions. Thought somebody was up here with you." O'Grady glanced around the hallway before venturing into the living room. "There's an escaped convict on the loose. I think hearing about the man sent Margaret's imagination into overdrive."

"Did you say there's an escaped convict around Dover's Mill?" Elizabeth asked.

"Reece Landry. Young fellow. Killed a guy down in Newell. Escaped after the sheriff's car took a bad spill off the road and into the side of a mountain near Deaton Crossing."

"Are you staying long enough for coffee?" Elizabeth nodded in the direction of the kitchen.

"No, child, I can't stay. Rod's itching to get back home. Got a date tonight, I guess. He's been cooped up during the storm."

"Are the authorities looking for this Landry man?"

"They used bloodhounds, but didn't have much luck. They figure the guy's probably frozen to death in the woods somewhere by now. The day he escaped they tracked him to the falls, but they didn't figure there was much point going on from there since the storm was getting worse. They saw where he'd fallen through the ice in the stream, but had no idea where he went once he got out of the water. Snow was falling so hard they couldn't see two feet in front of them, and the dogs seemed to be losing the scent."

"Do you suppose they'll be coming up this way soon?"

"Why are you asking me? I figure you already know the answer if you want to know."

Elizabeth smiled. "Humor me, O'Grady."

"Well, your aunt Margaret says they'll be at your door by tomorrow evening. And my guess is she's right. I heard they planned to search the woods for his body tomorrow, and they're already setting up roadblocks on all the major roads and doing a house-by-house search in Dover's Mill. If they don't find his body, they'll keep searching until they wind up in Sequana Falls." O'Grady removed his brown checkered wool cap with dangling earflaps. "Why are you so interested in what the sheriff's doing to find this Landry fellow?"

"Just curious." Elizabeth smiled.

O'Grady scratched his partially bald head, mussing the thin strands of white hair that stuck out around his ears. "I figure I can get back up here with the van in a few days and get deliveries back on schedule. Anything you need me to take down the mountain today? I can get Rod to help me load the back of his Explorer."

"No, there's nothing that urgent. Deliveries can wait a few more days."

"Any message you want to send Margaret?" O'Grady warmed his hands by the fireplace, then turned to face Elizabeth. "She sent you a message."

"Did she?"

"Yep. She said to tell you that you wasn't to leave Sequana Falls without letting her know."

Elizabeth stood deadly still, a chilling sense of foreboding rushing through her body. If Aunt Margaret had seen her leaving Sequana Falls, then there was every possibility that she would be going. She'd made no plans to leave the sanctuary of her home, and had no premonitions about her future travel plans.

"Tell Aunt Margaret that I'll call her if I decide to take a trip."

O'Grady gave Elizabeth a fatherly pat on the back. "Well, I'll report in to your aunt. You sure you're alone here?"

"I'm never alone with Mac around."

As he walked out of the living room, Elizabeth following him, O'Grady glanced at MacDatho, stretched out on the rug in front of the sofa. "Yeah, I guess he's a good guard dog. Don't figure nobody could get past Mac, could they? Not unless you gave him the okay."

Elizabeth opened the front door, waving goodbye to O'Grady as he crossed the porch, went down the steps and got into his grandson's Explorer. She watched until they disappeared down the road, then she turned and went back into the cabin.

Standing at the foot of the stairs, Elizabeth called Reece's name. When he answered, she told him that O'Grady was gone and it was safe for him to come down.

"I'm going to finish that shave I started earlier when I heard the phone ring," Reece told her. "I've still got a lot of beard left."

"I'll put on a fresh pot of coffee. Take your time."

Elizabeth hurried into the kitchen, ground some coffee beans and put them on to brew. Knowing what she had to do and that there was no time like the present, she went back into the living room, picked up the telephone and dialed Sam's Atlanta business number. As soon as she gave her name, she was put through directly to Sam.

Maybe Reece didn't trust Sam, but she did. Sam would never do anything to hurt her, and if she told him she believed Reece Landry was an innocent man, Sam would listen to her.

"Elizabeth, is everything all right?" Sam asked. "I've heard a bad winter storm hit the mountains. I tried to call, but your phone was out. I finally got in touch with Aunt Margaret."

"Did you also hear about an escaped convict named Reece Landry?"

"I'm afraid that bit of information hasn't been on the Atlanta news. What's this Landry guy got to do with your calling me?"

"Reece is here with me, at the cabin. He nearly died getting to me, but I took care of him and he's—"

"Dammit all, Elizabeth, are you telling me you're harboring a fugitive? Have you lost your mind? Has the man been holding you at gunpoint? Get off this phone now and call Howard Gilbert."

"I don't need to call the sheriff," Elizabeth huffed, shaking her head with disgust. Sam wasn't being as reasonable as she'd hoped he would be. "As a matter of fact, I'm trying to prevent the authorities from capturing Reece."

"Elizabeth, tell me what the hell's going on?"

"I've been trying to do that. If you'll just calm down and listen, I'll tell you what I want you to do." Elizabeth told Sam every detail of Reece's life that he'd shared with her up to the point where the sheriff's car had wrecked in the winter storm. "Reece never stood a chance, Sam. The sheriff's department never tried to find any other suspects."

"What makes you think this man is innocent?"

"My instincts."

"You've looked into his mind, is that it?"

"I've had visions about Reece for the past five months, but I didn't tell anyone. Not you or Aunt Margaret, although I think she suspected something." Elizabeth paused, taking a deep breath. "Reece has been in my heart and mind since the day his father was murdered. I know he's innocent, Sam. He needs your help."

"What do you want me to do?"

"Get as much information as you can about B. K. Stanton's death. We've got to prove who killed Reece's father, or he'll be put in prison for the rest of his life."

"Elizabeth, what are you not telling me?"

"I don't know what you mean."

"I asked if you knew Landry was innocent because you'd read his mind. You didn't answer me," Sam said.

"I can sense certain things about Reece, and pick up on some of his emotions, but . . . well, I can't read him the way I do most other people. He's able to form some sort of shield around his mind, around his emotions."

"Good God, Elizabeth, you're taking this guy on faith? You're risking your life without knowing for sure whether or not he's really innocent."

"He's innocent, Sam. I know he is. Please help us."

"I'll run a background check on Landry and I'll—"

"I thought I told you not to call Sam Dundee!" Reece stood in the doorway, his face flushed with anger, his amber eyes wild with fear.

"Reece, please try to understand...." Elizabeth gazed at Reece with compassion and a plea for understanding in her eyes.

"Elizabeth!" Sam shouted into the telephone. "Is that Landry? If it is, put him on the phone."

"Wait just a minute, Sam." Elizabeth held out the phone to Reece. "Sam wants to talk to you."

Reece stared at the phone as if it were a slithering snake ready to strike, then glared at Elizabeth. "I thought I could trust you, but the minute my back was turned you called Dundee."

Elizabeth shook the phone at Reece. "I didn't betray you. I'm trying to get Sam to help you prove your innocence. Sam has contacts everywhere. He owns a private security agency in Atlanta. His sources are unlimited."

Reece walked into the room slowly, glancing back and forth from Elizabeth to the phone in her hand. She shoved the phone at him.

"Talk to Sam," she said.

Reece took the phone. "Yeah?"

"Landry?"

"Yeah."

"I don't know exactly what's going on there," Sam said, "but I want to warn you that if you harm Elizabeth, you're as good as dead. Do I make myself clear?"

"Crystal clear."

"If Elizabeth believes you, then I'm willing to give you the benefit of the doubt. I'm checking you out, Landry, and if I find out you've been lying, I'll personally cut your heart out."

"And if you find out I've been telling the truth?"

"Then I'll do whatever Elizabeth wants me to do to help you. Now put Elizabeth back on the phone."

Reece handed her the phone. "He wants to talk to you again."

"Sam?"

"I'll call you tomorrow and let you know how much I've been able to find out. Until then, for God's sake, be careful."

Elizabeth breathed a sigh of relief. Sam was going to help them. "Thank you, Sam. You can't know how much this means to me."

"What I want to know is how much Reece Landry means to you."

"I'm not sure, but..." Elizabeth glanced at a scowling Reece. "Just call us tomorrow with whatever information you can find. Reece is going to have to leave soon, and he needs something to go on."

Returning the telephone to its cradle, she faced Reece. "Sam is going to help you."

"I think I should leave as soon as possible." Reece glared at her, the distrust glowing in his eyes. "I don't dare trust Dundee. For all I know he's calling the sheriff to turn me in right now."

Elizabeth grabbed Reece by the arm as he turned from her. "You don't have to leave. Sam isn't going to call the sheriff. He would never break a trust. He's an honorable man."

"I'll stay until morning," Reece said, all the while damning himself for a fool for taking a chance by trusting his beautiful witch. "On one condition."

"What condition?" Elizabeth asked.

"I want my gun back."

Elizabeth nodded agreement. "If I go get your gun and give it to you, you promise you'll stay until Sam calls tomorrow?"

"I'm probably a fool for agreeing, but I agree."

"I'll need to put on my coat. I hid your gun outside, between the compost bins." Elizabeth walked out of the living room, through the kitchen and onto the back porch. When she reached for her coat on the rack by the door, Reece grabbed her by the shoulders, twirling her around. She stared at him, uncertain what he intended to do.

"I would never hurt you. You know that, don't you? The gun is for my protection against the police."

Elizabeth swallowed the knot in her throat, but she couldn't slow the rapid beat of her heart. "I understand."

Reece traced the lines of her jawbone with his fingertips. "I don't want you to be afraid of me."

"I'm not afraid of you, Reece. I'm only afraid of what might happen to you."

Elizabeth pulled away from him, put on her coat and went out into the cold February afternoon alone. It was at that moment she made her decision. When Reece Landry left her mountain, she was going with him.

Chapter 5

"We're not going to discuss this anymore!" Reece stuffed cans of soup and sandwich spreads into the duffel bag Elizabeth had given him. "When I leave this mountain, I leave alone."

"But you don't know the back roads. If I'm with you, you're less likely to get caught. We could even get through the roadblocks with me driving. I could fill the back of the Jeep with flowers from the greenhouse and tell the police that I'm on a delivery run. You could hide under a blanket or something." Elizabeth handed Reece a loaf of bread and a carton of saltine crackers.

"You've seen too many movies. This isn't a game. This is for real. If you go with me, you could get yourself killed." Reece eyed the 9 mm lying on the kitchen table.

"And without my help, you could get yourself killed," she said.

Reece looked at Elizabeth, the woman who had saved his life only a few days ago, the woman who wanted to join him in his fugitive's journey. She wasn't small and fragile. She wasn't a whining, helpless female. Mother Nature had put Elizabeth Mallory together like a work of art—round, full-bodied, solid. She possessed an inner strength as well, a strength that attracted Reece as much as her physical beauty. Braless and with her hair tumbling freely down her back to her waist, Elizabeth presented a picture of earthy sensuality.

Elizabeth was the type of woman who could plow a field, cook three meals a day from scratch, shoot and skin her own game, give birth to a baby and be ready to fight off an Indian attack the next morning. Pioneer stock.

"Why are you looking at me like that?" she asked.

"I was just picturing you fighting off an Indian attack," Reece said.

"What?"

"Just thinking about how much you're probably like your ancestors who settled these mountains." Reece stuffed the stack of clean clothes Elizabeth had given him into the duffel bag. More of Sam Dundee's clothes.

"For your information, my ancestors didn't fight off the Indians. My Scots-Irish ancestors married Indians, they didn't kill them." Elizabeth laid her hand atop Reece's where he gripped the handle of the duffel bag. "If you let me go with you, I can get you to Newell safely, and . . . and I can help you find your father's murderer."

Reece looked her directly in the eye. "What do you intend to do, go through the whole town reading everyone's mind?" Reece pulled away from her, dropping the duffel bag to the floor.

"I could meet the people who knew your father. Possible suspects. Members of his family."

Picking up the gun, Reece slid it into the pocket of the leather jacket Elizabeth had given him. "I need to check the Jeep." He walked toward the door leading to the back porch. "You said it has a full tank of gas. That means I shouldn't have to stop on the way."

"Reece, please don't leave until after Sam calls." Elizabeth followed him to the back porch.

"I won't, if he calls in the next hour." Reece opened the door. A puff of cold air hit him in the face. Turning, he smiled at Elizabeth. "How will you explain about your Jeep being gone?"

"I'll think of something."

Elizabeth stood on the screened-in back porch, watching Reece until he rounded the side of the house. He would never agree to her going with him. She had to think of an alternative plan. Without her, Reece didn't have a prayer of finding B. K. Stanton's killer.

Reece could never understand the type of sacrifice she was willing to make for him, and it was probably best that he didn't know. Leaving the sanctuary of her home in the mountains meant having to face the world, to be bombarded with people's thoughts and feelings, to see into the futures of strangers. She had spent her entire life trying to control her abilities, and to some degree she had achieved that goal—but only to a degree. Often she had no control whatsoever over the visions, over the intense emotions coming from others, over the premonitions that sometimes only a look or a touch from someone triggered within her mind.

Her special talents were as much a curse as a blessing. Thank God her family had brought her to Aunt Margaret instead of trusting her future to scientists who would have used her as a guinea pig, or to charlatans who would have used her in money-making schemes.

She had chosen her solitary life here in her ancestors' Georgia mountains. Surrounded by nature, shielded from the thoughts and emotions of a town filled with people, Elizabeth found peace and purpose. Nothing and no one had ever tempted her to venture far from Sequana Falls since her college years, except one necessary visit to Sam six years ago to bring him home from Atlanta—a trip she wasn't eager to repeat.

And now she was preparing to go back out into the world, to follow a man she barely knew, to expose herself to the trauma of mixing and mingling with people. How could Reece Landry have come to mean so much to her in such a short period of time? But five months wasn't a short period of time, was it? For some people it was a lifetime. She had known Reece in her heart far longer than the few days he'd spent at her cabin.

A higher power had sent Reece to her. She knew that fact as surely as she knew Reece Landry was her destiny, and she

his. No one had ever needed her the way Reece did. Not only
did he need her to help him prove his innocence, he needed
the warmth and caring she could give him to vanquish the
loneliness he had endured his whole life.

Just as Elizabeth heard the telephone ring, she saw Reece
coming around the house, heading for the back porch.

"That's Sam calling," she told Reece, then ran inside,
racing toward the living room. Breathless and nervous, she
picked up the telephone. "Sam?"

"You sound funny. Is something wrong?" Sam asked.

"I was on the back porch. I ran." Elizabeth took several
deep, soothing breaths. "What did you find out?"

"You've gone and gotten yourself involved with a real
bad boy. Reece Landry's been in trouble since he was a kid."

"I know that. Reece told me all about his childhood run-
ins with the law. So what else did you find out?"

"Look, kiddo, there's a possibility that Landry murdered B. K. Stanton. A lot of people who know him agree
that he has a real killer instinct."

Elizabeth sighed. How could she persuade Sam that he
was wrong? "Reece may have a killer instinct, but he doesn't
possess the soul of a killer. You, of all people, should understand the difference."

Sam didn't respond. Elizabeth felt the hesitation, knew he
was having difficulty accepting a truth he could not deny.
Finally he said, "Point well taken."

Elizabeth sensed Reece's presence behind her before she
turned to face him. She mouthed the words "It's Sam."
Reece nodded.

"There are other suspects, aren't there?" Elizabeth asked.
"You must have found out something."

"Hey, I've had less than twenty-four hours to dig up information," Sam said.

"So tell me what you've found out."

"There's a chance Landry is innocent."

Smiling, Elizabeth glanced at Reece, the trust and confi-
dence she felt showing plainly in her expression. "Go on.
Tell me more."

"The whole thing was too neat, too pat to suit me. Landry's gun, no fingerprints on the gun, some of the tests were

inconclusive, eyewitnesses who caught him at the scene, a motive of hatred and revenge and the strange coincidence that Landry had been invited to Stanton's home that night, for the first time in his life." Sam paused for a moment. "I'd say the man was framed."

"Who could have framed him?"

"Now, that's the sixty-four-thousand-dollar question. But I'd say other members of Stanton's family are prime suspects. Especially the son, Kenny. Seems he and his father didn't get along, and Kenny hates Landry."

"Sam, Reece is going to need your help. He's planning on leaving today to go back to Newell. I want to go with him, but—"

"Dammit, Elizabeth, you aren't putting your life at risk by going with that man! Do you hear me?"

"The elephants in India can hear you."

Reece grabbed the phone out of Elizabeth's hand. "Dundee, you don't have to worry. I'm not taking her with me."

"Damn right you're not!"

"I'm borrowing Elizabeth's Jeep, but I'll make sure she gets it back, somehow. I don't want her involved in this any more than she already is. If you've found out anything that can help me, I'd appreciate you telling me now."

"From what little I've found out, I'd say there's a good chance you were framed. A smart man would turn himself in to the law before they shoot first and ask questions later. Your lawyer can appeal the case."

"What good would an appeal do if we don't have another suspect?" Reece asked.

"What chance do you have of discovering anything while you're on the run?"

"I'm not turning myself in," Reece said.

"Then you're a damned fool!"

"Would you turn yourself in if you were me?"

Sam grunted. "No."

Reece handed the phone to Elizabeth. "Sam, I'll call you back. Reece will be leaving soon, and I...we'll talk later and I'll explain things."

Hanging up the phone, Elizabeth turned to Reece. He stared at her, hoping she wouldn't ask again to go with him. As bad as he hated leaving her, he hated even more the possibility of anything happening to her because of him.

She stood there looking at him, those big blue eyes of hers pleading. She'd left her coffee brown hair loose today instead of French braiding it, and its dark, silky mass hung to her waist. She wore a pair of old, faded jeans that fit her round hips and legs like a second skin. Her nipples pressed against the ribbing of her beige sweater. Her golden skin glowed with youthful vibrancy and good health.

The temptation to scoop her up in his arms and carry her away with him became unbearable. He broke eye contact with her, wondering if she was messing with his mind, sending him subliminal messages of persuasion.

Reece took several tentative steps toward Elizabeth; she moved forward, reaching out for him. MacDatho inched his big body between them, accomplishing his obvious objective of separating them.

Elizabeth reached down, petting MacDatho's head, soothing him with her touch. She relayed a mental message to him that she needed a private goodbye with Reece. Mac nuzzled Elizabeth's leg, then removed himself from between Reece and her. Seating himself by the door, the wolf-dog waited patiently for Reece's departure.

Reece drew Elizabeth into his arms. She clung to him, running her hands up and down his back. "Don't go yet. Stay."

"I can't." He kissed her forehead. "If I stay here any longer, I not only jeopardize my own life, but yours, too. You've done more to help me than I could have ever asked of anyone."

Elizabeth wrapped her arms around his waist. "Since you won't allow me to go with you, to lead you off the mountain and safely back to Newell, I'll draw you a map of the back roads. The police won't have any idea that you'll know about the back roads."

Reece held Elizabeth away from him. "Draw me the map, but do it quickly."

She dashed over to the desk beneath the windows, fumbled inside the middle drawer and pulled out paper and pencil.

"If the deputies find any evidence that I've been here with you, tell them I held you at gunpoint. Tell them I threatened your life."

She held up the completed map, tears forming in the corners of her eyes. "Don't worry about me. I won't have to talk to any deputies. Besides, they'd never believe you held me at gunpoint for four days. Not in the shape you were in, and not with MacDatho around."

Reece took the map out of her hand, shoved it into his jacket pocket, then grabbed her by the waist, drawing her up against him. "Take care, huh, Lizzie. And don't shed any tears over me." He wiped the tears from her eyes with the tip of his finger. "I'm not worth crying over. I'm not worth anybody caring about me."

"You're wrong about that." She kissed his chin. "You are worth somebody caring." She kissed his jaw and then his cheek. "You deserve someone's tears." She kissed him lightly on the mouth. "You deserve to be loved, Reece Landry."

"Damn you, Lizzie. Don't do this to me!" His kiss consumed her with his brutal need, with his savage passion. All the loneliness, the pain, the anger that had been building inside him since the day he'd been born verged into one obsession. To have Elizabeth Mallory be that somebody. The somebody who'd care. The somebody who'd cry for him. The somebody who'd love him.

Feeling his desperation, Elizabeth tried to give him what he needed, to respond with an open heart. As her tears clouded her vision, she clung to him, whispering his name over and over again as he buried his face against her neck, his nose nuzzling her hair.

Mustering all the control he possessed, Reece released Elizabeth and stepped away from her. "Say a prayer for me, Lizzie."

More afraid than she'd ever been in her life, she stood motionless. She watched Reece walk to the door, pat Mac-

Datho on the head and pick up the large duffel bag from the floor before opening the front door.

When he walked out onto the porch, Elizabeth forced her legs to move. She lingered in the doorway while he got into the Jeep and drove down the road, away from Sequana Falls.

MacDatho waited patiently at her side, finally circling her as a signal that he thought it was time for them to go inside. Elizabeth glanced down at Mac, nodding in agreement, suddenly feeling the frigid air seeping through her clothing.

Twirling around, she ran inside, MacDatho at her heels. She knew what she had to do. If she hurried, Reece wouldn't have more than an hour or so head start. And it didn't really matter because she knew what roads he would be taking off the mountain, past Dover's Mill and all the way into Newell.

She was not going to let Reece face this ordeal alone. She was going to be at his side, offering him all the support she could give him. And Sam, even if he didn't know it yet, was going to help them uncover the real murderer.

Within twenty minutes she had packed her suitcase, doused all the fires in the fireplaces, checked both greenhouses, sacked a grocery bag filled with MacDatho's food and pulled Sam's antique car out of the barn they used as a garage and parked it in front of the cabin.

She dialed Aunt Margaret's number, mentally preparing herself to lie about her plans. "Aunt Margaret, I wanted to let you know that I've decided to go to Atlanta and spend some time with Sam."

"Is that so?"

"It's been a couple of years since I've been any farther than Dover's Mill, and I think now's the time to test the waters, so to speak, to see if I still have the same problems dealing with the enormous influx of thoughts and emotions I usually get from being around huge crowds of people." This is only a half lie, Elizabeth told herself. Maybe her aunt wouldn't see past the pretense.

"I suppose you'll be bringing that wolf of yours by here for me to take care of."

"I thought O'Grady could take care of him. Mac and O'Grady are old friends."

"Bring Mac by here on your way out of town and I'll see that O'Grady picks him up. And leave whatever instructions O'Grady will need to keep things running smoothly in the greenhouses until you return."

Elizabeth sighed. "Thanks, Aunt Margaret. I'm not sure how long I'll be gone."

"I suppose you'll be gone until you're either arrested for aiding and abetting a criminal or until you've helped the man prove himself innocent."

Why had she ever thought she could get away with lying to Aunt Margaret? The woman's psychic abilities were as keen as they'd ever been. No one kept secrets from Margaret McPhearson.

"He is innocent," Elizabeth said. "And he's out there all alone, with no one on his side."

"Be careful, Elizabeth. I feel great danger for you and for your man."

"Pray for us, Aunt Margaret. Please pray for us."

"I've been doing that since the night he came to you," Margaret told her niece.

"I love you."

"I love you, too, child."

After hanging up the phone, Elizabeth swallowed, wiped her eyes and said a brief prayer of her own. Aunt Margaret had understood. She wasn't so sure about Sam Dundee.

She dialed the Atlanta number and waited to be put through to Sam. Somehow she had to make him understand why she was going to follow Reece, and why it was imperative that he meet them in Newell.

"Elizabeth?" Sam's deep voice was brisk and a bit harsh. "Has Landry left?"

"He left almost thirty minutes ago. I let him take my Jeep."

"Thank God he's gone. You've done some crazy things in your life, but this has to be the craziest."

"Sam, I want you to listen to everything I have to say before you start screaming at me. Promise?" Elizabeth hated it when Sam made her feel like a naughty child. She sup-

posed that came from his having had the responsibility of
her guardianship for so many years. He couldn't stop acting like a big-brother protector.

"I don't like it already. What are you up to?"

"I'm going to follow Reece to Newell, and I'm going to
have to—"

"The hell you are! Now listen to me, young lady, you are
not to leave Sequana Falls. Do you hear me? I don't care
what all your special powers tell you about Reece Landry.
The man is an escaped murderer, and whether he's guilty or
innocent, the police aren't going to take that into consideration if he tries to resist arrest when they catch up with
him."

"I want you to meet me in Newell. Tomorrow. I'll call
you in the morning and tell you where to meet us."

"Elizabeth, don't do this!"

"My mind is made up. I've already packed my bags, told
Aunt Margaret and made plans for Mac to stay with
O'Grady."

"If Landry took your Jeep, how do you plan on following him? You aren't taking that old delivery van you let
O'Grady keep, are you?"

"O'Grady will need the van for deliveries and to make
trips up the mountain to keep check on the greenhouses
while I'm gone." Elizabeth sucked in a deep breath, calling
forth all her courage to tell Sam about her chosen mode of
transportation. "I'm taking your old Thunderbird."

"You're what?" Sam bellowed.

"You can pick it up tomorrow when you fly into Newell.
I promise I'll take good care of your baby."

"You are not going to take my '65 T-Bird down the
mountain in weather like this. The roads will still be icy in
spots. You could wreck the car and kill yourself."

"I'll call you in the morning and let you know where to
meet Reece and me. In the meantime, do whatever you can
from Atlanta to get the ball rolling. We're going to discover
who really killed B. K. Stanton, and we've got to do it as
quickly as possible. Reece can't stay on the run forever."

"Elizabeth, listen to me. Don't do this. It's crazy. You're
asking for trouble. You're—"

Elizabeth laid down the phone, cutting Sam off mid-tirade. He'd rant and rave for a while, but he'd eventually calm down, and when she called him in the morning to tell him where he could meet Reece and her, he would come prepared to help them.

"Come on, Mac. You're going to visit Aunt Margaret and O'Grady. And I want you to be a good boy for them."

Reece had followed Elizabeth's map and directions down to the last detail. He couldn't remember a time when he'd put so much trust in another human being, enough trust so that he literally put his life in her hands. She hadn't been kidding when she'd said she knew all the back roads off the mountain and through the surrounding towns. He hadn't run into one roadblock or seen anyone who even vaguely resembled a policeman, highway patrolman or sheriff's deputy. He'd pulled off the road halfway between Dover's Mill and Newell to relieve himself and enjoy one of the ham sandwiches Elizabeth had packed for him, along with coffee from a thermos she had prepared.

The sun eased lower and lower on the western horizon. Reece guessed the time was around three or three-thirty in the afternoon. With clouds building steadily in the sky, blocking part of the sun's last rays, night was sure to fall early today. He was less than fifteen miles from Newell. He couldn't risk going into town, taking a chance that someone might recognize him.

He knew where he'd spend the night. Flossie, the madam who'd once run the local brothel and had been his mother's friend, now owned a sleazy motel on the outskirts of Newell. Nobody would recognize the Jeep, and the type of clientele Flossie got at Sweet Rest Motel wasn't likely to call the police if they did recognize him. He'd be safe at Flossie's motel tonight, and he could make a few phone calls in the morning before he left. He needed to talk to his lawyer. Elkins was bound to be wondering where the hell he was, but he wouldn't risk telling Gary his exact location. Not yet. As much as he wanted to trust the man, he wasn't one hundred percent sure his lawyer wouldn't turn him in to the authorities.

He needed to call Chris. He didn't trust her entirely, either, but she was his half sister and she did profess to care about him and believe in him. She'd paid for his attorney, and would have posted bail if the judge had been willing to set bail.

And he would call Elizabeth. He'd call her tonight to let her know he'd made it home to Newell without a hitch. She'd be worried about him. It felt odd knowing someone actually cared about his well-being.

Maybe he'd give her another quick call in the morning before he went out to B.K.'s hunting lodge. It would be nice to hear the sound of her voice one last time.

Brushing aside the cotton-candy thoughts, Reece concentrated on the drive ahead. He turned off onto a dirt road that led through the woods and some unused farmland. It was the long way around to Sweet Rest Motel, but it was the safest. He'd be unlikely to run into any other vehicles.

He pulled the Jeep to a halt in front of the door marked Office in the parking area of the motel. The buildings were old, built of concrete blocks recently painted a rather nauseous shade of pink, the doors to each unit bright turquoise. Flossie didn't seem to be doing much business. Only one truck and one older model station wagon were parked in front.

Reece reached into his pocket for the money Elizabeth had given him. Two hundred dollars. It was all she'd had in cash, and she'd insisted he take it.

The woman behind the register wasn't Flossie but some young girl with huge breasts and frizzy, bleached-blond hair. He'd never seen her before, and he knew just about everybody in Newell. Hopefully she was a newcomer who wouldn't recognize a face that had been in all the newspapers and on TV.

"You need a room, handsome?" she asked.

"Yeah. Just for tonight. How much?"

"Thirty-five bucks. Local phone calls are free. And there's a TV in your room, with a pay-for-view box. Checkout time is eleven." She handed him a key. "You're in number nineteen."

Reece laid thirty-five dollars on the counter, then turned to leave.

"Hey, mister, you forgot to sign the register."

"You sign for me, honey."

"What's your name?" she asked, smiling.

"Whatever you want it to be." Reece opened the door.

"If you get lonesome later on, *Mr. Jones,* stop back by. I get off duty at nine. I could show you a real good time." She looked him over from head to toe, stopping to gawk at the way his jeans fit across his crotch.

"I'll keep it in mind." Reece went outside, looked around for number nineteen, then got into the Jeep. He parked in the slot in front of his room, got out, grabbed the duffel bag and locked the Jeep.

Unlocking the door to number nineteen, he flipped on the light switch. Two purple ceramic lamps, one on the night-stand, the other on the right side of the dresser, came on, casting a lavender glow over the mismatched furnishings.

Reece found the room to be pretty much what he'd expected. A double bed with an orange-and-purple flowered spread dominated the small space. A single chair rested under the window, which boasted curtains that matched the spread. Atop the left side of the dresser, an oak-veneer box that didn't match the bed's maple headboard or the metal rounds on the chair, sat the TV.

Reece dropped the duffel bag on the floor, removed the leather jacket he wore, tossing it on the chair, then fell across the bed sideways. The mattress sagged. The box springs moaned under Reece's weight. Within minutes he'd fallen asleep.

The ringing telephone wakened him. For a couple of seconds he wasn't quite sure where he was, then a quick look at the motel room reminded him all too vividly that he was back in Newell, already hiding out. Who the hell would be calling? No one knew where he was. He grabbed the receiver.

"Yeah?"

"Hi, there, Mr. Jones. This is Luanne, in the office. I thought I'd call and remind you that I get off work in about an hour."

Sitting up in the bed, Reece combed through his hair with his fingers. The image of huge breasts and red lips flashed through his mind. He needed a woman, but he didn't need one badly enough to risk having sex with someone who'd have no qualms about turning him over to the law in the morning. Besides, his taste in women had far surpassed Luanne's type years ago.

"Look, honey, I appreciate the offer, but—"

"I could run over to the State Store, get us a fifth and we could watch one of those sex movies on the TV."

"Luanne, I'm bushed. I'm afraid I wouldn't be much fun tonight. Some other time, okay?"

"Sure thing, Mr. Jones. You know where to find me. I work the evening shift here five nights a week."

Reece hung up the phone, crawled out of bed and went into the bathroom. What he needed more than anything else, even a woman, was a shower, a shave and a good night's sleep. Tomorrow his life as a fugitive would start all over again. For a few hours he could relax, here at the Sweet Rest Motel, under the guise of Mr. Jones. In the morning he'd head out for B. K. Stanton's hunting lodge. None of the family ever used the place during the winter months, after hunting season. And now that B.K. was dead, he doubted anyone would ever use the place again. Since Kenny hated hunting, he'd probably sell the place, with no objections from his mother or sister. As far as Reece knew, neither Alice nor Christina had ever set foot in the lodge.

Reece came out of the shower, dried off quickly, briskly rubbing his hair. He walked out of the bathroom, turned back the covers and sat on the bed. His stomach growled, reminding him that he hadn't eaten any supper. He didn't dare risk going out somewhere for food. Rummaging around in the duffel bag, he pulled out a pimento cheese sandwich and the thermos. The sandwich was soggy, the coffee lukewarm. Finishing both quickly, he lay down and closed his eyes.

He couldn't remember ever feeling so alone. Strange thing was that he'd spent most of his life as a loner, needing no one, wanting no one. Even the months he'd spent in jail before, during and after the trial, he'd never felt such intense loneliness. Anger. Frustration. Hatred. And even pain. But not overwhelming loneliness.

He knew damn well what was wrong with him. He'd spent a few days with a woman who had surrounded him with attention, a woman who'd cared for him when he was sick, who'd fed him and clothed him and shared her home with him. Elizabeth Mallory had pierced the barrier that protected him from loneliness. She'd made him want things he knew he could never have. She'd shown him life's goodness, when all he'd ever known was its evil.

He pictured her in his mind. That strong, sturdy body of soft, feminine curves. That mass of dark brown hair. Those pure blue eyes that looked inside him, as if they could see his very soul.

He heard her voice saying his name. *Reece. Reece. Where are you, Reece? I can't find you.*

His eyelids flew open; he sat upright in bed. What the hell was that all about? He'd felt her presence inside his head, felt her frustration at not being able to find him. Had he lost his mind? Elizabeth Mallory was over a hundred and fifty miles away, safe and secure in her mountain cabin.

Reece's hands trembled. Sweat beads dotted his upper lip. He found himself thinking about where he was, heard himself repeating the name Sweet Rest. Saw himself driving along the back road to arrive at Flossie's sleazy motel.

He flopped back down onto the bed. Dragging the lumpy pillow out from under his head, he turned on his side, beating the pillow with his fists.

He tossed and turned for what seemed like hours, but when he checked the electric alarm clock on the nightstand, he realized it was only nine-thirty.

He heard what sounded like a soft knock, but dismissed the noise as nothing more than another motel patron in the room next to his. The knock grew progressively louder until he realized that someone was knocking on his door. Damn, crazy woman! Luscious Luanne was no doubt standing outside with a fifth in a brown bag, her motor running and determined not to take no for an answer. He jerked a pair of clean jeans out of the duffel bag, slipped them on and zipped them. He glanced over at the 9 mm on the nightstand.

"I told you not tonight, honey," Reece said as he opened the door a fraction, keeping the safety chain latched. "Why don't you—"

Reece stared at the woman standing outside his motel door. She wasn't some cheap blond floozy carrying a fifth of whiskey. She was a blue-eyed brunette carrying an overnight bag.

"Elizabeth!"

"It's freezing out here. Let me in."

Removing the safety chain, he opened the door enough for Elizabeth to enter the room.

"What the hell are you doing here?" Reece asked, his voice a low growl.

"Well, hello, Elizabeth, so nice to see you. Glad you followed me over half the state of Georgia. Come in and make yourself at home."

"Don't get smart with me, Lizzie. What do you mean, you followed me?" Reece closed the door, locking it securely.

Elizabeth set her overnight case on the floor beside Reece's duffel bag. "I appreciate your letting me know where you were. I'd made myself crazy going all over Newell looking for my old Jeep. If you hadn't shown me how to get here, it could have taken me till morning to find you. I didn't dare ask anyone how to get to Sweet Rest Motel."

"I didn't let you know where I was. What the hell are you talking about?"

"You were thinking about me, weren't you?"

"You read my mind?"

"You let me read your mind, Reece. You opened up. You lowered your shield enough to let me in."

"I don't want you here. I told you that you couldn't come with me, didn't I?" Reece fumbled in the duffel bag, dragging out a pine green flannel shirt.

"Won't you sit down, Elizabeth?" she said in a mocking tone. "Why, thank you, Reece, I believe I will." She sat in the only chair, crossing her arms under her breasts.

Reece put on the shirt, leaving it unbuttoned, then grabbed Elizabeth by the shoulders, jerking her up out of the chair. His fingers bit into the plush material of her heavy wool coat.

"You're getting out of here, right now," Reece told her. "I don't want you here."

"Yes, you do. You want me and you need me." Elizabeth stared him directly in the eye, her look daring him to deny her statement.

"I can't let you stay with me! I'm running from the law, goddammit. If you stay with me, you could get killed."

"And if I leave you, you'll be all alone."

When she tried to touch his face, he released his hold on her and shoved her away from him. "I've been alone all my life. I like it that way. I don't want you around. You'll just get in the way. You'll be more trouble than you'll be worth."

"No matter what you say or do, I'm not going to leave you, Reece." Elizabeth tried again to touch him. He dodged her seeking hand.

"Get the hell out of my life, lady. Can't you get it through that screwy head of yours that I don't want you, I don't need you and I'm better off without you?" Reece saw her face pale, saw her jaw clench, noted the wounded look in her eyes. He couldn't allow himself to feel guilty about hurting her feelings. He had to think of Elizabeth, put her safety first, before his own needs. Every word he'd said to her had been a lie, but he'd lied to her for her own good.

Reece lifted her overnight case off the floor, handed it to Elizabeth and unlocked the motel door. "Go back to Sequana Falls where you belong. Forget you ever knew me."

Elizabeth accepted the overnight case. Reece opened the door. Cold night air swept into the room. Elizabeth quivered. Reece stood by the door, his gaze riveted to the floor.

Listening for her footsteps, he waited for her to walk past him. He waited and waited and waited. Then he heard the bathroom door close.

He slammed shut the outside door. "Elizabeth!"

Chapter 6

She ignored his constant beating on the door, dismissed his ranting words and made no effort to remove herself from the bathroom. Reece gave up, flipped on the television and sat at the foot of the bed. What the hell was he going to do with her?

He had never met anyone like Elizabeth Mallory. She was an enigma to him, a riddle without an answer. He'd left her in Sequana Falls, back where she was safe. He'd thought he'd never see her again. But here she was, in his motel room, locked in the bathroom and not listening to reason.

She was so damned sure she could help him, was determined to stay with him until they found B. K. Stanton's real murderer. Despite the fact that Elizabeth insisted that she possessed special psychic talents, Reece had his doubts. He was a man who didn't believe in anything if he couldn't see it, feel it, smell it, taste it or touch it; she expected him to believe that she could read minds, forecast the future and sense events occurring miles away.

One thing was for sure, she'd found him at this godawful motel on the seedy outskirts of Newell. But that feat hadn't necessarily taken any psychic powers. Maybe she'd simply gotten lucky. That's what he wanted to believe.

But he could not dismiss the nagging sense that Elizabeth had spoken to him from miles away, that she'd called out his name, that she had asked him where he was and told him she couldn't find him. Hell, when she'd showed up at his door he'd accused her of reading his mind. He didn't want to think she'd gotten inside him, that all this hocus-pocus stuff she'd been telling him was true, but dammit, he couldn't get the sound of her voice out of his head.

It didn't matter whether or not Elizabeth was psychic and might be able to use her powers to help him. He could not allow her to stay with him. He was a fugitive on the run, a convicted murderer. If she stayed with him, her life would be in danger. He wouldn't let her take the risk.

Besides, she'd just get in the way, he told himself. The woman didn't mean anything to him. He couldn't allow himself to care. He couldn't indulge in any weakness, and that's what caring about another person was—a weakness. His mother had loved B. K. Stanton. The man had been Blanche's weakness, and her mindless love for another woman's husband had destroyed her. No one, other than Blanche, had ever held a place in Reece's heart. He had never loved anyone, and he never would. That was a promise he'd made himself a long time ago, one he intended to keep.

Elizabeth took her time in the bathroom, dreading the thought of facing Reece again. He hadn't been happy to see her. No doubt he was out there now thinking of ways to make her leave. What he didn't know was that there was nothing he could say or do to make her go away. She had every intention of staying with him and helping him, whether he wanted her to or not.

She'd hung her heavy coat on the door rack, then stripped out of her jeans, sweater and shirt, peeling away the layers until she got down to her thermal underwear. She wasn't a femme fatale by any stretch of the imagination; her experience with men was quite limited. A more worldly wise woman would have come prepared with a slinky black negligee and a bottle of wine. She would have used her feminine wiles to seduce Reece, and thus bring him around to her way of thinking.

Elizabeth glanced down at her underwear. A splattering of tiny peach flowers gave the soft, beige cotton knit material a feminine appearance, but she certainly didn't look sexy covered from neck to ankles in her long johns. Well, it didn't matter how she looked because she had no intention of seducing Reece.

Regardless of what he said or did, she would not allow him to send her back to Sequana Falls. She had risked too much coming to him. No one knew he'd spent four days in her home, no one except Aunt Margaret and Sam, and they weren't going to tell anyone. If she hadn't followed Reece, she would have been safe—safe from the police if they caught him, and safe from the outpouring of emotions that always bombarded her whenever she went out into the world. Coming through Newell had been difficult, sensing random feelings, picking up fragments of thoughts, looking out the window at a middle-aged couple and knowing the woman would lose her husband in less than a year.

Come what may, whether he wanted her or not, she could not leave Reece. He needed her. Even though she couldn't see into his future any more clearly than she could reach into his mind, she knew she was meant to save him. Her own instincts told her that much. Aunt Margaret had sensed the same.

"You must save him, Elizabeth. No one else can," her aunt had told her when she'd left MacDatho in the old woman's care. "Only you can save him from himself."

Elizabeth washed her face, scrubbing away the light makeup she wore. Picking up her clothes, she eased open the bathroom door and glanced at Reece sitting on the edge of the bed. She couldn't hide in the bathroom all night; sooner or later she would have to face him. Now was as good a time as any.

A soft rapping on the outside door halted Elizabeth's first step out of the bathroom. Reece jerked around, his body tense, then he got up, walked to the window and pulled back the curtain. Elizabeth heard him laugh. He swung open the door.

"You're late," Reece said. "I expected you earlier."

Elizabeth didn't see the visitor until Reece moved out of the way, revealing a curvy blonde in a hot pink jumpsuit dotted with rhinestones, and with a white fake-fur jacket hanging around her shoulders. Holding up a brown paper bag, the woman pulled out a bottle of whiskey and offered it to Reece.

"Come on in out of the cold…er…uh…Luanne." Reece closed the door behind the woman, then accepted the liquor, slipping his arm around her waist and drawing her up against him.

"Now this is the kind of reception I was hoping for, Mr. Jones." Dropping her jacket on the floor, Luanne rubbed herself against Reece, her dark pink lips curving into a self-satisfied smile.

Elizabeth walked out of the bathroom, took several tentative steps across the carpeted floor and stopped to stare at Reece and the woman in his arms. Who was the woman and why had she come to Reece's motel room? Anger combined with jealousy, totally annihilating Elizabeth's sixth sense.

Elizabeth noticed that the blonde had caught a glimpse of her. Dropping her clothes on the floor, Elizabeth smiled and nodded her head. The woman Reece had called Luanne widened her eyes, staring at Elizabeth as if she thought she might be seeing an aberration.

"Look, honey, I'm interested in spending the night with you, but—" Luanne blinked several times when Elizabeth waved at her.

"And I'm interested in the same thing," Reece said. He knew that sooner or later Elizabeth was going to come out of the bathroom, and if she caught him in a compromising situation with another woman, she was bound to storm out of the motel and get her butt back to Sequana Falls and out of his life.

"Well, I'm not into these threesome deals, honey." Luanne kept staring at Elizabeth.

Without releasing his hold on Luanne, Reece pivoted just enough to catch sight of Elizabeth in his peripheral vision. "I wondered if you planned to stay in the bathroom all night. Come on out and meet a friend of mine. Lizzie, this is Luanne. Luanne, Lizzie.''

The two women sized each other up, each taking in every inch of the other's face and figure. Reece tried not to make comparisons, but the obvious stared him in the face. Elizabeth was a bigger, taller woman, with broader hips and shoulders. For all her bustiness, Luanne was small, with a fragile quality, whereas Elizabeth's body proclaimed her vitality and strength. Luanne wore heavy makeup, her hair was bleached almost white and her long fingernails were painted a bright pink to match her jumpsuit. Elizabeth's face was scrubbed clean and her long dark hair hung around her shoulders, hitting her at the waist. Her thermal underwear hugged her body, revealing every round, feminine curve. Her clear blue eyes glared at him, demanding an explanation.

Luanne was smoke; Elizabeth was the fire. Luanne was like a gaudy trinket that could be bought at the dollar store and discarded the moment it turned your skin green. Elizabeth was jewel-studded gold, priceless, and once possessed, the owner would rather die than ever part with it.

"Don't get in a huff, honey." Reece returned Luanne's endearment. "Lizzie showed up a while ago, uninvited."

Luanne grinned, first at Reece and then triumphantly at Elizabeth. "Is that right? Well, why don't you send her on her way? 'Cause I'm not staying if she does."

Reece set the whiskey bottle on the nightstand, then turned to Elizabeth and shrugged. "Well, Lizzie, you see how it is, don't you?"

Yes, by golly, she did see how it was. She saw clearly. Ms. Luanne Evans was a new acquaintance, not one of Reece's old friends. Luanne's mind was quite uncomplicated, and was wide open for anyone to pick up her rather raunchy thoughts. The woman certainly had plans for Reece. Elizabeth had no intention of allowing those plans to come to fruition. If any woman shared a bed with Reece Landry tonight, it was going to be Elizabeth Mallory.

Elizabeth sat on the bed. Reece frowned. Luanne pulled away from Reece, planting her hands on her slender hips.

"Look, Lizzie, maybe you're deaf or something, but the man said he wants me." Luanne glared at her rival.

Elizabeth scooted up in the bed until her back touched the headboard. Raising her arms behind her head, she stretched and yawned.

"Well, the only problem with that, Lu, is sometimes Mr. Jones says one thing when he means another."

Taking a few steps over to the bed, Reece reached down and grabbed Elizabeth by the arm. "I mean what I say, Lizzie. Get dressed, pick up your clothes and get the hell out of here. I've got plans for tonight."

Turning her nose up, Luanne smiled, then shook her head just enough to toss about her thick, teased hair.

Elizabeth slapped away Reece's hand. "I'm not leaving." She glanced over at a smug Luanne. "Besides, Luanne can't stay all night. When her boyfriend gets home from work around one in the morning, she'll have to be there or he'll come looking for her."

Luanne's mouth fell open. "How do you know when Joey gets home from work?"

"He's going to get home early tonight. From his job on the assembly line at Stanton Industries," Elizabeth said. "Around eleven-thirty. He's sick with a stomach virus."

"How do you know where Joey works and that he's going to get sick?" Luanne backed up against the wall, staring at Elizabeth with round, dark eyes. "What are you, some kind of fortune-teller?"

"I'm a witch. *Honey.*" Rising up on her knees, Elizabeth sat in the middle of the bed and pointed her finger directly at Luanne. "And if you stick around here, trying to put the make on my man, I'll cast a spell on you."

Luanne picked up her coat off the floor and hurriedly slipped into it. "I'm outta here. Just forget you ever knew me. Okay?" Glancing at the whiskey bottle, Luanne hesitated, then opened the door. "The drinks are on me." She rushed outside, slamming the door behind her.

Reece leaned over, bracing his hands on each side of Elizabeth where she sat on the bed. "You think you're cute, don't you?"

"I think I did what any sensible woman would have done under the circumstances." Tilting her head just a fraction, Elizabeth smiled at Reece. "I eliminated my competition."

"I had plans with Luanne. Plans that included getting rip-roaring drunk with her and—"

Elizabeth covered his lips with the tip of her index finger. "You didn't have any plans with that woman. You turned her down when she offered. She showed up here all on her own, just the way I did."

"How do you know?" Glaring at Elizabeth, Reece lowered his head until they were face-to-face, their breaths mingling. "You didn't read my mind!"

"No, I read hers. Minds like Luanne's are easy to read, but not very interesting."

"Damn you, Lizzie! I don't want you here with me. What do I have to do to make you understand?" He was too close to her. He needed to back off, to get away from her big blue eyes, her soft pink lips, her flowery scent, her womanly heat.

"Why are you so afraid of me?" Elizabeth slipped her arms up and around Reece's neck. "I would never hurt you. All I want to do is help you."

"I don't want your help." He prized her arms from around his neck and shoved her away from him.

Elizabeth fell back across the bed. She lay there staring up at Reece. "You don't want to need me, do you? You're afraid to want me, to need me, to care about me."

She wasn't reading his mind or picking up anything with her sixth sense, only with her feminine intuition. Reece was afraid of her, of the way she made him feel. And she had to admit the truth to herself—she was every bit as afraid of the way he made her feel. She couldn't remember a time in her life when she'd acted so irrationally, even when her actions were prompted by her psychic revelations. She had never felt so connected to another human being, never felt so essential to another's very existence. She had opened her home and her heart to a stranger, a man accused of murdering his own father, and she had followed that man halfway across the state of Georgia, determined to save him, not only from a wrongful conviction but from the pain and anger slowly destroying him.

"Don't send me away, Reece. Don't shut me out of your life."

Reece didn't want to think about what she'd said, about the truth of her words. Dammit, she was right. He was afraid of her, of the way she made him feel. That was the whole problem—Elizabeth Mallory made him feel more than anger and hatred, and Reece didn't want to feel anything else. He'd built his life on those two emotions. The thought of ever caring about another person scared the hell out of him.

For both their sakes, he had to get rid of Elizabeth. He had to make her see reason. Maybe the only way to do that was to show her what kind of man she was dealing with, what kind of man Reece Landry really was—a white trash bastard who didn't give a damn about anybody but himself.

"All right, honey, if you want to stay, stay." Grabbing her around the waist, Reece jerked her up off the bed, bringing her body tightly against his. "I had planned to enjoy Luanne's company all night, but you'll do just as well. After all, a woman's a woman."

Elizabeth stared at Reece, her blue eyes focused intently on his face as she tried to make sense of what he'd said. "Why would you say something so utterly ridiculous?"

Reece rubbed himself against her, his arousal hard against her softness. The feel of her, the scent of her, the warmth of her body created a heady seduction, prompting Reece's reaction to her nearness. He cupped her buttocks in his big hands, lifting her up and into the need pulsing between his legs.

Elizabeth squirmed, trying to free herself, but her movements ignited a strong reaction in Reece. Fondling her hip with one hand, he grasped the back of her neck, pulling her mouth to his, kissing her with bruising force. Moaning, Elizabeth opened her mouth for his invasion as she clung to his shoulders.

Reece devoured her lips. He pillaged her mouth with his tongue, all the while exploring her body with one hand as the other held her captive.

When he ended the kiss, Elizabeth laid her head on his chest, her arms draped around his neck. "Would . . . would it have felt like this with Luanne?"

Hell, no! Kissing had never made him feel the way he did right now. Women liked to be kissed, so Reece had learned the art of kissing quite young, but kissing had never meant more than part of the pleasant, necessary foreplay to entice a woman into bed. But after kissing Elizabeth, he was a minute away from exploding. If he hadn't ended the kiss, he would have taken her right where they stood. Hard and fast and hot.

"Like I said, a woman's a woman. Kissing is kissing." Reece grinned. "If you liked the feel of my tongue in your mouth, you'll love the way I'm going to feel inside you."

Elizabeth clutched Reece's shoulders. "I . . . I won't be used. If you think I'm willing to be just another woman in a long line of women, then you'd better think again."

"Nobody's forcing you to stay, Lizzie." Reece slid his hands into position under her breasts, lifting them. "All I'm saying is that I'm horny as hell. I need a woman, and if you stay, you're going to be that woman."

Elizabeth swallowed hard, wondering if Reece could possibly mean what he was saying. Swaying slightly, she closed her eyes, trying to focus, to concentrate on Reece's thoughts. Her mind ran into a solid wall of resistance.

"What's it going to be, honey?" Reece asked. "Are you going or staying?"

What was he trying to do? Scare her off? Make her dislike him? Despite the fact that she couldn't read his thoughts, Elizabeth felt certain that Reece would never do anything to harm her, and most certainly would never force her to have sex with him.

Pulling away, she turned her back to him and clasped her hands together. She couldn't allow Reece to run her off. She had to find the courage within herself to overcome whatever obstacles he put in her way.

"Go on home, Lizzie." Reece wanted to take the few steps that separated them and pull her back into his arms. He wanted to hold her and kiss her and find comfort in her embrace. He wanted to lay her down on the bed and make slow, sweet love to her all night. He wanted to wake in the morning and see her smiling at him, hear her saying his name.

Elizabeth turned to face him. "I won't allow your fear to keep me from helping you."

"Dammit, woman!" Anger. He knew and understood that emotion only too well. If he allowed the anger to consume him, to control his actions, he could drive her away. He couldn't let any other feelings influence him. Not now. Not when Elizabeth's life could depend on what happened between them tonight.

Without saying another word, Reece walked toward her. Elizabeth saw the anger and determination in his eyes, and for one split second she sensed something else in Reece—sorrow—and she held on to that fleeting emotion when he lifted her into his arms and tossed her down on the bed. She had no time to adjust her body or focus her mind before Reece came down on top of her, his big, hard body pressing her into the mattress. He gave his hands free rein to explore her body. He squeezed her breasts. He delved his hand between her tightly clenched legs, rubbing the side of his hand against her intimately. When she tried to roll away from him, he straddled her body, placing a knee on each side of her hips.

Elizabeth looked up at his hard face, into those lone-wolf amber eyes, and knew there was no way she could control this man, that she was completely at his mercy. "Don't do this, Reece. Stop trying to make me hate you."

Reece slipped his fingers beneath the edge of her thermal top, shoving it up over her stomach to the swell of her breasts. She grabbed his hands, momentarily stopping him, but he manacled her wrists in his grasp and lifted her hands over her head, flattening them on the pillow.

"I don't want you to hate me, honey. I want you to love me and love me and love me. All night long."

"No, Reece. Stop it. Now!"

He nuzzled her tummy with his nose, nudging the edge of her thermal top higher and higher until her round, full breasts were exposed. Elizabeth sucked in her breath, a surge of uncertainty and sensual longing combining within her.

She hated the way Reece was acting, but despite his deplorable behavior, her body ached with wanting, with the need for his touch.

"Great boobs, Lizzie. Just the way I like them. Big and firm." Leaning over her, he flicked one of her nipples with his tongue.

Groaning, she twisted and turned, struggling against his hold. "Don't, Reece. Please. Not like this."

Ignoring her pleas, he suckled her breast. She cried out from the pleasure of his touch and the pain in her heart. He released her trapped hands, ran his fingertips down her throat, over her breasts and into the waistband of her thermal bottoms. He eased the bottoms down enough to expose her navel and hips.

Reece forced himself to look at Elizabeth, to endure the hurt he knew he would see on her face. She stared at him, tears trapped in the corners of her eyes. The sight of those tears weakened him, but he forged ahead, sure he was right in what he was doing—saving Elizabeth from Reece Landry.

"You see how it is with me, Lizzie. I'm a sorry bastard who doesn't give a damn how you feel. I take what I want, and to hell with the consequences." He unzipped his jeans, lowered himself atop her and gave her a hard, forceful kiss. "I'm mean, honey. Mean enough to kill. I'm no good through and through."

Elizabeth tried to speak, tried to tell him that she didn't believe him, that somewhere buried beneath all that pain and anger and bitterness was a good man. A man who had been unloved and abused all his life, a man in desperate need of someone to care. But she couldn't form the words, couldn't get the sound past the knot of tears lodged in her throat. All she could do was cry.

Reece watched the tears well up in her eyes and spill over, streaming down her cheeks. Her chest rose and fell in quick, jerky undulations. Her mouth opened to release her gasping sobs.

He couldn't bear the sight of her tears. He knew she wasn't crying for herself, but for him. After the way he had treated her, she still cared. Damn her! He hadn't frightened her; he had hurt her. He hadn't run her off; he'd made her cry.

She lifted her hands up to him, touching the side of his face with her fingertips. Her touch burned him, like a cleansing fire cauterizing a wound. The pain surged through him. He fought the healing effects of her pure, loving concern. He couldn't care about this woman. He wouldn't!

Reece jumped off the bed, zipped up his jeans and reached for the bottle of whiskey on the nightstand. Opening the liquor, he tilted the bottle, placed it to his lips and took a choking swallow. He coughed several times.

"You're a fool to stay with me. Why the hell don't you leave while you still can?" He took another gulp of the whiskey, wincing from the impact as it seared a path down his throat.

Wiping away the tears she could not control, Elizabeth pulled up her thermal bottoms and jerked down the top, then got out of the bed. How could she ever make him understand that she couldn't leave him even if she wanted to? No one else could save him. Aunt Margaret knew and so did she. Even if someone else could prove his innocence and set him free, no one else could free him from the anger and hatred that had ruled his life. Only she could do that.

She laid her hand on his back. Every muscle in his body tensed.

Not turning around, Reece lashed out at her. "I could have raped you, Lizzie. Why the hell are you still here? Aren't you afraid to be in the same room with me?"

She wrapped her arms around his waist, holding him. His body remained rigid. "Don't you think I knew what you were trying to do?"

He covered her hands with his own where she held him tightly at the waist. "I was trying to get me some, honey, but you weren't cooperating." Prizing her hands from his body, he pulled away from her.

Elizabeth sighed. "You were trying to scare me away, trying to prove to me what a rotten, no-good skunk you are."

Reece turned around slowly. "You think you're so damned smart, don't you?"

"I'm not leaving, so you might as well cut the rest of this macho-idiot act!"

"You have got to be the most stubborn, bullheaded woman I've ever known!" Reece unzipped his jeans, pulled them off and tossed them on the floor.

Elizabeth stared at his naked body.

"If you want to stay, then stay." Reece lay down on the bed. "I've had a long, strenuous day and things are bound to be worse tomorrow. I'm going to get some sleep." He punched one of his pillows several times, bunched it into a wad and stuck it under his head. "You can do whatever the hell you want to do."

Reece turned out the nightstand lamp, pulled the covers up over himself and closed his eyes. Elizabeth stood in the middle of the motel room, her gaze riveted to Reece Landry. Why, of all the men on earth, had the good Lord in heaven sent her a man like this? A man who could shield his heart and his mind from her. A man who fought her efforts to help him every inch of the way. A man so scarred by his past that he was afraid to trust another human being.

Elizabeth turned back the covers and crawled into bed beside Reece, then pulled the covers up to her neck. Lying there quietly and unmoving, all she could think about was the way Reece looked naked. Big, tall, muscular. His arms, legs and chest covered with dark brown hair. He possessed an aura of strength and ruggedness, from his thick, overly long brown hair to his wide chest, to his impressive manhood.

Elizabeth shuddered at the thought of the way Reece had touched her, the memory of his lips at her breasts, his hands fondling her to the point of arousal. As the minutes passed, Elizabeth relaxed, her mind centered on the big, naked man lying beside her. She drifted off into sleep, succumbing to dreams of Reece Landry. His smile. His amber eyes. His naked, aroused body covering her.

Reece lay awake for hours, feigning sleep but unable to rest knowing that Elizabeth lay next to him. She'd fallen asleep quite some time ago. The sleep of the innocent. A clear conscience and a pure heart.

He'd done some damn fool things in his life, but his actions with Elizabeth tonight had to top the list. Had he actually been stupid enough to think she'd fall for his rapist act? He had spent four days alone with her in her cabin and had allowed her to get to know him, the real Reece Landry, the man he barely knew himself.

She hadn't bought the story of his rendezvous with Luanne and she hadn't believed him capable of brutalizing her. He had to face the facts. Elizabeth Mallory, for whatever misguided reasons, was determined to stand by his side, to march head-on into disaster, to go the limit to help him prove his innocence. What had he ever done to deserve the loyalty and trust of a woman like Elizabeth?

Did he dare believe what she believed? That they were predestined to meet? That she and she alone could save him?

Whether he believed or didn't wasn't the point. The point was that Elizabeth was in his life and in it to stay. Now, the question was, what the hell was he going to do with her?

Elizabeth snuggled against him, resting her head on his shoulder, cuddling her body into his. Swallowing, Reece opened his eyes and looked at her. She was asleep, and practically in his arms. Strange thing was that as many women as he'd bedded over the years, he'd never slept the whole night with one. Not ever.

A narrow ridge of illumination filtered through the window where the flowery drapes didn't quite meet, a combination of moonlight and fluorescent motel sign. Rising up on one elbow, Reece gazed down at Elizabeth. For a split second his heart stopped. She was so incredibly lovely, and he wanted her desperately.

Her dark hair looked like black silk in the shadowy room. Reece lifted a strand and brought it to his lips, then dropped it, watching it fall back to her shoulder. Her eyelashes were long and thick, her cheekbones high and only slightly rounded. And her lips—those full, luscious lips. The memory of how those lips had felt when he'd kissed her was enough to arouse him.

When she nestled more snugly against him, Reece slipped his arm under her, lifting her even closer to his side. Still asleep, she laid her arm across his chest, her fingers curling around his hair. He sucked in a deep breath.

He touched her cheek with his fingertip, tracing the lines of her face, slowly, lovingly. She moaned in her sleep, pressing her body into his. He leaned over and kissed her tenderly on the lips, then drew her securely into his arms.

Whatever tomorrow brought, Reece knew one thing for certain. He wasn't going to let anything or anyone hurt this woman. Not ever. And that included him.

Chapter 7

The jarring ring of the telephone woke Reece instantly. Instinctively reaching toward the nightstand, he grabbed the phone. Suddenly he realized that there was a woman in the bed with him, a woman lying there beside him, her head resting on his arm. Elizabeth! She opened her eyes and smiled at him.

"Answer the phone," she said.

Glancing from her sleep-fresh face to the phone in his hand, Reece growled at the caller. "Yeah?"

"It's Flossie, sugar."

"Flossie?" Reece sat upright in the bed.

"Look, you've got to hightail it out of there as fast as you can. Luanne just called me and said she remembered where she'd seen you—that Mr. Jones in number nineteen was that Landry fellow who killed old man Stanton."

"Dammit!" Reece jumped out of bed. "Can you trust her to keep her mouth shut?"

"Not hardly," Flossie said. "Not where there's money involved. Guess you didn't know that your half brother has put up a fifty-thousand-dollar reward for information leading to your capture."

"Hell!" Reece held his hand over the bottom half of the phone and turned to Elizabeth. "Get our stuff together. Quick. We're leaving."

"Look, sugar, I tried to persuade Luanne that she was wrong, but she said she planned on calling the sheriff just in case she was right. They're liable to show up here any minute now. I'll do whatever I can to stall them, but—"

"Thanks, Flossie. I owe you one," Reece said.

"You don't owe me nothing, sugar. I just wish you hadn't come back to Newell. They're all out to get you, and the Stantons won't rest until you're back behind bars."

"I won't let that happen."

"You got some place you can go?" Flossie asked.

"B.K.'s old hunting lodge."

"I wouldn't go there. The sheriff might not check it out, but you don't need to take any chances. Kenny's liable to remember you've been to the lodge. You need some place the law would never look."

"What about your old place on Lilac Road?" Reece asked.

"That place has been condemned for nearly a year," Flossie told him. "Besides, the sheriff is bound to check out any place you've ever been connected with."

Reece hadn't thought beyond his plan to hide out at B.K.'s cabin, but he realized that Flossie was right. Any place the law could connect him to would be suspect.

"I've got it! The Burtons' summer house up at the lake in Spruce Pine."

"Perfect," Flossie agreed. "Get going, boy, and good luck. If there's anything I can do to help you, just let me know."

"I've got a friend with me." Reece watched Elizabeth stuff their belongings into their bags. "If she ever needs anything, Flossie, I'd appreciate your looking out for her."

"Sure thing, sugar. What's her name?"

"Elizabeth." Reece hung up the phone, grabbed his jeans and shirt as Elizabeth threw them across the bed, and dressed hurriedly. By the time he was fully clothed, she was pulling on her boots.

Reece grabbed her by the shoulders. "Do you still feel the way you did last night? Are you still determined to stay with me and help me prove who killed my father?"

"You know I am."

"Okay, then, listen carefully. I'm going to take your Jeep and drive out to Spruce Pine. An acquaintance of mine took me to her parents' summer house up there once. No one ever uses the place in the winter." At least, he hoped no one would be using it while he and Elizabeth were there. Tracy Burton Stanton occasionally used her parents' summer cottage during the off-season as a hideaway to take her lovers. She'd taken him there once.

"I'll follow right behind you," Elizabeth said.

"The place is pretty isolated, so we should be safe there, at least for a few days." Reece knew Tracy would never tell a soul that her brother-in-law knew where her parents' summer house was located. After all, she'd have to explain why she'd taken him there. "Don't follow me right away. Just in case. Do you understand?"

Elizabeth nodded her head.

"After I leave, you drive around to the office and tell Flossie who you are. She'll give you directions to the Burtons' summer place. She's been up there a few times herself, entertaining old man Burton and his friends."

"Can you trust this Flossie?" Elizabeth wondered what sort of woman the former madam was, and why Reece was acting out of character by letting the woman know his whereabouts.

"A man would be a fool to trust Flossie with his money or his heart, but he can trust her not to turn him in to the law." Reece cradled Elizabeth's chin in the curve of his thumb and index finger. "We'll need some supplies. Stop at a store on the way and get whatever you think we'll need to last a few days. Once we're safely hidden away, we'll plan our strategy."

"I'll follow your instructions." Elizabeth threw her arms around him, hugging her fiercely. "I'll meet you as soon as I can."

Reece pulled out of her embrace. "I've got to go, Lizzie." He threw his bag over his shoulder, opened the door and walked outside.

"Please be careful." She stood in the doorway, watching him get into the Jeep and drive away.

Elizabeth closed the motel door behind her, walked out to Sam's vintage T-Bird and put her bag in the trunk. She glanced toward the office, near the main entrance to the motel. Four sheriff's vehicles screeched into the driveway. A man she assumed was the sheriff emerged from the first car and went inside the office. Elizabeth got into her car and drove around toward the office, parking and waiting until the sheriff came out and walked around to the car directly behind him. Elizabeth was too far away to hear what was being said, but she knew they were discussing Reece. She sensed the high tension, the raised level of adrenaline in the officers forming the search party.

She kept hearing the words *murderer, Landry, own father, dead or alive* tumbling around in her mind, and knew the officers were intent on capturing Reece at any cost.

The sheriff led the pack as they pulled up outside room nineteen, several men emerging from their vehicles, their guns pulled, as the sheriff lifted his bullhorn and called for Reece Landry to surrender.

Elizabeth's mouth felt dry, her hands damp. Her stomach twisted into knots. Hatred. The sheriff's deputies hated Reece Landry. They hated him not only because he had escaped but because they thought of him as a bad seed, a man capable of murdering his own father.

Clasping the key to number nineteen in her moist hand, Elizabeth marched into the office. The woman behind the desk glanced up at her.

"You checking out, sugar?" the six-foot redhead asked.

"Are you Flossie?" Elizabeth stared at the woman whose striking burgundy red hair had been draped into a French twist.

Flossie eyed Elizabeth, raising her black-lined, thinly tweezed eyebrows. "Yeah, sugar, I'm Flossie."

"Then, yes, I'm checking out." Elizabeth laid the key on the counter and waited for a response from Flossie.

Flossie picked up the key, then dropped it into the waste-basket under the counter. ''What's your name?''

''Elizabeth.''

''Elizabeth, huh? Well, has our friend left yet?''

''Only a few minutes ago.'' Elizabeth looked at Flossie, wondering if she dared trust her.

''Are you in a hurry or you got time for a cup of coffee?'' Flossie nodded toward the coffee machine sitting at the end of the counter. ''Might be a good idea for us to talk, and you could wait around and see what happens when Sheriff Bates finds out his man has slipped through his fingers.''

''Luanne saw me last night,'' Elizabeth said.

''Well, we'll just skip the coffee, but I don't think you have to worry about Luanne telling the sheriff much about you. I don't know what you said or did to her last night, but you convinced her you were a witch. She won't tell anybody but me because she's afraid they'll think she's crazy.'' Flossie's wide red lips spread into a big grin.

''Thanks for everything, Flossie.''

''You'd best be leaving, sugar.''

Elizabeth reached out across the counter, taking Flossie's age-spotted, ring-adorned hand into hers. The two women exchanged knowing glances.

I've got to help this girl get away. She's important to Reece, and that's a first. Maybe she'll stand by him and he'll get himself out of this mess. Sensing Flossie's thoughts, Elizabeth breathed a sigh of relief.

''You know he's on his way to the Burtons' summer house by the lake. I need directions so I can go to him after I pick up some supplies.''

Flossie looked past Elizabeth, out the glass front of the office. ''They're busting in room nineteen right now.''

Turning her head, Elizabeth watched as the deputies broke down the door and stormed inside.

''Tell me how to get to Spruce Pine, to the summer house.''

''Take Highway 40 until you get to Midget Creek. There's a four-way stop. Take a left and keep going until you see a sign that says Oden's Bait and Tackle Shop. About a mile past Oden's is a turnoff on the right. Take it and stay on that gravel road until it forks in two different directions. Take another right. It'll turn into a dirt road before you reach the cottage. The house is pretty well hidden in a grove of trees."

"I'll find it. Thanks."

Flossie came out from behind the counter, sizing up Elizabeth. "I hope you love that boy, sugar. I hope to God you love him, 'cause if ever a man needed to be loved, Reece Landry does."

Did she love him? Elizabeth asked herself. Did she? She cared about him, longed to be with him, was willing to suffer going out into the world to help him, was taking a chance on being arrested for aiding and abetting a criminal.

"I care about him. I care a great deal." Elizabeth rushed outside into the cold morning air. Glancing toward room nineteen, she saw the sheriff and other officers standing around in a circle, discussing Reece Landry's second escape.

She slipped into the T-Bird, started the engine and drove out onto the highway. Within five minutes she turned onto Highway 40 and began looking for a minimart of some kind, one that had a pay telephone. About two miles up the road she pulled off at Joe's Market, asked the attendant at the full-service pump to fill the T-Bird and went inside to shop for supplies. Only a few customers wandered around, most of them people who'd stopped for gas. Elizabeth filled a hand basket with sandwich fixings, canned soups, milk and cereal and coffee, along with assorted items she thought they could use. She placed the basket on the checkout counter, then retrieved a six-pack of beer and a six-pack of cola from the wall cooler.

The middle-aged woman at the checkout counter smiled as she added up Elizabeth's purchases. "You new in town or just passing through?"

"Just passing through right now, on my way to meet a friend." When Elizabeth heard the bell hanging above the door tinkle, she turned to see a highway patrolman entering.

"Hey, there, Pete," the checker said. "Are you here for your regular?"

"Just coffee right now, Carolyn." The patrolman poured himself a cup from one of the two pots behind the counter, handed the checker the correct change and took a sip of the hot liquid. "I haven't got time for lunch. They've called an all-points bulletin for us to be on the lookout for Reece Landry. The night clerk over at the Sweet Rest thinks a customer who came in yesterday evening was this Landry guy."

"You mean he's here in Newell?" Carolyn rolled her big brown eyes heavenward. "Didn't know the man personally, but I can't imagine anybody in his shoes being fool enough to come back here, knowing he'd be recognized."

"Well, whoever this Mr. Jones was that spent the night in room nineteen, he got away this morning, and so did the woman who spent the night with him."

Carolyn grinned at Pete while she continued checking Elizabeth's groceries. "Yeah, well, I heard that Landry had a way with the ladies. Good-looking guy…uh…from what I could tell from his pictures in the paper. I remember something coming out during the trial that Kenny Stanton's wife said Landry was after her hot and heavy."

"Kenny Stanton's wife is a real looker. Can't blame Landry for giving it a try." Pete laughed, tipped his hat to Carolyn and Elizabeth, then walked toward the door, his disposable coffee cup in his hand.

"Do y'all know who the woman was with Landry?" Carolyn called out just as Pete opened the door.

"Got no idea, and the only description is sketchy. A brunette."

"Probably some hooker, if he was at the Sweet Rest."

"Yeah, more than likely."

Elizabeth watched the patrolman get into his car and drive away. Turning to the checker, she forced a smile. "Is this Landry man in trouble with the law?"

"Child, Reece Landry's been in trouble with the law all his life." Carolyn began sacking Elizabeth's groceries. "But he's an escaped convict now. He was convicted of murdering his own father, but he escaped on his way up to Arrendale less than a week ago."

"Why would he come back here?" Elizabeth picked up amusement in the woman's mind and heard words like *framed* and *innocent* and *inheritance* in her thoughts.

"I'd say he's a fool." Carolyn handed Elizabeth two sacks, then picked up the third. "I'll help you to your car with this one."

"Thanks."

Carolyn followed Elizabeth toward the door. "Reece Landry claimed he was innocent, and a few folks around here believed him. He wasn't old B.K. Stanton's legitimate son, if you know what I mean."

Elizabeth opened the door. "Weren't there any other suspects?"

"Plenty, but the sheriff didn't follow through on anything once they arrested the man the Stanton family wanted out of the way." Carolyn followed Elizabeth to the T-Bird and handed her the third sack after Elizabeth placed the others on the back floorboard. "If you come through this way again, stop by."

"I'll do that." Elizabeth slid behind the wheel of Sam's antique T-Bird, turned and waved at Carolyn.

Her round cheeks rosy from the winter wind, Carolyn waved back as she curved her lips into a friendly smile. Elizabeth had the oddest sensation that Carolyn knew she was somehow connected to Reece Landry, and like Flossie, Carolyn hoped that Elizabeth truly cared about Reece.

Elizabeth drove the car to the edge of the parking area where a pay telephone was located. Glancing back toward the market, she saw that Carolyn had returned inside. Elizabeth rummaged in her purse for a quarter.

Dialing the operator, she gave Sam's phone number and asked that the charges be reversed. Within seconds Sam came on the line.

"Are you in Newell?" he asked.

"I'm at a minimarket outside town at a pay phone," Elizabeth told him.

"Where's Landry?"

"We're in separate cars. He's taken the Jeep on out to a summer house in Spruce Pine. He thinks it's a safe place to hide out while we're searching for the real murderer."

"Are you all right, Elizabeth?"

She smiled, knowing full well that Sam wanted to ask about his precious '65 Thunderbird. "I'm fine and so is your car. It could get muddy when I drive out to the cottage. The place is located on a dirt road."

"Give it up, kiddo, and go home. I promise I'll do everything I can to help Landry."

"I want you to come to Newell, today, and meet us at the cottage. We have to form some sort of strategy. Reece is confused and not thinking straight or he never would have come back here. A woman at the motel recognized him and called the sheriff this morning."

"What motel?" Sam asked.

"The motel where Reece and I stayed last night."

"My God, Elizabeth, tell me you're not sleeping with that man!"

"I'm not sleeping with Reece." She grinned, remembering waking this morning in Reece's arms. "Well, I did sleep with him last night, but—"

"I'll kill him!"

"Calm down, Sam. We just shared the same bed. I'm still as pure as the driven snow."

"This is no joking matter. Landry may not have killed his father, but he's no saint. As a matter of fact, he's a real bad boy and has the reputation to prove it."

Elizabeth sighed. Sam should know better than to try to convince her to do anything she didn't want to do. "I'm not leaving him."

"What's going on, Elizabeth? Really?"

"I think I may be falling in love with Reece."

Sam groaned. "Do you think he loves you?"

"No," Elizabeth admitted. "Reece doesn't know what love is, but he will. He needs me, Sam. Even Aunt Margaret says I'm his only hope, that no one else can save him from himself."

"Why do you need Aunt Margaret to read Landry's mind, to see into his future? Isn't your crystal ball working?"

"Now who's trying to be funny?" Elizabeth asked. "I can't see into Reece's future. I haven't picked up any images about what's going to happen to him. And I told you I can't get inside his head, except every once in a while. When he lets me.''

"Well, I'll be damned. A mind you can't read and a future you can't predict. You really are taking him on faith, aren't you?"

"I care so much about Reece, about what happens to him. He's lived a very hard life. He deserves some happiness.''

"Look, kiddo, you've got yourself involved in this man's problems and you're sexually attracted to him. But don't just assume you're falling in love with him." Sam cleared his throat. "Sexual attraction isn't love, and neither is caring about someone. You could easily be mistaking your desire to set things right in Landry's life with love.''

"I know." Elizabeth realized far better than Sam did that she was totally confused where her feelings for Reece Landry were concerned. "That's why I said that I think I'm falling in love with him. I've never been in love before, and I'm not sure.''

"Take things slow and easy.''

"Sam, please fly out of Atlanta as soon as you can. We really need your help. I'll give you the directions to the cottage.''

"Even if Landry is innocent, we may not be able to prove it,'' Sam told her. "Have you ever considered that possibility? Are you willing to stay on the run for the rest of your life?''

"Reece *is* innocent, and together the three of us are going to prove it.''

"Have you told Landry that you're involving me in this, that I'm coming to Newell?''

"No, not yet. Why?''

"Because he may not like the idea of me trying to help him," Sam said. "I don't think Landry trusts me any more than I trust him.''

"Well, that's plain stupid. You trust me and Reece trusts me, and I trust both of you, so it stands to reason that the two of you should trust each other.''

"Yeah, sure. Now give me the directions to that summer house."

Elizabeth gave him the details and wished him a safe trip.

"Kiddo, you be careful."

"I will, Sam. I promise."

She replaced the telephone slowly, her hand lingering on the cool plastic. She'd loved Sam all her life. He was her brother, her uncle, her father figure and her friend. She wanted Sam to like Reece, to trust him. And she wanted Reece to feel the same way about Sam.

Reece paced back and forth on the front porch of the Burtons' summer house, the February sun warming him as surely as the winter wind chilled him. Where the hell is she? he wondered. She'd had more than enough time to pick up a few supplies and get to the cottage. What if the sheriff had picked her up? What if she'd been in an accident? What if she'd changed her mind and decided not to join him?

If she had any sense at all, she was on her way back to Sequana Falls and as far away from him as she could get. In the cold light of day she might have realized what a mistake she'd made following a fugitive, a man balanced between life and death.

A hard knot formed in his gut. He slammed his fists down on the pristine white wooden banister surrounding the porch. Dammit, he didn't want to care whether she was on her way to him or on her way back to Sequana Falls. He didn't want it to matter, but it did. There was something addictive about Elizabeth Mallory, about the way she looked at him, the way she put her strong arms around him, the way she said his name. In less than a week she'd gotten under his skin. She'd made him want her near. No other woman had ever done that.

Reece glanced up at the blue-gray sky, heavy white clouds floating past, the sun noonday high. In the distance he heard a car. His heartbeat accelerated. Maybe it was Elizabeth; maybe it was the sheriff. He went inside the cottage, positioning himself beside one of the huge front windows, and waited for the car's approach. Peering around the side of the window, he saw the black '65 Thunderbird round the curve in the dirt road.

Elizabeth! She'd come to him. She hadn't deserted him. A spiral of sweet, unadulterated joy sprang up inside him and spread through his body and mind, and even invaded his heart.

Swinging open the front door, he rushed out onto the porch, but stopped himself from running into the yard to meet her. His heartbeat roared in his ears. Excitement raced along his nerve endings.

He wasn't alone.

Elizabeth flung open the car door, stepped outside and waved at Reece. Dear Lord, he was so handsome, so big and virile and utterly beautiful standing there on the gingerbread-trimmed porch, Sam's old jeans clinging to his lean, muscled hips and legs. She wanted to run to him, throw her arms around him and tell him how glad she was to be with him.

Did she love Reece Landry, a man she'd met less than a week ago, yet a man she'd known in her heart for months? Her feelings for Reece were complicated, her empathy for him, her desire to help him and the sexual attraction she felt all mixed together. She knew one thing for certain—she had never felt about another man the way she felt about Reece, and the intensity of those feelings frightened her.

Reece headed straight for her. "I was beginning to wonder if you'd come to your senses and gone back to Sequana Falls."

For one brief instant Elizabeth felt Reece's fear—he'd been afraid that she had left him. Swallowing down the overwhelming emotions choking her, Elizabeth smiled, secure in her knowledge that, despite how much Reece protested, he truly wanted her at his side.

"It took a while to get the supplies. The checker was talkative. And a highway patrolman came in the store and they started discussing you and your second escape."

Reaching inside the car, Elizabeth picked up a grocery sack and handed it to Reece. "Can you carry two?" she asked.

Nodding, he accepted the second sack. Elizabeth took the third and they walked toward the cottage. She glanced around, taking in the two-story white frame house with dark green shutters and roof. A wraparound porch, graced with carved banisters, circled the house.

"Why did you decide to come here instead of your father's hunting lodge?" Elizabeth asked, wondering who owned this lovely summer cottage.

"Flossie pointed out that the sheriff might have the hunting lodge under surveillance, since Kenny would alert them that I knew how to locate the lodge."

"You spent time with your father at his hunting lodge?"

"Yeah. Once. B.K. liked roughing it, liked hunting. He took Kenny and me up to his lodge to do some hunting last year." Reece led Elizabeth up the porch and inside the house.

Just as she had suspected, the interior had been perfectly decorated by someone with good taste and money. Pastel, spring colors dominated the living room. Fragile lace curtains had been pulled back to expose the row of French windows facing the front porch. Sturdy white wicker furniture held thick cushions and pillows covered in blue, rose and cream floral prints. A brass screen stood in front of the fireplace, which had been painted a pale cream and was adorned with a simple wooden mantel. A cheerful fire burned brightly in the fireplace.

Elizabeth followed Reece into the kitchen, an open area adjacent to the living room. The stainless steel appliances were modern and matched the sink and countertops. White hexagonal tiles covered the floor and glass-fronted white cabinets lined the walls. "I didn't realize that you ever socialized with your father and his family."

Reece helped Elizabeth unsack the supplies and place them in the empty cupboards, storing the beer and colas in the double-wide refrigerator.

"I didn't socialize with the family. Not really. I was never invited to their house, but B.K. saw to it that I attended some of the same social functions." Reece retrieved one of the beer bottles, snapping the lid with a decorative metallic opener attached to the side of the refrigerator. "The hunting trip wasn't socializing. It was a contest B.K. contrived to see which one of his sons was as rough and tough and mean as he was.''

Elizabeth watched Reece put the beer bottle to his lips and pour the liquid into his mouth. "Are you saying that your father deliberately encouraged a rivalry between you and his other son?''

After downing a third of the beer, Reece set the bottle on the counter and wiped his mouth. "I'm saying that B. K. Stanton's legitimate son was a disappointment to him. Kenny lived the good life. Never had to get his hands dirty. He's a spoiled, weak mama's boy."

"Everything you're not."

"Everything that B.K. and Alice Stanton's wealth and social positions made him, and yet, he wasn't what B.K. wanted." Looking toward the front of the cottage, Reece gazed out the windows. "Are your bags in the trunk of your car?"

Elizabeth nodded. When Reece walked past her, she reached out, laying her hand on his chest. "Your father discovered that you were more of a man than his other son, is that it? He found that you possessed the qualities he admired, the qualities he couldn't find in Kenny."

Reece glanced down at her hand. "Yeah. I'm the exact opposite of my big brother. And our father finally saw how he could use those differences to his advantage. He thought that if he threw me up in Kenny's face often enough, Kenny would eventually grow a backbone and become the son B.K. wanted." Reece walked away from Elizabeth and out onto the porch.

A stinging warmth of pain spread through her when she realized how deeply Reece had been affected by his father's manipulation. She met him at the door when he returned with her bags.

"There is one bedroom downstairs and two upstairs. They're all pretty much the same. I'll put your bag in here." Opening the door to the downstairs bedroom, Reece walked in, tossed the bag on the old iron bed and turned quickly, his body colliding with Elizabeth's. He grabbed her by the shoulders to steady her.

"Looks like we won't need to share a bed tonight," she said. The memory of waking in the early-morning hours to find herself snuggled into Reece's arms warmed Elizabeth with the hope of what lay ahead for them.

"Not unless you ask me real nice," he said.

"Oh?"

Reece laughed. "I'll have to hunt up some more firewood, since our only source of heat is the fireplace. There used to be some electrical heaters the Burtons kept for cool autumn nights, but since they use this place mostly in the summer, I don't think they keep the heaters around anymore. If you get cold in the night, you can always come get in bed with me."

"I'll keep that in mind." She smiled, trying to imitate his jesting. But talking about sharing a bed with Reece reminded her just how much she had liked awakening in his arms this morning. Reece was a virile man, and if they shared a bed again, he would probably expect them to have sex. Was she ready for such an important step in their relationship? More importantly, was Reece ready?

"Did you have any problems finding this place?" Reece asked.

"No problems. Flossie's instructions were perfect."

"The sheriff didn't try to stop you or question you, did he?"

"I left before they gave up searching the motel for you."

Reece turned toward the fireplace, warming his hands. He'd thought twice about building a fire in the fireplace, since a helicopter might spot the smoke, but he'd been listening to news on the radio and there had been no mention of a search outside Newell. Roadblocks had been set up and a manhunt begun, but the law figured Reece Landry was either on his way out of town and they'd catch him at a roadblock or that he was hiding out in one of his old haunts and a door-to-door search might reveal his whereabouts. The police had no reason to come snooping around Spruce Pine, no reason to connect him with Tracy Burton Stanton's parents or their summer house.

"Lizzie, you shouldn't be here with me. You shouldn't be involved in this."

"I thought we'd already settled that argument once and for all," Elizabeth said. "I'm staying and that's all there is to it."

"I'm no good, Elizabeth." Reece kept his back to her, his focus on the fire in front of him. "If you stay with me, I could get you killed, or at the very least, break your heart."

Elizabeth refused to acknowledge the possibility that Reece was right. Together they would prove Reece's innocence and come through this nightmare. And she would save Reece, save him from himself. If he broke her heart in the process, she would survive.

"Are you hungry?" she asked. "I'm starving. I haven't had a bite to eat since I stopped for a hamburger on the way to Newell yesterday."

Reece slapped his hands against his hips, then rubbed them up and down his thighs. He turned to face her. "Yeah, sure. I'm hungry."

"Let's fix lunch. I can open a can of tomato soup and make some grilled cheese sandwiches."

"I'll do the soup," Reece said. "You fix the sandwiches."

Elizabeth spread out the bread, cheese and margarine on the stainless steel counter. "Whose place is this, anyway?"

"It belongs to Albert and Edna Burton." Reece placed the can of soup under the can opener.

"How do you know these people?"

"What difference does it make?"

"Just curious, I guess." Elizabeth spread margarine on the bread. "I have a feeling you're hiding something from me."

Reece jerked a metal pot from a bottom cupboard. "I know the Burtons' daughter."

"Is she one of your old girlfriends?"

"No." Reece poured the soup into the pot, then filled the empty can with water and added it to the mixture.

"Why are you being so secretive?" Elizabeth laid the sliced cheese on the bread.

Reece set the soup pot on the stove, adjusted the heat and turned to face Elizabeth. "Albert and Edna Burton's daughter married Kenny Stanton."

"This house belongs to your sister-in-law's parents?"

"Yeah."

"How did you know about this place? Did Flossie tell you about it?" Elizabeth remembered what Carolyn, the checkout clerk at the minimart, had said about Tracy Stanton accusing Reece of coming on to her hot and heavy. Had Reece had an affair with his brother's wife? Had they shared a secret rendezvous at her parents' summer house?

"Like I told you, Flossie had entertained Albert Burton and some of his friends out here when Mrs. Burton was otherwise occupied."

Reece handed Elizabeth a frying pan he'd pulled out of the cupboard where the cooking utensils were stored.

"What about you? Obviously you know your way around this kitchen. You've been here before, haven't you? You've been here with Tracy Stanton."

"I checked the kitchen out while I was waiting for you. As a matter of fact, I gave the whole house a once-over." Reece placed his hands on Elizabeth's shoulders. She laid the sandwiches in the skillet and placed the skillet on the stove.

"What kind of relationship do you have with your brother's wife?"

"I don't have a relationship with Tracy."

"Then why did she make the statement at your trial that you were after her, and I quote, 'hot and heavy'?"

"Because she was still angry with me for turning her down." Reece released Elizabeth's shoulders. "Tracy was after *me* hot and heavy. She invited me up here to her parents' summer house one weekend over a year ago."

"You met her here?"

"Yeah. I was curious. I knew what she wanted, and I have to admit that the idea of cuckolding Kenny tempted me."

"What happened?"

"We kissed." Reece closed his eyes, remembering how close he'd come to carrying his brother's wife to bed. "We both got pretty steamed up, but then I put a stop to things. Tracy Burton Stanton might have money and education and generations of blue-blooded breeding, but I realized that she wasn't any different from the girls who used to work for

Flossie." Reece laughed, the sound a mirthless grunt. "The only difference was she gave it away for free."

"You didn't make love to Tracy Stanton?"

"I don't make love to women," Reece said. "I have sex with them. But I didn't have sex with Tracy."

"I'm glad," Elizabeth said. "I'm very glad."

"Yeah? Well, funny thing is, Lizzie, so am I."

Thirty minutes later Elizabeth and Reece sat at the small kitchen table, an oak antique flanked by four Windsor chairs, and sipped on second cups of coffee and nibbled on oatmeal raisin cookies.

"One of the reasons it took me a while to get here is that I stopped at a pay phone and called Sam." Elizabeth glanced at Reece. He stared at her, his amber eyes void of any emotion.

"Even when you're on the run with another man, you still have to check in with Dundee?" Reece set down his cup with a resounding thud, warm coffee spilling out onto the tabletop. "What sort of hold does that guy have over you?"

Elizabeth stared at Reece in disbelief. He was jealous. Reece was jealous of Sam. She suppressed her laughter. "Sam's family. He's been like a big brother to me most of my life." She reached across the table, placing her hand atop Reece's fist. "Sam was a DEA agent for years, then something happened that made him want out, and he formed his own private security agency in Atlanta. He knows a lot about investigating people and protecting them."

"Sounds like good old Sam is the answer to our prayers." Huffing, Reece jerked his hand away from Elizabeth.

"Sam's coming to Newell. Today."

"What the hell for?"

"He's already set things in motion to investigate B. K. Stanton's death and discover other suspects. He'll have his first real report for us this afternoon."

Tightening his jaw and clenching his teeth, Reece breathed deeply. "It may have slipped your notice, but we don't have a telephone out here."

"Sam isn't going to phone me. He's coming out here to the cottage."

Reece jumped up, knocking his chair backward in the process. "You told Dundee where we were? You gave him directions to this place?"

"Yes, I did. And I don't see why you're so upset."

Reece glared down at her. "You don't see why I'm..." Reece's amber eyes glowed with yellow fire. "You betrayed me, Lizzie. Surely you aren't stupid enough to think that Dundee wants to help me. All he wants is to get you away from me, to keep you safe. He's probably already called the sheriff."

Elizabeth scooted back her chair and stood. "I would never betray you, Reece. Never. Sam won't call the sheriff, and he will help you."

"Because he loves you!"

"Yes, because he loves me, and he knows my instincts are seldom wrong."

"I hope you're right about Dundee, because if you're wrong..." Reece walked out of the kitchen, through the back door and into the small clearing behind the house.

If he had any sense at all, he'd take Elizabeth's Jeep and get the hell out of Newell. He'd leave her behind, her and her big brother Dundee. Did he dare stay and trust a man he didn't even know, a man whose primary interest in him was the woman they had in common? And could he really trust Elizabeth? Just because every time he looked at her, he wanted to take her didn't mean he could trust her.

What the hell was he going to do? Would he be a fool to stay and put his life and his freedom in Elizabeth Mallory's hands? Or would he be a bigger fool to run away from his one chance to prove himself innocent and from the one woman who'd ever really cared about him?

Chapter 8

Elizabeth sat alone inside the Burtons' summer house. Reece had been outside for the past couple of hours. First he'd parked Sam's '65 T-Bird at the back of the house, beside the Jeep, then he'd taken off into the woods, saying only that he was going to take a walk down by the lake.

For the twentieth time she checked her watch, wondering when Sam would arrive and how long Reece was going to stay outside sulking. She wasn't accustomed to being alone; MacDatho was nearly always at her side. She wished she could have brought him with her, but where a lone woman might go practically unnoticed, no one would forget a huge black wolf-dog.

The back door creaked. Elizabeth tensed. Turning her head just a fraction, she saw Reece enter the kitchen.

"It's getting colder out there," he said. "I thought I'd make some fresh coffee, but it looks like you've already done that." He glanced at the freshly filled coffeepot.

"It's going to snow before dark." Elizabeth turned back around, focusing her attention on the fire.

"Does that mean Dundee will be snowed in here with us?" Reece picked up a clean coffee mug from the dish drain, grabbed a dish towel off the wall rack and lifted the coffeepot.

"There will be a light snow, just an inch or two. Sam should be here soon."

"Maybe he couldn't get a flight out of Atlanta." Reece poured the mug full of coffee, returned the pot to the coffeemaker and walked into the living room, sitting in a chair to the left of the wicker sofa where Elizabeth sat.

"Sam flies his own plane. A small twin-engine Cessna. He probably rented a car at the airport and is on his way here now."

"Quite a man, our Mr. Dundee." Reece leaned over, resting his hands between his spread knees, the warm mug secure in his grasp. "Former DEA agent, owns his own business, flies his own plane. I can hardly wait to meet this guy."

"He's anxious to meet you, too." Tilting her chin up, Elizabeth glared at Reece. "You see, you're the first man I've ever run away with, and Sam doesn't trust you any more than you trust him."

"Sounds like he's very protective when it comes to screening the men in your life." Reece sipped his coffee. "Does he warn off all men you show an interest in or just the ones who are escaped convicts?"

"There haven't been any men in my life for Sam to screen." Elizabeth bowed her head, looking down at her lap where she'd laid her clasped hands. "You're the first."

Reece strangled on his coffee. The mug in his unsteady hand hit the wooden floor. "Damn!"

Elizabeth jumped up, rushed to the kitchen for a towel and returned to mop up the spilled coffee. Reece knelt beside her, picking up the broken pieces of the ceramic mug. He threw the shards into the fireplace. Elizabeth wiped the floor clean.

She rested on her knees in front of him. He laid his hand on her shoulder. She froze at his touch.

"Clarify things for me, will you, Lizzie?" Taking her hands in his, Reece lifted her to her feet, took the soaked towel from her and threw it across the room toward the kitchen area. "My mind has gone into overdrive here and

I'm thinking some pretty crazy thoughts. I don't think you said what I thought you said. Or at least, I don't think I understood you right."

"What didn't you understand? That Sam has always considered himself my protector? That Sam doesn't trust you? That there have never been any men in my life for Sam to screen?" Elizabeth's hands trembled.

Reece pulled her to him, holding her hands between their bodies. "How old are you, Elizabeth?"

"Twenty-six."

Reece sighed. "Well, you've had boyfriends, dated, had a few experiences over the years. Right?"

"I dated some in college."

Reece grinned. "Good. Then I did misunderstand when you said I was the first."

Elizabeth looked into his eyes, those lone-wolf amber eyes. They were so warm, so intensely inviting. "I dated several silly boys who were scared off once they found out I could read their minds. Sam worried about me when I went away to school, but he didn't worry about me getting in trouble with boys. He knew how difficult it would be for me to control all the energy I'd receive from other people. He doubted any boy could sweet-talk me into something I didn't want to do, since I would be able to perceive his motive."

"Okay, so you dated silly boys in college who couldn't deal with your hocus-pocus routine. What about after college? There had to have been men who didn't give a damn that you were psychic."

"Does it bother you, Reece? That I'm psychic? That usually I can predict the future, that sometimes I'm aware of events occurring miles away, that often I can read people's minds?"

Dropping her hands, Reece grabbed her face and pulled her to him. "I'm on the run with a virgin, aren't I, Elizabeth? There really hasn't been another man in your life, has there?"

"You're the first, Reece."

Looking at her face, flushed and glowing with emotion, gazing into those pure, honest blue eyes was almost more than Reece could bear. "Of all the men on earth, baby, why me?"

"You came to me, Reece, in my mind. I felt your pain and anger and hatred. I sensed your loneliness. I could see you locked in a tiny cage. You invaded my life." Tears filled her eyes. "You became the stranger in my heart."

"Elizabeth?"

"It was meant for me to save you. I'm the only one who can. Aunt Margaret knows it. I know it." Tears spilled from her eyes, streaking her cheeks. "You know it, too, Reece. In your heart."

"Can you read my mind? Can you see into my future?"

"I can't see your future, Reece. I've tried. Something is blocking my vision. Aunt Margaret says it's because our futures are entwined and I have never allowed myself to look into my own future. I've been too afraid." She slipped her arms around his waist. "And I can't read your mind. I told you that you shield your thoughts and your emotions from me most of the time. Every once in a while I pick up on a few things."

"Do you know what I'm thinking right now, Lizzie? What I'm feeling?" His lips took hers in a wild yet tender kiss, his mouth covering hers, tasting, licking, savoring the sweetness of her innocence.

He cradled her head in one hand and ran his other hand down her back, pushing her forward, holding her against his arousal. Elizabeth clung to him, her arms lifting, her hands caressing the corded muscles in his back. When he slipped his tongue inside her mouth, she moaned, bunching the material of his shirt into her fist.

Reece ended the kiss quickly, his body still throbbing with need. He heard a car. Gulping for air as she pulled away from him, Elizabeth glanced toward the windows. The afternoon sun hung low in the cloudy sky. A gray Buick Regal stopped in the driveway in front of the cottage. Sam Dundee, all six feet four inches of him, emerged.

"It's Sam." Elizabeth wiped the loose strands of her hair away from her face, took a deep breath and rushed to the front door.

Reece followed her, halting directly behind her when she opened the door and stepped out onto the porch. So that is Sam Dundee, Reece thought. About an inch taller than me, fifteen pounds heavier and a good five or six years older. And by the looks of his suit, overcoat, shoes and gold watch, a hell of a lot richer.

When Elizabeth started to go to Sam, Reece grabbed her by the shoulders, holding her in place on the porch in front of him. She stopped immediately, relaxing in his grasp.

Reece stared at Sam when the other man reached the bottom of the porch steps. Their gazes locked. Steel blue-gray eyes met cold gold-amber. Reece recognized the look in Dundee's eyes, the expression on his face. One strong warrior always recognized another.

"Come on inside, Sam," Elizabeth said. "It's freezing out here." She pulled away from Reece's hold; he let her go.

Sam walked up the steps, reached out and took Elizabeth into his arms. The blood ran cold in Reece's veins. He didn't like seeing Elizabeth in another man's arms, especially a man like Dundee. It took every ounce of his willpower not to jerk her away.

"Thanks for coming." Elizabeth hugged Sam, thankful, as she had always been, that he was a part of her life.

"You knew I would." With his arm around Elizabeth, Sam turned to Reece. "You must be Landry."

"Yeah. And you must be the guy that Lizzie thinks can walk on water."

Sam grinned, squeezed Elizabeth's shoulder and held out a hand to Reece. Reece accepted the greeting, a quick, hard handshake, each man putting the other on notice. *Elizabeth Mallory is important to me.*

"Lizzie, huh?" Sam laughed. "Never thought of you as Lizzie."

Elizabeth laughed. "Come on, you two, let's go warm ourselves in front of the fire."

Reece waited for Elizabeth and Sam to enter the cottage, then followed them. After laying Sam's overcoat on the back of the wicker sofa, Elizabeth motioned for him to sit.

"Would you like a cup of coffee?" she asked him.

Sam sat down, then glanced over at Reece. "Let's talk business, Landry."

"Now, Sam." Elizabeth sat beside her big-brother protector.

"I don't like Elizabeth being here. Every minute she's with you, she's in danger," Sam said. "I'll do everything I can to help you prove your innocence, but your best bet is to surrender to the sheriff and let me find some evidence that will warrant your lawyer getting you an appeal."

Reece crossed the room to stand in front of the fireplace. "Have you already called the sheriff? Told him where he can find me?"

"I don't work that way, Landry. For whatever reason, Elizabeth has taken on your problems. She's determined to help you, and I'm determined to help her and protect her."

"The last thing we need is for you two to argue," Elizabeth said.

"I think Landry needs to know where I stand." Sam unbuttoned his charcoal gray pin-striped coat, exposing the pristine whiteness of his shirt, his tie a crimson stain against the purity. "If Elizabeth believes you're innocent, then I'm willing to do whatever it takes to find the real murderer. I think you should turn yourself in, but I haven't betrayed you and I won't. I don't like Elizabeth's involvement with you because I think you can get her in big trouble. I don't want her to stay with you. I want her to leave here with me this afternoon."

"I'm not leaving." Elizabeth placed her hand on Sam's where he'd rested it on the back of the sofa. "Tell us what you've found out, and then we'll all work together to figure out where we go from here." She glanced up at Reece. "Sit down."

Reece took the chair to the left of the sofa, the one closest to Elizabeth. Leaning back, he folded his arms across his chest. "Let's hear it. What has the great man found out?"

Elizabeth scowled at Reece. "Go ahead, Sam. Don't pay any attention to Reece. I haven't had a chance to work on his manners yet."

"How much have you told Elizabeth?" Sam asked Reece.

"About what?" Reece widened his eyes, a mocking grin on his face.

"About your past. About your life."

"She knows I'm a worthless bastard who's been convicted of murdering his father," Reece said.

"I know the whole story." Elizabeth felt torn between her need to comfort Reece and her need to make Sam understand her feelings.

Sam glanced at Elizabeth, then at Reece. "All right. Then it's safe to say it won't come as a surprise to hear that Reece Landry has a few enemies in Newell, enemies with money and power who are very pleased that he was convicted of B. K. Stanton's murder."

"That's all you've found out?" Reece chuckled.

"You've also got a few friends, including your sister. She's the one person who might be able to help us." Standing, Sam shoved his hands into his pants pockets. "Just from my preliminary inquiries I think there's a good possibility that you were framed, and I think your brother and his mother could be our prime suspects. After all, they, and your sister, Christina, stood to lose a lot of money if you weren't convicted of murder."

"What do you mean?" Elizabeth asked.

"My old man made a new will shortly before he was killed," Reece said. "But he didn't bother telling anyone, including me. The only person who knew, other than B.K. himself, was the family lawyer, Willard Moran." Reece tossed his head back, blew out his breath and looked up at the ceiling. "I think that's the reason B.K. asked me to come by his house that night. The night he was shot."

"He named you in his will?" Elizabeth wanted to put her arms around Reece, to comfort him, to share the pain he felt.

"B. K. Stanton left Reece one-third of everything he possessed." Sam paced back and forth in front of the fireplace. "After thirty-two years he was finally acknowledging Reece as his son."

Reece sat up straight, looked across the room and out the windows, his gaze not really focused. "Damn generous of him, wasn't it?" Reece laughed. "The really funny thing is that I think he did it because he knew how furious it would make Kenny and Alice."

"Look, bottom line here is that Stanton's whole family had reason to kill him," Sam said. "He and Kenny never got along. B.K. completely controlled his son's life. He even handpicked Tracy Burton for Kenny's wife.

"The man had been betraying Alice with other women most of their married life. It was no secret that she despised her husband." Sam glanced over at Elizabeth, never slowing as he paced back and forth. "And the whole town knows that Christina Stanton never forgave her father for paying off her fiancé to dump her about ten years ago because B.K. didn't think the man was good enough for his daughter." Sam stopped pacing, then looked down at Reece. "And your stepfather had motive to kill Stanton. From what I've learned, Harry Gunn had threatened to kill his wife's former lover on more than one occasion."

"Good old Harry." Reece shook his head. He didn't know who he'd hated the most over the years—B. K. Stanton or Harry Gunn.

"So, it looks like we've got ourselves a full cast of suspects," Sam said. "I've set up an appointment with Gary Elkins in the morning. He's eager for us to work together. Your lawyer believes you're innocent."

"Does he?" Reece asked, glancing up at Sam. "Since Christina's money paid for his services, I was never quite certain where his loyalties lay."

"You don't trust anybody, do you, Landry?"

Reece stood, facing Sam. Two big, tall men sizing up each other. "Something tells me you're not the trusting sort, either, Dundee. You sure as hell don't trust me with Elizabeth, do you?"

Elizabeth jumped up off the sofa, standing in front of Reece and Sam, her body separating the two men, the three of them creating a human triangle. "We're going to have to trust one another. It's the only way we can prove Reece's innocence."

Sam turned, taking Elizabeth by the arm. "He's right about my not trusting him with you, kiddo. You shouldn't be in the middle of this mess. I want you to come with me, today. We'll both stay in Newell, if that's what you want, and I'll do whatever it takes to find Stanton's killer.''

"Why don't you two talk this over," Reece said. "I need some fresh air." He grabbed his coat off the rack by the door and went outside.

Elizabeth turned to Sam. "Why did you have to ask me to leave again? I'd already told you that I'm staying with Reece." Never before had she been forced to choose between Sam and another man. Never before had she had reason to go against Sam's wishes.

Sam took Elizabeth by the shoulders, pulling her into his arms, stroking her hair the way a parent would comfort a child. "I'm worried sick about you, kiddo. I'm scared something really bad might happen."

Elizabeth hugged Sam, feeling, as she always had, safe and secure in his arms. "I understand how you feel, but I want you to understand how I feel. I really do think I'm falling in love with Reece. I know it's crazy for me to love him, but—"

"Elizabeth, Elizabeth." Sighing, Sam took her by the shoulders again.

"He needs me, Sam. There's just so much pain inside him. Anger, pain and fear." Reaching up, Elizabeth cradled Sam's cheek in her palm. "Remember the agony you were in six years ago when you came off your last assignment for the DEA? That's the shape Reece is in now, but for different reasons."

Elizabeth felt Sam flinch, saw the memories glaze his eyes. "It wasn't your fault, Sam. You didn't have a choice. You did what you had to do. But I have a choice. I'm not leaving Reece."

Sam swallowed, squeezed Elizabeth's shoulders and forced a smile. "He doesn't deserve you, kiddo."

Elizabeth flung her arms around Sam, hugging him fiercely. "I love you, you know that, don't you?"

"And I love you, too, little girl."

Reece stood on the front porch, the afternoon sun dimmed by the clouds, small, damp snowflakes beginning to fall. He had meant to stay out here, to give Elizabeth time alone with Sam Dundee, but the more he'd thought about the possibility she might leave him, the more determined he'd become to ask her to stay. He'd opened the door just a fraction and had seen Elizabeth in Sam's arms. He'd heard her tell him she loved him.

A knot of intense agony sprang to life in Reece's gut. Why the hell should he have trusted this woman any more than he'd ever trusted another?

She'd leave with Dundee. She loved Dundee. He didn't care, dammit! It didn't matter! He had lived his whole life without Elizabeth Mallory. He'd be just fine without her. He didn't need her. Reece gripped the top rail of the porch banister, his knuckles turning white from the strength of his hold.

The front door swung open. Sam Dundee came outside alone. Reece waited for the second set of footsteps, then, when he didn't hear any, decided Elizabeth was probably getting her bags.

Sam walked over and stood by Reece. "It's snowing."

"Y'all better leave soon, otherwise, you and Lizzie could get snowed in here with me."

"Elizabeth says there won't be more than an inch of snow." Sam bent over, clasping the banister with both hands.

"You believe in her psychic abilities?" Reece asked.

"Yeah, I believe," Sam said. "I've known Elizabeth since she was six years old and my brother married her mother. They moved to Sequana Falls, into Elizabeth's grandparents' home, so that she could be near her great-aunt, who also has psychic talents."

"Aunt Margaret?"

"Margaret has been Elizabeth's guide, her teacher and her protector."

"I thought being her protector was your job!"

"Margaret's and mine." Sam turned to Reece.

Reece faced Sam. "If you've got something to say to me, then say it."

"Elizabeth has risked more than you know to follow you, to stay with you, to help you."

"So, when she leaves with you, she won't be risking herself anymore, will she?"

Sam grinned. "She's not leaving with me."

"What?"

"You chose the wrong time to walk in on us," Sam said. "And you misunderstood what you saw and heard. I noticed you standing in the door. Elizabeth didn't. Odd that she can't read you clearly."

Reece held his breath, wanting to believe and yet afraid to believe what Sam was saying. "She's not leaving with you?"

"Elizabeth and I are family." Sam grasped Reece's shoulder in his big hand. "Elizabeth and I are not lovers. We aren't in love."

Reece nodded his head, acknowledging what Sam had said. "She shouldn't stay with me."

"She won't leave you."

"You couldn't persuade her to go with you?"

"No. She's staying with you because she believes she's the only one who can save you," Sam said. "She'll risk being caught with you and charged with aiding and abetting a criminal, she'll risk the possibility of being killed if she gets caught in the cross fire if the law finds you, and she risks her sanity by going into town and facing people whose thoughts and emotions she can't control."

"What do you mean, people's thoughts and emotions she can't control?" Reece stared at Sam, noting the concern in his expression.

"Elizabeth reads minds, she picks up on the energy that comes from people's thoughts and from their emotions. Often she can predict their futures or see into their pasts just by touching them. Sometimes she can control these energies. Other times she can't. When she can't control them, can't shield herself, then she's bombarded with too much input."

"That's the reason she lives secluded in the mountains, isn't it?" Reece asked. "So she won't be exposed to too much psychic energy coming from other people."

"She almost had a nervous breakdown when she went away to college. We learned then that she didn't dare risk living in a city or even a large town."

"Will she be all right out here? Away from town?"

"She probably would be if she stayed, since she only occasionally picks up anything telepathically at distances, the way she did with you. But she doesn't intend to stay out here," Sam said. "She's meeting me in town tomorrow at Gary Elkins's office."

"Why?"

"She knows it's possible that if she can meet everyone involved with B. K. Stanton, she might be able to read them and discover which one of them is the murderer."

"No, I can't let her do that," Reece said. "I won't let her put herself at risk for me."

Elizabeth opened the front door and stepped outside. "You two finished with your man-to-man talk?"

"Just about." Sam released the banister, stood up straight and smiled at Elizabeth.

"It's too cold out here for y'all to stay much longer. For goodness' sakes, it's snowing." Elizabeth walked over and stood between Sam and Reece.

"I'll see you in town in the morning." Sam gave Elizabeth a quick peck on the cheek, then walked down the steps and out to his rental car. "You take good care of my T-Bird."

"We could swap," Elizabeth suggested.

"No need to do that, kiddo. You keep the Thunderbird." Sam opened his car door, glanced up at Elizabeth and then over at Reece. "She's worth a king's ransom, Landry. Remember that."

Sam got in the Regal, started the engine and drove away without a backward glance. Elizabeth slipped her arm around Reece's waist. He pulled her close. She laid her head against him.

"You should have gone with him, Lizzie."

"I couldn't leave you."

A sharp, breathtaking pain hit Reece straight in the gut. He couldn't let this happen—he couldn't let Elizabeth care for him, and he didn't dare feel anything more than sexual attraction for her. He wasn't a man accustomed to women like Elizabeth—honest, caring and loyal, with a purity of soul that frightened him.

"You're putting yourself in danger by staying with me."
Reece pulled away from Elizabeth, turning to look down
into her crystal-clear blue eyes. Eyes that spoke so elo-
quently without words. Eyes that told him how much she
cared, how deeply she longed to share his misery and lighten
his burden.

"You don't really want me to leave, do you?"

"Besides the fact that you could get injured accidentally
if the law finds me, you're sure to be in big trouble unless we
can convince them that I kidnapped you." Reece walked the
length of the porch, leaned back against the wall and gazed
out at the forest, trees and brush blanketed with a light
dusting of newly fallen snow.

Elizabeth stood near the steps, looking across the porch
to where Reece rested his back against the house. Why was
it so difficult for him to accept the fact that she wanted to
stay with him, to help him, to comfort him? Surely the good
Lord wouldn't have sent Reece to her if he hadn't meant the
two of them to be together.

Reece kept his gaze focused on the scenery. "Sam told me
what you're risking, emotionally and mentally, by leaving
Sequana Falls, by exposing yourself to so many other people's thoughts and feelings."

"Sam told you?"

"He thought I had a right to know."

"He shouldn't have told you."

Reece turned around slowly, admitting to himself that he
had to face Elizabeth and yet not wanting to look into those
all-too-knowing blue eyes of hers. Why now, God, why
now? he asked himself. Why send someone so special into
my life when my whole world has crumbled around me?
Why offer me something that I can never have, something
I'm not worthy of, something I didn't dream could ever be
mine?

"You're going to wind up getting hurt, one way or another, because of me." When he saw her take a tentative step
forward, he held up a hand to warn her off. "I can't give
you what you want. I'm no good for you, Lizzie. What do
I have to say or do to get through to you?"

"I thought we'd settled this argument." She wanted desperately to run to him, throw her arms around him. She couldn't; he wouldn't accept her. Not now.

"When you go into Newell and meet with Gary Elkins, you're going to be exposed to hundreds of people, maybe thousands. How can you deal with that kind of attack on your mind?"

"It's not as bad as Sam led you to believe." Elizabeth knew she was trying to convince herself as much as Reece. "When I went away to college I was only in my teens and I hadn't been able to train my mind to shield itself."

"Can you shield your mind now?"

"To some extent," Elizabeth said. "Every living thing gives off energy. I read the psychic energy people emit. Sometimes that energy is so strong I can't block it."

"Can you read everybody? Do you pick up on everybody's psychic energy?"

"Almost everyone. Some people shield their minds and their emotions without realizing they're doing it. But no one can shield themselves all the time."

"You can't read me all the time, can you?"

"No, I can't. You won't admit your true feelings even to yourself. You won't allow anyone to get close to you. You've closed your mind and your heart to others because you're afraid."

Reece walked toward her, his gaze locked with hers, his amber eyes hypnotizing her the way an animal often does his prey as he moves in for the kill. Elizabeth stood perfectly still—waiting—her heart racing wildly, her breathing shallow and quick. He reached out, circling the back of her neck with his big hand, drawing her forward until her lips were at his throat. She tilted her head, staring up at him, excitement and uncertainty shining in her eyes.

"Why is it that you can read other people so clearly, that you can see into other people's futures, but not mine?"

Tears formed in Elizabeth's eyes. Her bottom lip trembled as she forced herself not to cry. "I told you that I can't read your future because our futures are entwined, and I have always refused to look into my own future. You see, Reece, I have my own fears."

He brought her face closer to his, their lips almost touching. "You can get inside my head, Lizzie. You've done it before. I heard you calling my name when I was at the motel and you were trying to find me. I told you where I was and how to get there, didn't I? And I realize now that all those months I stayed in jail, before and during the trial, I kept getting these odd feelings that someone was trying to talk to me, to comfort me, to let me know I wasn't alone. I thought I'd been caged for so long I was going crazy."

Tears escaped from Elizabeth's eyes, falling like life-giving raindrops. Reece kissed her eyes, kissed her tears, tasting her heart's blood. Dear God in heaven, forgive me, he thought, but I can't be strong any longer. I can't walk away from this precious gift. I'm only human.

"What am I thinking, Elizabeth?"

Sweet, tingling warmth spread through her, quickly turning to hot excitement. Desire poured from Reece's mind, desire so intense she felt it in every cell of her body. She shivered from the power of his thoughts.

"You . . . you want to make love to me." Elizabeth trembled, her body softening, her legs weakening. She swayed into Reece. He covered her mouth with his, taking her with tender fury. Wanting as he had never wanted in his life. Hungry for love. Desperate to claim this woman as his own.

Reece lifted her into his arms, his lips caressing her throat. Wrapping her arms around his neck, Elizabeth gave herself up to the moment, to the destiny neither of them could deny.

Chapter 9

Carrying her into the cottage, Reece held her close, secure in his arms, as he marched straight through the living room. He kicked open the partially closed bedroom door. Elizabeth tightened her hold around his neck, a sudden sense of fear mingling with the anticipation she felt.

Reece was going to make love to her. Now!

He lowered her slowly onto the old iron bed, laying her on top of the crocheted lace bedspread. With her arms still around his neck, she beckoned him downward. He spread his legs, placing his knees on each side of her hips, towering above her, gazing down into her flushed face.

Elizabeth had never known true desire before, had never wanted a man with desperate, mindless passion. Removing his coat, Reece threw it on the floor. Her feelings frightened her, making her wonder if she was prepared to give herself to Reece, to not only abandon her body, but to place her heart and soul into his safekeeping. By his own admission, he was not a man who knew much about love. Would he use her and then discard her after she'd served her purpose?

Elizabeth looked into his eyes, focusing, trying to connect with his mind. She perceived a need and a longing so incredibly intense that her own mind reeled from the power. Whatever else Reece felt was overshadowed by his masculine need to possess, to take, to dominate.

Elizabeth's hand trembled when she reached up to touch his face. "I'm afraid, Reece. I'm so afraid."

No! his mind screamed. Don't be afraid of me. Don't deny me. Not now. I'll die if you don't let me love you.

Shuddering from head to toe, Elizabeth blinked back tears. Dear God, she'd heard his thoughts!

"I'm not going to deny you anything," she told him. "Not now or ever. I want you to make love to me. I want to become yours. But . . . I haven't . . . this is my first . . ."

Circling her wrists, Reece lifted her hands from around his neck and lowered them to the pillow resting above her head. She trembled, her body arching up against his.

"I want to take you right now. Hard and fast." Reece rubbed his arousal into her aching femininity. "I hurt with wanting you, Elizabeth."

Desire, fear, love and uncertainty swirled around inside her. She nodded her head in understanding, giving him permission to do with her as he would.

Tightening his hold around her wrists, he lowered his head to her breasts, nuzzling her through her sweater. When her nipples beaded, he bit them through the heavy cotton material.

"I could do anything I wanted to do to you and you couldn't stop me." Reece stared down at her, his face void of emotion. "I'm bigger than you. Stronger than you. And folks around here will tell you that I can be a mean son of a bitch. You have every reason to be afraid of me."

Elizabeth opened her mouth to speak, but no words came out, only a gasping breath.

He released her hands. "But I don't want you to be afraid of me. I want you to believe me when I tell you that I'd never hurt you. I'd never do anything you didn't want me to do."

She did believe him. She knew in her heart of hearts that Reece Landry would never harm her, that despite all the pain and bitterness inside him, he wanted and needed the love only she could give him.

"I trust you," she said.

He groaned, covering her body with his, burying his face in her neck. "Ah, Lizzie, I want to wait, to take my time, to make it good for you, but I don't know if I can. I'm close to losing it right now."

"It's all right, Reece. We have all night, don't we? The first time won't be the best for me, anyway, will it? So let me do the giving this time and you do the taking. Then next time, you give to me. You can—"

He covered her lips with a hot, hungry kiss, his body moving urgently against hers. She felt his hands at her breasts, kneading her through her sweater, then lifting the garment with great haste. Trying to help him, she rose up enough to accommodate the removal of her sweater. His mouth descended, taking one nipple, sucking, savoring, tormenting, while he pinched at the other nipple with his fingertips. Elizabeth moaned into his mouth, writhing as a savage warmth unfolded deep within her.

While Reece fought with the zipper on her jeans, Elizabeth unbuttoned his shirt, spreading it away from his body. She ran her hands over his chest, loving the feel of his springy chest hair, his tight male nipples, his hard muscles, his hot flesh.

Reece brought her zipper down, then tugged on her jeans until he pulled them over her hips and down her legs. He tossed them on the floor. He removed her panties with such haste that he ripped the thin cotton lace.

All the while he removed her clothes, he kept kissing her, tasting her mouth, running his tongue over her naked body, suckling her breasts, delving into her navel. Elizabeth explored Reece from neck to waist, glorying in the joy she found in his very masculine body, covering him with hot, excited little kisses.

Reece unbuckled his belt, unzipped his jeans and jerked them off, throwing them atop Elizabeth's on the floor. She slipped her hands beneath his shirt, scoring his back with her fingernails, delving beneath the waistband of his briefs to cup his buttocks. Reece groaned, his swollen manhood pulsating against the triangle of dark curls guarding her femininity. He jerked his briefs off and kicked them onto the floor.

"I can't wait, baby. I can't wait!" Reece clenched his teeth, grabbed her hips and lifted her up, seeking and finding the heaven between her thighs.

Elizabeth clung to his shoulders, her body arching to accept his invasion, welcoming him. Reece plunged into her, hesitating when he felt her tightness; then when she clasped his buttocks and pushed him into her, he completed his possession, taking her completely. She cried out, the sound an indrawn gasp. Reece stopped, waiting for her to accept him. Nothing had ever felt this good. Nothing!

Elizabeth was his now. She belonged to him. No other man had ever known the ecstasy of her sweet body.

"I hurt you, didn't I?" Despite the winter chill that filled the house, sweat beaded across Reece's forehead and on his upper lip.

Elizabeth rose enough to kiss his chest, his neck and then his chin. "I'm fine. You're the one who's hurting. Please let me take away that hurt, Reece."

On the brink of orgasm, Reece needed no further inducement. Her words prompted him to action, his big body tense as he thrust deeper and deeper into her satiny, gripping heat. Within seconds he cried out, spilling himself into her, shuddering with release.

Elizabeth ached with need, with wanting something she had never known with a man, wanting Reece to be the first and the only one to give her pleasure. When he fell to her side, holding her against him, Elizabeth stroked him, petting his chest, his hips and his thighs.

"Thank you, Lizzie."

She snuggled against him, unable to speak, unable to do anything more than cling to Reece.

Evening shadows fell across the room. Only the dreary gray gloom of cloud-obscured light came through the windows. She could see his body, naked except for his shirt, big and hairy and muscled, his flesh a natural light olive hue. His partially erect manhood lay nestled in a bed of brown hair. She had an irresistible urge to touch him, to circle him and discover the feel of his masculinity. When she reached for him, Reece grabbed her hand, bringing it down on his stomach, trapping it beneath his own.

They lay side by side, their heads resting on the pillows. Glancing over at him, she smiled. "Reece?"

"Are you all right, Elizabeth?"

She saw the concern in his eyes, the fear. "Yes, I'm all right. It's just that I want more. I want to touch your body, to taste you. I'm aching inside, Reece."

Reece lifted himself up on one elbow. "Keep talking like that, Lizzie, and I'll be ready in a couple of minutes."

She ran her hand down his chest, stopping just a fraction above his manhood. "My breasts are so tight and heavy."

Reece looked at her large, firm breasts, noting how rigidly her nipples stood out, as if begging for his mouth. He flicked one nipple with his tongue. Elizabeth squirmed, moaning and reaching out, circling Reece.

Reece clasped her hand, covering it with his own, showing her how he liked to be touched, what movements gave him the most pleasure.

"My whole body throbs," Elizabeth said. "I have this tingling sensation down here." With her unoccupied hand she covered herself, indicating the area. "I took away your pain, Reece, now I want you to take away mine."

Reece removed his shirt, tossing it atop their other clothes on the floor, then reached up and tugged down the spread and blankets. Elizabeth lifted up as Reece pulled the covers down enough so that they could slip underneath. He slid his arm behind her back, dragging her up against him.

"Warm?" he asked.

She nodded.

"Comfortable?"

"I would be if I weren't hurting so much."

"Do you want me to take you again, right now?"

"Yes."

Reece laughed. "The first time was for me. The second time is going to be for both of us."

Elizabeth kissed his chest. Reece shoved her slightly away from him, turning her over on her side.

"What are you doing?" she asked.

He rubbed her shoulders, lifting her long hair aside to kiss her neck. "I'm making love to you, Lizzie. Slow, sweet, passionate love."

"Oh."

"Just relax, baby, and let me take you where you want to go."

He kissed and licked and caressed every inch of her back side, from her neck to the heels of her feet. Elizabeth squirmed and moaned and begged Reece to stop tormenting her, but he continued with his magic foreplay, teaching her what an incredibly sensuous woman she was. Her body, though tense with need and anticipation, became pliant in his hands, warm, quivering putty to be molded to his specifications. By the time he turned her around to face him, she was crying with her need, pleading with him to take her, to ease the agony that had built inside her.

Reece spread her legs, positioning himself between them, but he did not take her. Instead, while she clung to his shoulders, biting her nails into his muscles, he lowered his head and took one of her nipples into his mouth. She arched up off the bed, her femininity open and waiting for his possession. With every stroke of his tongue, every touch of his fingertips, Reece brought Elizabeth closer and closer to the brink.

"Please, Reece. Please . . ."

"You're almost ready."

"I *am* ready!"

His fingers sought and found her moisture, hot and dripping with desire. "You are ready, baby. So very, very ready."

When he entered her with one swift, firm plunge, she took him into her, accepting him fully, clinging to his shoulders, wrapping her legs around his hips. She met him thrust for thrust, giving and taking in equal measure, reveling in the feel of him buried deep within her, savoring the fullness of him that made her complete.

"Ah, Lizzie . . . so good, baby. You're so good."

"Love me, Reece. Love me!"

He took her hard and fast then, with a frenzy she equaled with her acceptance, her raging hunger to find fulfillment. Their bodies moved in unison, to the undulating rhythm of mating. The tightness within her released, exploding shards of breathtaking pleasure through her whole body, the throbbing spasms of her climax continuing on and on until satiation claimed her. Reece followed her over the precipice, falling headlong into an earth-shattering climax, his body jerking as he jetted his release into her receptive body. He groaned with pleasure, falling on top of Elizabeth, whose own body still pulsed with the aftershocks of such a fierce loving.

He rested heavily atop her, his big body damp with sweat, even though the covers lay at their feet. Elizabeth clung to him, her own body damp from their lovemaking. She felt as if she were still a part of him, still connected. She could not bear to let him go.

Reece eased off her, cradling her in his arms, never wanting to release her, wanting to keep her at his side forever. Reaching down, he pulled the covers up and over them. He kissed Elizabeth on the forehead.

"I don't think I could bear to lose you, Lizzie. Not now." He hadn't even realized he'd spoken aloud until he heard the sound of his own voice.

Draping her arm across his stomach beneath the covers, she cuddled closer to his side. "I'm yours. Now and forever. Don't you know that, Reece?" *Don't you know that I love you?*

She felt his body go rigid, and knew only too well that he wasn't ready for her confession of love.

"It's all right," she told him. "I won't leave you."

They lay there together, in each other's arms, as evening turned to night. Elizabeth slept, warm, safe and content, protected in the embrace of the man she loved. Reece lay awake for a long time, thinking about his life and wondering if there was any chance that he could change. Was it possible for a hard-hearted, cold bastard like him to ever learn to love, really love, the way Elizabeth deserved to be loved?

Finally Reece allowed sleep to claim him, but even in his dreams he could not escape the fact that Elizabeth Mallory cared for him. And more than anything, yes, perhaps even more than revenge against the Stantons, he wanted to be able to return her feelings.

Elizabeth awoke to the sound of the winter wind whipping around the edge of the cottage, creating a keening whine. Opening her eyes to the morning sunlight filling the room, she glanced at the empty side of the bed and wondered where Reece was. The silence in the house chilled her far more than the frigid temperature in the room. Holding the covers around her to protect her from the cold, Elizabeth crawled over to the edge of the bed, leaned down and picked up her jeans and shirt from the floor, leaving her panties. She slid the garments under the covers and dressed as quickly as possible, then sat on the side of the bed to put on her shoes.

She glanced into the kitchen when she emerged from the bedroom. Coffee brewed in the coffee machine; two clean cups waited on the counter. When she entered the living room Elizabeth felt the warmth from the roaring fire and also a distinct chill coming from across the room. She saw that the front door stood wide open, freezing air pouring into the cottage.

Approaching the door, she noticed Reece standing on the porch, his back to her. She walked across the room and out the door, stopping just inches away from Reece.

"It's a beautiful morning," he said, not turning around. "But it's damned cold. Are you wearing your coat?"

Elizabeth eased up behind him, slipping her arms inside his coat and around his waist, hugging him to her. "You can keep me warm."

In an instant he whirled her around and into his arms, opening his coat to pull her up against him. She smiled at him, loving the look she saw in his eyes, those lone-wolf amber eyes that told her how glad he was to have her near.

"What time is it?" she asked, wrapping her arms around him, burying her face in his chest.

"Probably around seven-thirty." He rubbed her back with up-and-down strokes, warming her with his touch.

"How long have you been up?" She kissed his neck.

"Not long. About twenty minutes." He nuzzled the side of her face with his nose. "I've made coffee." Reece turned her around so that they stood with her back to his chest, facing the front of the cabin. "You were right about the snow. There's less than two inches."

Elizabeth glanced at the white-glazed scenery, a light dusting of snow producing a fairyland effect on the bare trees and brush, tipping the evergreens with a thin layer of ice. The wind howled, blowing snow in every direction, creating the illusion that it was still falling from the sky. Like tiny, delicate diamonds, translucent in the sunlight, the snow danced in the wind.

"It is a beautiful morning." Turning in his arms, Elizabeth looked at Reece, absorbing the pure pleasure of being so near to him. "The most beautiful morning of my life."

He took her face in his hands, gazing into her eyes, his look pleading with her for understanding. Then he kissed her, soft, delicate, gentle kisses.

"Morning always comes, doesn't it?" She smiled at him. "I understand. No matter how magical the night might have been, today we're back to reality."

"I'm sorry, Lizzie. I wish—"

She covered his lips with her fingertips. "It's all right, Reece. I know what lies ahead of us, what we'll have to face. I suppose I just wanted a few more minutes of pretending everything is the way I want it to be."

"Come on back inside." He ushered her across the porch and into the cabin, closing the door behind them. "You're freezing, babe." He brought her cold hands up to his lips, cupping them and then blowing his warm breath over them.

"How about breakfast? Toast and some scrambled eggs?" She pulled away from him.

He caught her around the waist, pulling her up against him. "What time are you supposed to meet Sam at Gary Elkins's office this morning?"

"Ten o'clock."

Releasing Elizabeth, Reece shrugged off his coat and tossed it onto a nearby chair. "Toast, eggs and coffee sound good." Reece sat on the sofa.

"Fine. I'll go fix breakfast." She started toward the kitchen.

"Breakfast can wait." Reece glanced over his shoulder at Elizabeth, who turned and looked back at him.

"I suppose it could, but if we're both hungry, why should we wait?"

"I'd say that depends on what we're hungry for, wouldn't you?"

Elizabeth swallowed hard, wondering if she could dissolve the knot in her throat. She took several tentative steps across the room, halting directly behind the sofa.

"What are you hungry for?" she asked.

Before she knew what was happening, Reece reached out, grabbed her and pulled her over the back of the sofa and into his arms. She squealed. He sprawled out the full length of the long wicker couch, resting her body atop his.

"I'm hungry for you, Elizabeth. I didn't get enough of you during the night."

She straddled his lean hips, pushing one of her knees into the padded sofa back and balancing the other on the edge of a seat cushion.

"I'd rather devour you first and save the eggs and toast until we've worked up a real appetite for food." Elizabeth unsnapped his jeans and released his zipper, finding him naked beneath his pants.

Reece undid her jeans and tugged them down her hips. She lifted her body up enough from him to jerk the jeans past her knees and down to her ankles. Just as she started to kick them onto the floor, Reece tumbled them both onto the heavy, braided rug in front of the fireplace.

"Reece!" Her jeans fell off her feet.

He eased his own jeans down over his hips, anchoring them at midthigh, then he pulled Elizabeth on top of him, positioning her just where he wanted her. She adjusted her knees on each side of his hips, lowering herself onto his arousal. He surged up and into her as she took him into her body.

He urged her breasts toward his mouth, taking one nipple between his teeth, nibbling, then stroking it with his tongue before suckling greedily. He allowed her to set the pace, to create the rhythm. Elizabeth took charge, building the tension higher and higher not only in herself but in Reece, allowing the primeval woman within her to dominate, to take her own pleasure as surely as she gave it to her mate.

There before the blazing fire, Elizabeth took Reece, glorying in her own feminine power and accepting the fact that he possessed equal dominion over her. When their bodies burned with a fire hotter than the one that warmed the cottage, they shattered into simultaneous releases so intense that the aftershocks rocked them again and again.

Elizabeth lay on top of Reece's sweat-damp body, exhausted from appeasing a hunger far greater than any she'd ever known. After endless moments Reece helped her to her feet and led her to the bathroom, where they shared a long shower, making love again before dressing and returning to the kitchen for breakfast.

Elizabeth waited for Sam outside the renovated nineteenth-century antebellum cottage on Main Street where Gary Elkins's office was located. She felt a bit underdressed in her jeans, sweater and winter coat, but she'd packed light when she'd left Sequana Falls, thinking of nothing except following Reece.

At precisely ten, just as the town clock struck the hour, Sam Dundee stepped out of his rental car. Elegant in his dark suit and overcoat, Sam approached Elizabeth, giving her a quick hug.

An attractive young receptionist greeted them when they entered the office, which had been decorated by someone with excellent taste and a flair for making an office practical and at the same time pleasantly appealing. "May I help you?" The receptionist smiled at Sam and Elizabeth, her warm brown eyes revealing her genuine friendliness.

"We have an appointment with Mr. Elkins. I'm Sam Dundee." Sam assisted Elizabeth in removing her coat, then took off his overcoat and hung both items on a wooden rack near the entrance.

"Yes, sir. Mr. Elkins is expecting you." Getting up from her tidy desk, the young woman led Sam and Elizabeth toward a heavy wooden door to the right of the reception room. She knocked, then entered, announcing Mr. Elkins's ten-o'clock appointment.

Gary Elkins rose from a button-tufted hunter green leather chair, rounded his enormous antique oak desk and held out his hand to Sam.

"Won't you come in, Mr. Dundee? I'm eager to find out how you can help me prove Reece Landry innocent of B. K. Stanton's murder. You said that you were contacted by a psychic who claims she had a vision about Reece, that she believes in his innocence."

Elizabeth watched Gary Elkins as he shook hands with Sam and motioned for the two of them to sit, his gaze scanning Elizabeth quickly before he offered his hand to her.

"And is this lovely young lady the psychic you told me about?" Elkins asked.

Gary Elkins's white-blond hair was thin, his blue eyes pale and his complexion ruddy. Standing beside Sam, he looked like a kid, but then few men were as big as Sam Dundee.

"This is my niece, Elizabeth," Sam said. "She's quite involved in this situation."

"I see." Gary Elkins released Elizabeth's hand, motioned for them to be seated in the two Queen Anne wingbacks that flanked his desk, then returned to his chair.

Elizabeth felt immediate warmth, honesty and goodheartedness coming from Gary Elkins. She sensed that not only were the man's credentials as a lawyer irreproachable, he was also a decent human being. She knew that she and Sam wouldn't be putting their trust in someone who might betray Reece.

Sam glanced over at Elizabeth. Smiling, she nodded, reassuring Sam that they could confide in Gary Elkins. Sam returned the smile and the nod, then faced Reece's lawyer.

"Not only do Elizabeth and I believe that Reece Landry is innocent, but we think he was framed for his father's murder," Sam said.

Gary Elkins's eyes widened. "I see. Well, I agree with you, but I'm afraid that there's no evidence to substantiate that fact."

"I intend to uncover that evidence, Mr. Elkins." Sam leaned back in the chair, crossing his legs as he relaxed.

"Is your niece the psychic who had a vision about Reece?" Elkins glanced at Elizabeth.

"I am psychic, Mr. Elkins, but...I...I know Reece, personally," Elizabeth said. "And I know he didn't kill his father."

"I'm afraid I don't understand." Elkins frowned. "I thought I'd met all of Reece's friends during the trial."

"Look, Elkins," Sam said, "what I'm about to tell you will remain confidential. Understand?"

"Yes, I understand."

"When Landry escaped after the wreck nearly a week ago, he broke into Elizabeth's cabin in Sequana Falls—"

"He didn't break in," Elizabeth said. "The door wasn't locked."

Sam gave Elizabeth a hard stare, then turned his attention back to Reece's lawyer. "Landry was in pretty bad shape. Elizabeth nursed him back to health and the two of them became friends. He told her the facts about Stanton's murder and the trial. Elizabeth believed him, and so do I."

"Why didn't you go to the sheriff?" Elkins asked. "Why did you come to me?"

"Because Reece doesn't trust the sheriff's department, and I believe he's right in his distrust. But he wasn't sure about you, and I decided to find out for myself whether or not you were truly on Reece's side." Elizabeth scooted to the edge of her seat, clasping her knees with her open palms.

"Do you know where Reece is now?" Elkins looked directly at Elizabeth. "If you do, then I urge you to contact him and tell him to turn himself in. If the local authorities find him, they'll kill him."

Icy chills pelted Elizabeth's body. "They'll—"

"Landry isn't going to turn himself in," Sam said. "I've talked to him, tried to convince him to give us a chance to dig up some new evidence, to wait for his appeal to go through."

"Look, I don't know who you people are or why you've chosen to believe Reece, but he needs all the help he can get. So do I." Elkins slammed one hand down atop his desk.

"Dammit, the Stantons possess a great deal of power in Newell and the local sheriff knows the family wants Reece apprehended dead or alive."

The outer door swung open and a tall, slender brunette entered. "Not all the Stantons want Reece dead."

"Christina!" Elkins jumped up, rounded his desk and rushed over to the woman who'd just entered his office.

"Is this the man who has information about Reece?" Christina Stanton asked. "Is she the psychic?"

Gary Elkins slipped his arm around Christina's shoulders, closed the office door behind her and led her into the room. Sam stood, offering the woman his seat. She shook her head and turned her attention to Elizabeth.

"Chris, these people say they want to help Reece. They know where he's hiding," Elkins said.

Elizabeth held out her hand. "I'm Elizabeth Mallory."

Christina stared at Elizabeth's hand for a few seconds before accepting it in greeting. The moment Elizabeth touched Reece's half sister, she felt the woman's anguish and frustration.

"You really do want to help your brother, don't you, Ms. Stanton?" Elizabeth asked.

Looking directly at Elizabeth, Christina pulled her hand away. Her eyes glazed with tears. She nodded her head. "Yes, I do. I know my mother and brother are convinced that Reece killed Daddy, but I don't think Reece is capable of murder."

"Neither do I," Elizabeth said.

Christina glanced from Elizabeth to Sam to Gary Elkins.

"Reece broke into Ms. Mallory's cabin when he escaped after the wreck," Elkins said. "They became acquainted and she and her uncle, Mr. Dundee, want to help Reece."

"Do you know where Reece is?" Christina asked.

"I'm afraid I can't tell you where he is." Elizabeth sensed Christina's fear. "But I can tell you that he's all right."

"Chris, honey, please sit down." Elkins led her to the empty chair Sam had just vacated. "When I spoke to Mr. Dundee yesterday, he told me that he owns a private security agency in Atlanta and he has a great deal of experience in preventing crimes. He's a former DEA agent." Elkins glanced up at Sam. "I've got all that straight, haven't I, Mr. Dundee?"

"You've got it right." Sam sat on the edge of Gary Elkins's desk. "Ms. Stanton, what we need is another suspect, someone else who would have had motive and opportunity to kill your father."

"Oh, Mr. Dundee, my father had a lot of enemies. Personally, I think Reece's stepfather, Harry Gunn, killed Daddy. The man hated Daddy."

"Ms. Stanton, do you believe in psychic abilities?" Sam asked.

"What?"

"Elizabeth is a psychic," Sam said. "She can read the psychic energy from people."

"Are you saying she can read minds?" Gary Elkins asked.

"Sometimes." Sam stood, towering over Christina Stanton. "If Elizabeth could meet your family and others who knew your father, then she might be able to pick up on something that could help us. She might be able to clue us in on a suspect."

"This is crazy!" Gary Elkins walked between Sam and Christina, boldly glaring up at Sam. "We want to help Reece, but if you think we're going to be fooled by some charlatan act—"

"You and Christina are in love." Elizabeth stared directly at the couple. "Neither of you have had the courage to admit your feelings to the other."

Gary's mouth fell open; Christina gasped, tears springing to her eyes.

"Gary is afraid you don't find him attractive," Elizabeth said. "And, Christina, you're afraid to trust another man after what happened with your fiancé."

"I don't believe this!" Elkins said.

Standing, Elizabeth walked over to Christina. Gently pushing Gary Elkins out of the way, she took Christina's hand. "The two of you will marry someday, and you'll be happy."

"Now, see here!" Elkins said.

Christina held fast to Elizabeth's hand. "No, Gary. I believe her." Christina looked up at Elizabeth. "What can I do to help you help Reece?"

Gary Elkins slumped down beside Sam on the edge of his desk.

"I want to meet your family," Elizabeth said. "Introduce me to them as a psychic who has had a vision about your father's murder and tell them that I'm convinced Reece is innocent. They mustn't know that I've met Reece, that we're personally acquainted."

"When do you want to meet my family?"

"As soon as possible."

"This evening," Christina said. "You can have dinner with us."

"Why don't you and I leave Sam and Gary to discuss what they can do, and in the meantime, you and I can become better acquainted." Elizabeth squeezed Christina's hands, then helped her stand.

Christina glanced at Gary Elkins, a weak smile trembling on her lips. "Gary, I think you and I need to have a nice, long talk very soon."

Elkins's ruddy complexion flushed a blotched pink and red. "Yes, Chris, we do."

Christina turned to Elizabeth. "Do you have your car with you, Ms. Mallory? I'm afraid I had Mother's chauffeur drop me by here."

"Call me Elizabeth. May I call you Chris?"

"Yes, please do."

Elizabeth waved goodbye to Sam, and ushered Chris out the door.

Three hours later Elizabeth sat across the table from Chris at Calahan's, a downtown restaurant located in a restored building. Their table was on the second floor, in the non-smoking section by the windows looking down on Main Street.

In the time since they had left Gary Elkins's office Chris had given Elizabeth a tour of Newell, including a ride down Lilac Road where Reece had grown up. Elizabeth had felt an instant rapport with Christina Stanton, and had no doubts that the woman was sincere in her desire to help her brother.

Elizabeth watched Chris play with the piece of apple pie on her plate. "Are you sure it's a good idea for me to go home with you after lunch?"

"I'm sure," Chris said. "Mother had some sort of charity do at the country club, so she'll be out until around four. Kenny's at work, trying to keep things going at Stanton Industries, and finding out he can't fill Daddy's shoes."

"You want to run Stanton Industries, don't you, Chris?"

Chris turned her head sharply, staring at Elizabeth with round eyes. "How did you… I forgot, you're psychic. You really did read my mind, didn't you? You knew exactly what I was thinking."

Elizabeth wiped the corners of her mouth with the white linen napkin, then laid it on the table beside her empty dessert dish. "Your father must have been a very old-fashioned man, one who didn't believe his daughter should be left in charge of his business."

"Daddy didn't have any problem with me working at Stanton Industries, giving me an honorary position to pacify me." Chris scissored through her piece of pie with the prongs of her fork. "But he wasn't too thrilled when I started coming up with ideas, making suggestions, actually taking my job seriously."

"I'd bet you have a degree in business. Right?"

"Can't you just read my mind?" Chris smiled.

Elizabeth picked up her coffee cup. "I only pick up on strong emotions, usually, and I try very hard not to tune in to every thought of the person I'm with."

Chris laughed. "Yes, I have an M.B.A."

"And Kenny?"

"Kenny didn't go for his M.B.A. after getting his B.S. because Daddy thought it best for him to learn to run the business by running the business."

"What happened?"

"Reece happened."

Elizabeth sipped her coffee. "Reece worked at Stanton Industries, and he and Kenny didn't get along."

"That's the understatement of the year. Reece and Kenny hated each other. Kenny was so jealous of Reece he couldn't see straight."

"Why? Because he knew Reece was your father's illegitimate son?"

"Oh, it went a lot deeper than that." Chris shoved her pie plate away from her, dropping her fork on the table, the edge hitting the plate with a clink. "Daddy was a manipulator. He deliberately pitted Reece against Kenny. He saw that Reece was smart and quick to learn, that he was hungry for acceptance and success. He used that against Reece, and against Kenny."

Elizabeth had wondered how much his inheritance would mean to Reece, how deeply his need for revenge against the Stantons ran. Once the real murderer had been found, would Reece stay on in Newell, accept his share of Stanton Industries and seek his place as a member of society? If he did, was there any hope for her to have a future with Reece? She couldn't live in Newell. She could never become a part of the world he would live in as part of the Stanton family.

"Do you think Reece would like to be in charge of Stanton Industries?"

"I'm not sure," Christina said. "I know he feels cheated by my father's unwillingness to recognize him as his son. I think Reece wanted Daddy's acceptance more than he's willing to admit."

"I understand that your father changed his will shortly before his death," Elizabeth said. "Who knew that your father left Reece one-third of his estate?"

"As far as Gary could find out, no one other than Willard Moran, our family's lawyer, knew about the new will."

"How long before his death did your father have his lawyer draw up a new will?"

"Three days."

"Reece thinks that your father asked him to your house the night he was killed because he planned to tell him about the new will."

Sighing, Christina rubbed her forehead. "Uncle Willard suggested to the sheriff that Daddy had told Reece before...that Reece actually killed Daddy for the money. The district attorney tried to use Uncle Willard's testimony at the trial.''

"When can I meet Uncle Willard?" Elizabeth asked.

"He will be dining with us tonight. He's been very supportive ever since Daddy died. I'm not sure Mother would have survived half as well without him."

"So, I'll not only meet your mother and brother, but Uncle Willard, as well."

"And don't forget Tracy!"

How could she forget Tracy? After all, she and Reece were hiding out in the woman's parents' summer house. "You don't like your sister-in-law, do you?"

"You didn't have to read my mind to figure that out, did you?" Chris laughed.

"How did Tracy get along with your father?"

"Tracy got along better with Daddy than she does with Kenny. Daddy handpicked Tracy, you know. Old family. Old money. But Daddy didn't realize the good breeding that was supposed to come along with old families and old money was sadly lacking in our dear Tracy."

Elizabeth reached across the table, touching Chris's hand where she clutched her napkin. "Do you think a member of your family could have killed your father?"

Chris breathed deeply, letting out her breath on a long sigh. "As much as I despise Tracy, she had no motive. Kenny feared Daddy and sometimes hated him, but he also worshiped him. And Mother...well, Mother and Daddy lived separate lives. She knew he had his women, and she chose to look the other way. I suppose she hated him for it, but I doubt she would have killed him, not after all these years."

"And we know that Reece didn't kill him," Elizabeth said.

"I'm not sure how much good it will do for you to meet the family this evening."

"If I can pick up on anything, something I learn might help Reece."

"Let's go, then, and we'll see what we can find in my closet that might fit you. Mother would die if you came down to dinner wearing jeans."

Elizabeth grinned. "Thanks, Chris. I'm afraid I left Sequana Falls in such a hurry I didn't consider I'd need anything to wear other than jeans."

Chris stood, placing the straps of her bag over her shoulder. "Lunch is on me."

"I'll leave the tip."

When Elizabeth opened the driver's side door of Sam's '65 T-Bird, she saw a note lying on her seat.

"What's that?" Chris asked as she got inside the car.

Elizabeth picked up the note and opened it. A key fell out. Holding the key in her hand, she read the note silently to herself. Sam had left her the name of his motel, the room number, a key and a message to meet him after her dinner with the Stantons.

"It's from Sam."

Elizabeth started the engine and drove down Main Street. The bright sun had melted most of the snow, leaving a grimy slush along the roadside. Following Christina's instructions, Elizabeth maneuvered the car out of town and toward the highway. Glancing in her rearview mirror, Elizabeth noticed an older model Chevrolet, the paint faded, rust splotching the surface and the vinyl top ragged. The car had been behind them since they had pulled out of the parking lot at Calahan's.

Elizabeth turned left onto the highway; the Chevy followed. She couldn't make out the driver's identity, but she could tell that he was the sole occupant.

"Chris, do you know someone who drives an old, ragged blue Chevrolet?"

"Why?" Chris started to turn around.

"Don't look right now, but I think somebody's following us."

"Who would be following us?"

"I have no idea." Elizabeth speeded up just a little. The car behind her speeded up enough to keep them in sight. "Turn toward me and act as if you're talking, then catch a quick glimpse of the car behind us."

Chris followed Elizabeth's instructions. Gasping, she jerked around quickly. "It's Harry Gunn!"

"Reece's stepfather?"

"The man is scum. No, he's worse than scum. He makes my skin crawl."

"Why would he be following us?"

"I have no idea . . . unless—"

"Unless what?" Elizabeth asked.

"Unless he's been following me to see if I'd lead him to Reece. He knows that I hired Gary to defend Reece, that I offered to put up bail for him before the judge denied bail. Harry Gunn knows that I'm one of the few people in Newell who believes Reece is innocent."

"So Mr. Gunn thinks if he follows you, you'll lead him to Reece, and he wants Reece handed over to the sheriff. Right?"

"Harry Gunn would like to see Reece dead." Chris pulled her shoulder bag across her stomach, holding it close to her beige wool coat. "I think Reece's stepfather killed Daddy and framed Reece. He hated Daddy even more than he hated Reece."

"I want to talk to Mr. Gunn," Elizabeth said.

"No! You mustn't. He's dangerous!" Chris clutched Elizabeth by the arm.

Elizabeth pulled the car off the road into a service station located in the middle of a minimall. Killing the engine, she opened her door. The old Chevy pulled in on the opposite side of the service station.

"Stay here," Elizabeth said. "If I can get close enough to him, I should be able to sense something. If he killed your father, maybe I can pick that up."

"Elizabeth!" Flinging open the door, Chris jumped out, following Elizabeth as she marched toward Harry Gunn's old car.

The man was slumped down in the seat, the bill of a ball cap covering his eyes. Elizabeth knocked on the window. Harry Gunn shoved the ball cap up and looked out the window at Elizabeth. Her stomach flip-flopped. The man, probably no more than his mid-fifties, appeared much older. His gray hair had thinned to baldness in the front, his complexion was sallow and a week's growth of scraggly beard covered his face.

Harry Gunn rolled down his window. "Yeah? Something I can do for you?"

Overwhelmed by the smell of liquor and stale body odor, Elizabeth stepped back, bumping into Christina.

"I don't know where Reece is," Chris said. "Stop following me or I'll call the police."

When Harry Gunn laughed, he showed a mouthful of yellowed, chipped teeth. "Go ahead and call 'em. I'll tell them you're hiding that bastard half brother of yours."

Elizabeth sensed the hatred. She felt the evil, the cruel, malevolent energy surrounding Harry Gunn. Seldom, if ever, had she felt such wickedness. She could not probe past the wickedness into Harry's thoughts.

"Reece Landry is an innocent man," Elizabeth said. "He has friends who will not allow him to pay for a crime he didn't commit."

"Who are you, sister? You don't look like any of the Stantons' highfalutin friends or any of Reece's good-time gals."

"She's my friend, and... and a psychic who had a vision about Daddy's murder. She's come to Newell to help us find the real murderer," Christina said. "She believes in Reece's innocence."

"Well, then, she's as big a fool as you are." Gunn grinned, tobacco spittle dripping from the side of his mouth. "Reece is no good. He never was. I tried my best to beat some sense into him, but all he ever gave me was trouble. He killed B.K., all right. The whole town knows it. And I'm just sorry they didn't give him the death sentence."

Harry rolled up his window, started the old Chevy's engine and backed out of the service station.

Chris grabbed Elizabeth by the arm. "Can you imagine being raised by a man like that? Reece's life must have been a living hell."

Elizabeth covered Chris's hand, patting her gently. "I believe that man is capable of anything, even murder!"

Chapter 10

Elizabeth felt uncomfortable wearing Christina Stanton's designer dress, and even more uncomfortable surrounded by the emotions of a family who despised Reece Landry. A sense of panic began growing inside Elizabeth during the formal dinner when Christina introduced her as a new friend and a psychic who had predicted she would marry Gary Elkins. Tracy and Kenny had seemed amused, Alice Stanton disgusted at the thought and Willard Moran unconcerned.

Dinner conversation had been light, inconsequential and unrevealing as far as Elizabeth was concerned. Everyone seemed curious about exactly who she was and why Christina had invited her into their home.

After-dinner coffee was served in the elegant, austere living room, where Alice Stanton sat on the gold brocade Sheraton sofa and stared at Elizabeth.

"Where do you live, Ms. Mallory?" Alice asked, her faded blue eyes shaded by half-closed lids. "Would I possibly be acquainted with any of your people?"

"Elizabeth is—" Christina said.

"I'm from a small town in the northern part of the state." Elizabeth didn't have to be psychic to sense Mrs. Stanton's snobbery or her discomfort at having an undesirable stranger in her home. "And I'm quite sure you wouldn't know anyone in my family."

"How long have you been practicing this psychic stuff?" Tracy Burton Stanton, long and lean, with huge brown eyes and a halo of strawberry blond curls, smiled at Elizabeth, who wondered how someone with such a sharp, hawk nose could turn it up with such expert ease.

Christina gasped, then glared at her sister-in-law, silently chastising her for being rude to a guest.

"I've been psychic all my life, Ms. Stanton, but my abilities became very apparent when I was about six years old." Elizabeth held the delicate china cup and saucer in her hand, wishing she had declined the offer of coffee.

"How did you and Chris meet?" Kenny sipped his coffee with the same precise movements his mother used, an almost feminine flair to his actions.

"In Gary's office," Christina said, glancing at Elizabeth for approval. "She . . . Elizabeth had a vision recently. A vision about Daddy's murder."

"What?" The cup in Alice Stanton's trembling hand quivered.

Murmurs rose around the room. Kenny set his cup on a nearby table. Tracy sat up straight, her eyes widening, her face turning pale. Seated beside Alice on the sofa, Willard Moran placed his arm around her shoulders.

Overwhelmed by the whirlwind of emotions Christina's revelation had stirred up, Elizabeth gripped the arm of her Queen Anne chair and very slowly set her cup on the marble-topped mahogany coffee table. She tried desperately to sort through the myriad feelings coming from the people in the room, but the strength of their emotions collided, creating chaos in Elizabeth's mind.

Standing beside Elizabeth's chair, Christina glanced down, then leaned over and whispered, "Are you all right?"

"I can't separate their emotions. Their energies are mingled together." Elizabeth breathed deeply, willing herself under control. The bombardment began to ebb as she shielded herself.

"What sort of vision did you have about Daddy's death?" Kenny, short and squarely built like his mother, stood behind the sofa, stroking the fine brocade cloth with the tips of his perfectly manicured fingernails.

"I won't have this sacrilege in my house." Alice Stanton, her sagging, hound-dog cheeks flushing profusely, straightened her spine and shrugged off Willard Moran's comforting arm. "This psychic business is evil and I'll have none of it."

"Calm down, Alice." Tracy laughed, obviously amused at her mother-in-law's discomfort. "You're overreacting a bit, don't you think? After all, we know what happened to B.K. What could this woman—" Tracy glanced over at Elizabeth, a smug smile on her face "—possibly tell us that we don't already know?"

"Tracy's right, my dear." Grasping Alice's hand, Willard patted her tenderly. "We all know that Reece Landry killed poor B.K."

"I don't want that man's name mentioned." Jerking her hand out of Willard's, Alice entwined her fingers in a prayerlike gesture. "He's caused this family more than enough grief. And now he's running around free, possibly still in Newell."

"Don't fret so, Mother. The authorities will apprehend him, and he'll spend the rest of his life rotting in Arrendale." Kenny clutched the back of the sofa, his fingers biting into the cushion.

"Reece Landry didn't kill B. K. Stanton." Elizabeth saw, heard and felt an immediate reaction. Disbelief and fear dominated the room. Elizabeth tried to zero in on the fear. She felt it strongly, emanating from the area around the sofa where Alice Stanton sat beside Willard Moran, and Kenny stood behind them.

"Of course he did," Willard said. "Alice and I walked in on him only moments after he'd shot B.K. We discovered him kneeling over B.K.'s body. His hands were covered with blood."

Very slowly, as if she were in a trance, Elizabeth stood, her eyes slightly glazed as she stared across the room at the fireplace. "B. K. Stanton was shot twice while he was standing behind his desk in his study. I can't see the murderer, but I can see Reece Landry rushing into the room, after the shots were fired. I can see him being struck over the head and falling to his knees.''

"Those are the lies he told in court!" Kenny shouted. "The man's a conniving, money-hungry bastard! He hated Daddy. He hates this whole family.''

Elizabeth felt Kenny's hatred—intense, all-consuming, bitter, resentful. She also felt his fear. A little boy's fear that his father didn't love him, didn't approve of him, that another brother might prove to be the father's favorite.

"Not all of us hate Reece,'' Christina said. "And not all of us believe he killed Daddy.''

"Is that what this is all about, Chris?" Tracy asked. "You're so determined to prove Reece innocent that you've hired some phony psychic to say that she's had a vision about who really killed B.K.? Don't you think it's odd that she can't see who the murderer is?''

"Each time I have the vision, I see more and more,'' Elizabeth lied, and prayed her deceit didn't show on her face.

"What do you mean, you see more and more?'' Willard Moran stood, his sharp blue eyes narrowing as he glared at Elizabeth.

"I believe it is only a matter of time before the real killer's identity is revealed to me.'' Elizabeth sensed more fear, greater fear—a mother's fear. She glanced down at Alice Stanton. The woman was afraid Kenny had killed his father!

"That's nonsense, and no court of law would take anything you have to say under consideration.'' Bespectacled, ruddy-faced Willard Moran smoothed his thick white mustache with his thumb and index finger. "Reece Landry was tried and convicted and that's all there is to it. The man will be apprehended and punished.''

Elizabeth focused on the Stanton family's lawyer. Finding him in complete control of his very logical mind, she prodded harder. Sensing only a determination to protect Alice Stanton, Elizabeth probed his emotions. Moran's emotions were so totally centered on his devotion to Alice that all other feelings were subdued and thus shielded from Elizabeth's search.

"You shouldn't be doing this." Alice frowned, shaking her head sadly as she stared at her daughter. "Reece Landry...killed B.K. and we all know it. You betrayed this family by hiring Gary Elkins to defend that man, and now you're so desperate to free your father's murderer that you've hired some woman to pretend she's had a vision that can prove Reece innocent."

"I haven't hired Elizabeth," Christina said. "She does possess psychic abilities and she does know that Reece is innocent."

"I will not listen to another word," Alice said, tears forming in her eyes. "I do not wish to be rude, young woman, but I want you to leave." She glanced at Elizabeth briefly, then focused on her clasped hands resting in her lap. "Immediately!"

"I'm sorry that my presence has upset you, Mrs. Stanton." Elizabeth nodded to Christina. "I'll say goodbye now."

Chris escorted Elizabeth out into the foyer, halting at the front door. "I'm sorry. I guess I was hoping—"

"Don't apologize." Elizabeth squeezed Chris's hand. "I didn't sense anyone's guilt, but I was able to shift through all the emotions whirling around tonight and conclude several things."

"Like what?" Chris asked. "Anything that can help Reece?"

"I'm not sure, but perhaps." Elizabeth wondered just how honest she should be with Chris. "Your mother is afraid Kenny killed your father."

"Oh, God! I have to admit that I've had the same doubts myself, but I still believe Harry Gunn killed Daddy. That man is an animal."

"What about Mr. Moran?"

"Uncle Willard?"

"He loves your mother. He's quite devoted to her." Elizabeth opened the front door. "He'd do anything for her. Anything."

"But why would Uncle Willard kill Daddy? He had no motive."

"Well, someone killed your father, and we know it wasn't Reece. That leaves your brother, sister-in-law, mother and Willard Moran."

"And Harry Gunn."

"Yes, Harry Gunn."

Elizabeth glanced down at the mauve silk dress she'd borrowed. "I'll have Sam return the dress to Gary Elkins's office tomorrow."

"Don't worry about the dress." Chris followed Elizabeth outside onto the front portico. "When you see Reece . . . tell him . . . well, tell him that . . ."

"He doesn't accept love easily, does he?" Elizabeth smiled at Reece's sister. "I think he knows you love him. It's just that he's known so little love in his life that he doesn't trust the emotion. Not in himself, and most definitely not in anyone else."

"You know Reece so well to have met him only a week ago."

Ah, but I've known him for months. "We won't give up on him, will we?" Elizabeth hugged Chris, then walked down the brick steps and toward her car.

"Your coat," Chris called out. "Did you leave it upstairs?"

"I put it in the car with my jeans and sweater before dinner." Elizabeth waved goodbye, then hurried quickly to her car, the winter wind chilling her.

Just as she grasped the door handle on the T-Bird, she felt a tap on her shoulder. Whirling around, she came face-to-face with Tracy Stanton.

"Ms. Stanton! You startled me."

"If Chris hired you, then I'll pay you double for telling me the truth."

"Chris didn't hire me." Sensing Tracy's bitterness and anger, Elizabeth braced herself against the side of Sam's antique car. "I am a psychic, and I honestly do believe that Reece Landry is innocent."

"Damn that man!"

"Why do you dislike your brother-in-law so much, Ms. Stanton?"

Tracy's shrill laughter scraped across Elizabeth's nerves. "I don't dislike Reece. As a matter of fact..."

Tension coiled inside Elizabeth like a deadly snake waiting to strike. A green snake filled with jealousy. Tracy Stanton cared about Reece. She loved him, in her own selfish way.

"You love Reece."

"You said his name as if you know him." Tracy scanned Elizabeth's face. "Is that what this is all about? You're one of Reece's women?"

"I can assure you, Ms. Stanton, that I'm not one of Reece Landry's women." Liar! Liar! Her conscience screamed at her. You've lain in his arms. You've kissed his hard mouth. You've known the pleasure of his possession.

"Then let me warn you, Elizabeth Mallory. Reece Landry is deadly to the female sex. He's the kind of man we all dream about."

When Elizabeth stared at Tracy, showing her confusion, Tracy laughed. "He's all man, if you know what I mean. I used to lie up there—" Tracy nodded toward the second floor of the Stanton mansion "—on my silk sheets and dream about what it would be like to have Reece Landry make love to me."

"Ms. Stanton, I really don't think—"

Tracy manacled Elizabeth's wrist, her sharp fingernails biting into Elizabeth's flesh. "I wish I'd known that B.K. was leaving Reece a big piece of the golden pie. I wouldn't have ended our affair so quickly. I would have chosen him instead of Kenny. Stanton Industries is what Reece has always wanted, you know."

"Either you're lying to me or to yourself," Elizabeth said, jerking free of Tracy's hold. "You never had an affair with Reece Landry. He wouldn't have sex with you. He wouldn't betray his brother."

Her brown eyes wild, Tracy glared at Elizabeth. "You really are psychic, aren't you?"

"And you're very good at lying, aren't you, Tracy? You lied to the police and you lied in court, didn't you?"

"You can't prove a thing." Tracy backed away from Elizabeth, her walk unsteady. "Uncle Willard told us that nothing you say is evidence. Isn't that what he said?"

"I feel very sorry for you, Tracy Stanton." Elizabeth opened the door and got inside her car. As she drove away, she didn't look back at either Tracy or the Stanton mansion.

Elizabeth turned her car into the parking area of the Plantation Inn, an expensive motel on the outskirts of Newell. She parked the T-Bird near the entrance. With trembling hands she opened the car door and stepped outside, her legs unsteady. The confrontation with Tracy Stanton had topped off the evening to perfection, weakening her considerably. There would be no way she could keep her condition from Sam; he would detect the symptoms immediately, having seen them in the past.

She knew he would be furious, but that couldn't be helped. She had to give Sam her impressions of the people she had met tonight, several of the most likely suspects in B. K. Stanton's murder. Although she hadn't picked up on specific guilt from anyone, the only person she had completely ruled out was Christina.

A sense of relief washed through her when she realized that Sam's room was on the ground floor. Fumbling in her purse for the key, Elizabeth heard voices coming from inside and wondered if Sam wasn't alone. Listening carefully, she realized that the voices were coming from a television newscast.

Inserting the key, she turned the lock and opened the door. The room lay in semidarkness, the only light coming from the television screen and the bathroom. She scanned the room quickly. Sam was nowhere to be seen.

"Sam," she called out, closing the door behind her.

The bathroom door opened; Reece Landry stood in the doorway.

Already weak from her ordeal with the Stantons, Elizabeth swayed, clutching at thin air as she felt her knees give way.

"Lizzie!" Reece rushed across the room, grabbing Elizabeth just as she crumbled onto the floor. Lifting her in his arms, he carried her to the bed.

She stared up into his worried face, reaching for him, barely able to lift her arms. "What are you doing here?"

"Waiting for you." Reece laid her gently on the bed, sitting beside her, holding her hand. "What's wrong? What happened?"

"Nothing's wrong. I'm fine." She tried to sit up, but her head began to spin. This was all her fault. She had overreacted to the venom inside the Stanton home, the riot of emotions ranging from hatred to desperation. She had tried to shield herself, but in her zealousness to discover any possible leads, she had allowed herself to become too immersed in her psychic readings.

"You're not fine. Something happened. I want to know." Reece ran his hands up and down her arms, grasping her shoulders and anchoring her to the bed.

"Where's Sam?"

"He's not here." A twinge of anger shot through Reece. Why did she need Sam? What could Dundee do for her that he couldn't? "What's wrong, Lizzie? Tell me. I want to help you."

Elizabeth smiled at Reece, recalling the numerous times she had pleaded with him to allow her to help him. Now the situation was reversed, if only temporarily. Lifting her hand, she stroked his cheek.

"I'm exhausted . . . from trying to read their thoughts, from trying to pick up on anything that could—"

Reece covered her lips with his fingertip. "You never should have gone home with Christina. My gut instincts told me it was dangerous. Damn, Lizzie, this is my fault. Sam tried to tell me what could happen to you."

"I'm all right, Reece. I was just trying too hard. I didn't protect myself."

"You shouldn't be in the middle of this mess. You should be home in Sequana Falls all safe and sound."

"And I will be home all safe and sound, once we find out who really killed B.K." Elizabeth tried to sit up; Reece shoved her back down on the bed.

"I don't want you to do anything except lie there and rest. Sam should be back in a few hours." Reece kissed her on the forehead, then stood. "I have to go see somebody before I go back to Spruce Pine. I want you to stay here with Sam tonight. You'll be safe."

An old Western movie came to life on the television. Blurs of vivid color danced across the screen. The beat of Hollywood-style Indian war drums echoed through the room.

"Where is Sam?"

"He's following up a lead I gave him." Elizabeth widened her eyes, questioning Reece. "I had told Sam that Tracy was Kenny's alibi and vice versa, but my bet was Tracy wasn't with Kenny when B.K. was shot. I figure she was with some guy."

"She spends more time with her lovers than with her husband, doesn't she?"

"I didn't sleep with Tracy. I told you that. I was tempted, mainly because she belonged to Kenny, and then when it came right down to it, Kenny was the reason I didn't."

"You hurt her deeply when you rejected her." Elizabeth sat up on the edge of the bed, removed her coat and tossed it on a nearby chair. "She thinks she's in love with you."

"Did you two have a nice little chat tonight?" Reece surveyed Elizabeth from the top of her head to the tips of her mauve pumps. "Where did you get those clothes?"

"Yes, Tracy and I had a *nice* little chat. And these clothes belong to Christina. The shoes are a little loose, but a close fit." Elizabeth kicked off the high heels. "So Sam is trying to find the guy you think Tracy was with when B.K. was shot?"

"He's already found him. He's meeting him tonight and going to try to persuade him to admit the truth."

"Sam has been very busy." Elizabeth rubbed her temples, willing the tension to subside, breathing deeply as she relaxed.

"Sam came out to the cottage this afternoon to tell me what he'd found out. He knew I'd be going nuts waiting around out there. He understood why I needed to come into Newell with him, why I needed to see you after you met Chris's family."

"I can't believe Sam let you take such a risk!"

"Sam understood, dammit! He advised me against coming, but he knows I've got to be involved in solving my own problems, that I can't sit out there in Spruce Pine while you and he take all the risks."

Standing, Elizabeth walked slowly toward the bathroom. Reece hurried to her side when she leaned against the doorpost. "Where the hell are you going?"

"I need to wash my face and get something to drink."

"Come on and sit down." Reece led her back to the bed. "I'll get you a washcloth and a glass of water."

"How does Sam think he'll be able to persuade Tracy's lover to admit she was with him the night B.K. was murdered?" Elizabeth asked, sitting down on the bed.

"By paying him to tell the truth, the same way I'm sure Tracy paid him to lie," Reece called out from the bathroom. "Sam said he'd cover the expense and I could pay him back out of my inheritance."

"By all means, you and Sam be sure to keep tabs on who owes what. You wouldn't want to be indebted to each other," Elizabeth mumbled.

"What?" Reece came out of the bathroom carrying a damp washcloth and a glass of water.

"Nothing. I was just talking to myself."

Reece set the glass on the nightstand and handed Elizabeth the washcloth. "Will you be all right here by yourself until Sam gets back?"

"Where are you going?" Elizabeth ran the washcloth over her face, savoring the feel of the cool moistness on her skin.

"B.K.'s secretary, Claire Roberts, lied under oath during the trial. When Gary questioned her about a fight Kenny and B.K. had the day B.K. died, she claimed Kenny and his father hadn't argued, that the two got along beautifully."

"Hadn't anyone else heard their argument?"

"Yeah. Me."

"So it was your word against this Claire Roberts's. Why would she have lied?"

"All I can figure is that Kenny threatened her somehow, probably threatened to fire her. I know Claire liked me.

She's a good, decent woman. If I can talk to her, I might be able to persuade her to tell the truth.''

"You can't mean you're going to see her tonight!"

"She'd never admit the truth to Sam, but she just might be honest with me. It's worth a try." Taking the washcloth from Elizabeth, Reece handed her the glass of water.

Clutching the glass, Elizabeth stared at Reece. "What makes you think she won't call the sheriff the minute she sees you?"

Reaching out, Reece tilted the glass up to Elizabeth's lips. She drank several sips, then set the glass down on the nightstand. "Besides, you shouldn't be out running around all over Newell. Have you forgotten that the authorities are in the middle of a manhunt for you?"

Reece flipped off the television. "If I stay in Newell, sooner or later I'll get caught. I've got to do everything I can before that happens to find some sort of evidence to clear myself, or at least to throw suspicion on someone else."

"Let Sam do the investigating. He's an expert. And he's not an escaped convict the police can shoot on sight."

"Sam and I can do twice as much working together."

Elizabeth slid off the bed, standing in her bare feet. "Then the three of us should be able to get three times as much done, shouldn't we?"

"Stay out of this, Lizzie. You've done more than enough for me already. Look at yourself. You're wiped out. You need to rest, to steer clear of people."

Elizabeth slipped Christina Stanton's mauve pumps back on and reached for her coat. "I'll drive you to Claire Roberts's house. You can lie down in the back seat. Maybe no one will stop us."

"You're staying here."

"I'm going with you."

"Dammit, what do I have to say or do to convince you that I don't want you in danger because of me? Not only is the law apt to take potshots at me, I've got dear old Harry scouring Newell trying to find me. Sam told me that folks are laying odds that Harry finds me before the sheriff does."

Elizabeth walked over to Reece, placed her hand in his and looked him in the eye. "I'm all right. I can't stay here, waiting and wondering. Please understand. I want to help you."

Reece brought her hand to his lips, kissing her knuckles. "What did you think of the Stantons?"

"They're all afraid of you," Elizabeth said. "Chris wants us to prove your innocence. She considers you her brother. Kenny hates you, and Tracy wants you. Alice Stanton is afraid Kenny killed his father, and Willard Moran would do anything for Alice."

"The Stantons in a nutshell." Clutching her hand, Reece brought it to his chest, holding it against his heart. "All my life I wanted to be a part of that family. I wanted everything that Bradley Kenneth Stanton had, and if we can prove my innocence, everything I ever wanted can be mine. A big house. An expensive car. Stanton Industries."

"Your revenge would be complete if you could claim your inheritance, wouldn't it?" Elizabeth knew only too well that if Reece claimed what was his and stayed in Newell, they would have no future together. She could never exist in an artificial world of power and prestige. Even if she could control her psychic abilities, she would never fit into the Stantons' wealthy life-style. And she'd found out tonight that she still didn't possess the power to completely shield herself, that other people's thoughts and emotions could harm her, even eventually destroy her.

"The sweetest revenge against Kenny and Alice, but especially old B.K. himself, would be to walk into the Stanton Industries boardroom and tell them that I'm taking over. With Chris behind me, I could do it."

"Chris would back you. She would think the family owed it to you." Elizabeth felt a sense of uneasiness, remembering how much Chris wanted the CEO job herself. What would Reece do if he realized that the job Kenny now possessed and he longed for himself was destined to belong to their sister?

"I need to talk to Claire, to see if she can help. If I can't prove my innocence, I can never claim my inheritance."

"Then let's go see Claire Roberts," Elizabeth said.

"Please stay here."

"I'll drive," she said. "You lie down in the back seat. Just give me the directions."

Within fifteen minutes Elizabeth parked Sam's '65 Thunderbird in Claire Roberts's driveway in front of her neat, redbrick house. They hadn't met another car along the tree-lined street.

"There's a light on in the front of the house and a station wagon parked under the carport." Elizabeth glanced over her shoulder at Reece, who sat up in the seat.

"You stay out here." Reece shoved up the seat on the passenger side and opened the door. "I'm not sure what kind of reception I'll get, but if I could persuade Claire to tell the truth about Kenny's fight with B.K., the sheriff might think about reopening the case."

"I'll be all right." Elizabeth tried to smile. "You do what you have to do."

"If you see anything suspicious or if the police drive by, then just back out of the driveway and ride around for a while. I don't want you—"

"Getting in trouble because of you." Elizabeth shook her head. "This conversation is getting ridiculous."

"I'll be back as soon as I can."

Reece couldn't shake his guilt. Elizabeth Mallory had no business smack-dab in the middle of his problems. If the police caught her with him or found any proof that she was involved in keeping his whereabouts a secret, she was sure to be brought up on charges.

But what was a man to do with a woman like Elizabeth? He'd never known anyone like her. She was determined to help him. She had convinced herself that she was destined to save him, and the funny thing was, she'd half convinced him.

Of course, once they found out who killed B.K. and everything had been set right, she'd go back to Sequana Falls. And he would claim his inheritance.

Reece rang the doorbell. The porch light came on. Claire Roberts, short and matronly plump, eased open the door. Her expressive brown eyes widened. She clutched the storm door handle.

"I need to talk to you, Claire. Please." Reece saw the fear in her eyes and hated that she was afraid of him.

"What are you doing here, Reece? The sheriff's department, the police . . . everyone's looking for you." Lowering her eyes, staring down at the floor, Claire bit into her bottom lip. "You have to go. I can't talk to you."

Reece clasped the outside door handle. "I don't know why you lied in court about Kenny and B.K.'s argument, but I need you to tell the truth. I know you don't want to see me spend the rest of my life in prison for a crime I didn't commit."

"Oh, Reece, I'm so sorry. I . . . I . . ." Tears welled up in Claire's eyes.

"Did Kenny threaten you?" He shouldn't be feeling sorry for Claire, considering that her testimony at the trial proved him to be a liar, but he knew she was a good person.

Claire unlocked the storm door, opening it slowly. "I had no idea that my testimony would hurt your case. Kenny said that he wanted to protect his family, his mother in particular, from any more sordid news coverage. He said . . . he was under no obligation to keep me on as his secretary when he took over the reins at Stanton Industries."

"He threatened to fire you?" Reece glanced around, wondering how long he could stand on Claire's porch without one of her neighbors noticing.

"I have two daughters in college. I've raised them all on my own since my divorce when they were small. I have to have a job."

"Claire, could we talk inside?" Reece asked.

"What? Oh, yes, Reece, come in. I'm sorry that I lied, but I did what I felt I had to do."

Claire opened the door and allowed Reece inside her house. He closed the door behind him.

"Your older daughter is attending college on a Stanton scholarship, isn't she?" Reece wondered how many Stanton employees' sons and daughters had been awarded a full-tuition scholarship paid for by Stanton Industries. He'd been B. K. Stanton's son, but he'd put himself through school.

"Kenny could have taken away Shelly's scholarship and could have seen to it that Lauren didn't get one. He made himself very clear when he told me that he didn't want anyone to know about the argument he'd had with his father."

"Claire, I understand the predicament you were in, and I can't really blame you, but...I need your help." Reece stood in the living room, only a couple of feet away from the front door. He didn't want to push his way into Claire's home. He didn't want to frighten her.

"I know you didn't kill Mr. Stanton," Claire said. "In the years I worked with you at Stanton Industries, I had a chance to see what sort of man you are. You aren't a murderer. But then, neither is Kenny."

"I'm not asking you to accuse Kenny of murder," Reece said. "All I'm asking is that you tell the truth."

"Kenny warned me only this morning about keeping quiet." Claire clasped her hands together. "He's out of his mind with worry since you escaped."

"Kenny won't be calling the shots at Stanton Industries if I'm proven innocent of B.K.'s murder. Christina and I will have the majority shares. We'll make sure your job is protected and your daughter's scholarship."

"Hearing you put things like that makes me so ashamed." Claire wiped the tears from her face with her hand. "I knew I should have told the truth. I wanted to go to your lawyer and tell him what I'd done after the trial, but I was so afraid."

Reece took Claire by the shoulders. She stared at him, wringing her hands, her chin quivering. "Will you go to the sheriff tomorrow and tell him the truth?"

"I...I..."

They both heard the car pull into the driveway. Reece released his hold on Claire's shoulders. "Are you expecting someone?"

"No, I..." Claire eased back the sheer curtains over the picture window and peered outside. "Oh, my goodness, it's Kenny. He just got out of his car, and he's talking to some woman."

Every nerve in Reece's body tensed. Some woman. Hell, the woman had to be Elizabeth.

"What's he doing here?" Claire trembled, her hand clutching the sheer curtains.

"He's checking up on you. Making sure you keep your mouth shut."

"Who's the woman with Kenny?"

"She's not with Kenny. She's with me. She drove me over here to see you tonight."

"Oh, dear. How will she ever explain being at my house?"

Standing directly behind Claire, Reece glanced out the window. Elizabeth stood beside Sam's T-Bird. He heard her voice, loud and strong and clear.

"Well, hello, Mr. Stanton. What are you doing here?"

"Ms. Mallory, our visiting psychic." Kenny surveyed Elizabeth from head to toe. "I'm here on business, to pick up some papers from my secretary. What are you doing here? I wasn't aware that you were acquainted with Claire Roberts."

"I'm not acquainted with Mrs. Roberts." Elizabeth glanced toward the house, hoping Reece was aware of Kenny's arrival. "I had another vision. One that involved the woman who lives here."

"What sort of vision?" Kenny asked.

"A vision of a terrible argument between you and your father. Mrs. Roberts witnessed the argument. I came here to question her about my vision, and find out what she knows."

Even in the darkness, Elizabeth saw Kenny's face collapse, but she couldn't help admiring his control. He didn't move a muscle.

In her peripheral vision Elizabeth noticed the front door of Mrs. Roberts's house open. Surely Reece wouldn't be foolish enough to walk outside at this precise moment.

"Mr. Stanton, is that you?" Claire Roberts stood on her porch, staring out at the two people in her driveway.

"Yes, Claire, it's me." Turning around, Kenny faced Claire. "I've stopped by to pick up those papers I need for tomorrow morning's meeting, but it seems I'm not your only visitor."

"Who's that with you?"

"Elizabeth Mallory, some young woman who claims to be a psychic and says she's had visions about B.K.'s death. Christina brought her to the house for dinner tonight."

"Why did you bring her here with you?"

"I didn't," Kenny said. "She was here when I arrived."

"I see. Well, I'm afraid those papers you want aren't ready yet. Perhaps if you can come back in an hour."

Kenny walked up the sidewalk, stopping at the bottom of the front steps. "I'll just come inside and wait for you to finish up with that report if you don't mind, Claire. There's no need for me to drive all the way back home, is there?"

"I'd like to speak to you tonight, Mrs. Roberts." Elizabeth rushed over, stepping in front of Kenny. Reece had to be inside the house, and undoubtedly Claire Roberts had no intention of telling Kenny. Did that mean Reece had persuaded B.K.'s secretary to tell the police the truth, to admit that she had lied under oath?

"Couldn't this wait until tomorrow, Ms. Mallory?" Kenny glared at Elizabeth, his round, full face slightly flushed.

"It's all right," Claire said. "Why don't you both come on in."

Once inside the house, Elizabeth glanced around the living room, wondering if Reece had exited through a back door or if he was hiding in another room. She could tell that Claire Roberts was nervous simply by the hesitant way she walked, the way she kept wringing her hands, the way she repeatedly glanced toward the darkened hallway.

Reece was at the end of that hallway, impatiently waiting. Elizabeth sensed his unease. She tried to reassure him by sending him a telepathic message, hoping he would open his mind to hers. She could almost hear him saying, "Be careful, Lizzie. Be careful."

"I really won't take up too much of your time," Elizabeth said. "Like Mr. Stanton told you, I'm a psychic, and I've had several visions concerning B. K. Stanton's death. I am convinced that Reece Landry is an innocent man."

"I agree," Claire said. "I've never, not for one moment, thought Reece capable of murder."

"Who are we to say?" Kenny balled his meaty hands into tight fists. "After all, Reece was convicted of Daddy's murder. He was the only real suspect. The only one with a motive. Everyone knew he hated Daddy, that he hated our family."

Ignoring Kenny, Elizabeth turned all her attention on Claire. "You were present when B. K. Stanton and Kenny had a terrible argument the day Mr. Stanton was killed, weren't you?"

"How did you—" Claire gasped.

"This is utter nonsense!" Kenny's baritone voice sounded overly shrill in the stillness of Claire Roberts's living room. "Don't say another word, Claire."

Elizabeth glanced at Kenny. "By threatening Mrs. Roberts, you make it appear that you have something to hide."

"Why the hell did you have to show up?" Kenny's hound-dog cheeks, so similar to his mother's, sagged. His thin lips drooped at the corners. "Everything is as it should be. Reece Landry is a worthless bastard. He hated Daddy."

"But he didn't kill him." Elizabeth's voice was a mere whisper, but the conviction of her words filled the room.

"Yes, he did!" Glaring at Elizabeth, Kenny walked toward her slowly. "Landry killed Daddy. He killed him!"

"You may hate your brother, Mr. Stanton, but you know he wouldn't have been the only suspect if your family hadn't bribed and threatened witnesses to keep quiet. Somehow you persuaded Mrs. Roberts to lie about an argument you had with your father." Elizabeth sensed the fear and anger building to a boiling point within Kenny Stanton. "You . . . you threatened to kill your father that day, didn't you?" Elizabeth was as shocked by the realization as Kenny was by her pronouncement. The memory had been crystal clear in Kenny's mind.

"He might have threatened to kill his father," Claire said, "but he didn't any more kill Mr. Stanton than Reece did."

"No, you mustn't!" Kenny's eyes glazed over, his vision unfocused as he stared off into space. "We've always been good to you, Claire. Why would you betray us?"

"I'm not betraying anyone anymore." Claire slumped down on the sofa. "I lied in that courtroom because I was afraid, but I can't keep quiet any longer if I can help Reece by telling the truth."

"What are you saying?" Kenny staggered about as if he were drunk.

"I'm going to the sheriff in the morning and tell him what I did."

"You can't!" Kenny turned quickly, his eyes fixed on Elizabeth. "This is all your fault. You and your damned visions. No one is going to do anything to help Reece. I won't allow it. Do you hear me? I won't allow it!"

"Did you kill your father?" Elizabeth backed away from Kenny, slowly but surely easing toward the front door.

"Did I... Is that what this is all about?" Kenny opened his clenched fists, then reclosed them. "Is that what your crazy visions showed you? That I killed Daddy?"

"Mr. Stanton...Kenny..." Easing herself up off the sofa, Claire held out her hand. "No one is accusing you of anything."

"She is!" Kenny pointed at Elizabeth. "You're no psychic. You haven't had any visions. You're in this with Reece, aren't you? You're just another stupid woman who fell for his tough-guy image, aren't you?"

Sensing Kenny's deep frustration, Elizabeth backed up against the door, uncertain how close he was to losing control. "You're talking about your wife, aren't you? Reece Landry didn't have an affair with Tracy, despite what you may think or what she might have said. Don't let your jealousy blind you to the truth about your brother."

"That man is not my brother." Kenny reached out for Elizabeth, grabbing her by the shoulders, jerking her forward. "You're as big a fool as every other woman I know when it comes to Reece Landry, but you've made a big mistake trying to help a convicted murderer." Grabbing Elizabeth around the waist with one fleshy hand, Kenny circled her neck with his other hand, pressing his fingers against her windpipe.

"If the police don't catch Landry, then Harry Gunn will," Kenny said. "And that old man's crazy enough to kill anyone who gets in his way. You know how crazy he is? He's been taking turns following Chris and then Tracy all around

Newell. Ever since he heard Reece was back in town, he figured Chris or Tracy would lead him to Reece.''

"Kenny, please let Ms. Mallory go." Claire took a tentative step forward. "She may want to help Reece, but that doesn't mean she wants to harm you."

Kenny tightened his hold on Elizabeth, his fingers biting into her neck. She tried not to panic, but she felt Kenny's desperation, all his pain focused on her because she was Reece Landry's woman.

"Kenny, please..." Elizabeth said. She knew what was going to happen, and wished she could prevent the inevitable. Reece would never allow Kenny to harm her. At this precise moment she sensed Reece preparing himself to attack. And when he did—

"I was Daddy's only son," Kenny said. "Everything was mine. Daddy, Stanton Industries and Tracy. Then Reece came along."

"I know how difficult it must have been for you, but surely you realize that your father played you and Reece against each other for his own perverse reasons. You mustn't blame Reece—"

Kenny roared with laughter, the laughter of a man on the edge of a breakdown. "Don't blame Reece for sleeping with my wife, for taking my father away from me, for stealing part of my inheritance." Kenny shoved Elizabeth up against the wall. "When I found out about Tracy and Reece, I should have killed her. I should have killed them both."

Kenny's fingers closed around Elizabeth's throat, choking her. She grabbed at his shoulders, shoving him, at the same time kicking his leg. If only Reece would stay put, she could handle this situation. Kenny didn't have a weapon, and she felt certain she was strong enough to fight him off.

Just as she raised her leg, aiming directly for Kenny's groin, he released her. Reece jerked Kenny away from Elizabeth, tossing him to the floor as easily as he would have thrown a pillow. Kenny glared up at his brother, pure hatred in his eyes. Elizabeth slumped against the wall, coughing several times, then gulping in air.

"You slimy little son of a bitch!" Reece stared at Kenny, at his father's firstborn, at the soft, pampered, weak and spoiled heir to the throne.

Lying flat on his back on the floor, Kenny looked toward Elizabeth. "I was right, wasn't I? You're just one more of Reece Landry's conquests." Then Kenny grinned as he stared up at Reece. "What's the matter, Landry? You don't want me to touch your woman? That's not fair, is it, since you've done a lot more than touch my wife?"

Reece, his legs spread apart, clenched his hands open and closed as he stood over his brother, wanting more than anything to beat the hell out of Bradley Kenneth Stanton, Jr. "You're too blinded by hate to see the truth. God, I feel sorry for you. To think I envied you all my life."

Elizabeth grabbed Reece by the sleeve of his jacket. "Don't do what you're thinking. He's not worth it."

"You'd better listen to your lady friend," Kenny said, shoving himself up into a sitting position. "Unless you intend to kill me and Claire both. After all, she'd be a witness to my murder."

Elizabeth tugged on Reece's sleeve. He glanced at her quickly, exchanging a brief message of understanding, then looked back down at Kenny. "Claire is going to tell the sheriff the truth about your fight with B.K.," Reece said. "And the man Tracy was with when B.K. was killed is going to blow your alibi, so, big brother, you'd better be prepared to do some explaining."

"You think you're so damned smart, don't you?" Kenny's mouth widened into a self-satisfied smirk. "Well, I didn't kill Daddy. And Claire isn't going to tell the sheriff anything, and neither is that muscle-bound twenty-year-old Tracy was screwing the night you murdered Daddy."

Elizabeth saw Claire pick up from the end table a heavy brass flower vase filled with an arrangement of silk roses. Elizabeth glanced at Reece, and knew he was aware of Claire's movements.

"The Stantons own this town," Kenny said. "We make the rules. Nobody goes against a Stanton and wins. You should know that, Landry."

Claire Roberts walked up behind Kenny, who sat on the floor smiling at Reece and Elizabeth, a cocky glint in his eyes. Lifting the large brass vase, Claire brought it down on top of Kenny's head. He fell sideways, unconscious. The brass vase thumped silently onto the floor; the peach silk roses scattered across the sea of blue carpet.

Claire knelt beside Kenny, feeling for a pulse. "He's fine. I just knocked him out."

"You most certainly did," Elizabeth said, slightly stunned by the other woman's actions.

"Reece, you have to get away as fast as you can," Claire said. "I'll have to call the police before Kenny comes to, but I'll wait as long as I can to give you a head start."

"Claire?" Reece stared at B. K. Stanton's secretary.

"I'll tell the police everything. The truth about Kenny's quarrel with his father, the fact that he threatened to kill B.K. And…and I'll tell them that you were here tonight. I'm through with lying. For Kenny or for you."

"That's fair enough," Reece said. "Thank you, Claire."

"Go on. Get out of here." Bracing her hand on a recliner at her side, Claire lifted herself up from the floor.

Slipping his arm around Elizabeth, Reece led her out the front door and to Sam's T-Bird.

"Get in the back and lie down," Elizabeth told him. "I'll drive us to Spruce Pine as quickly as possible."

Reece opened the car door. "We need to talk to Sam before we go back to the cottage. He should know what happened here, that Kenny's going to tell the police you're helping me. And I need to find out if Sam was able to persuade Tracy's lover to admit the truth."

"It's too dangerous to go to Sam's motel. Once Kenny comes to—"

"We're going to the motel," Reece said. "And Sam's going to get you out of Newell as fast as he can."

"No! I won't go. I won't leave you."

"Dammit, Lizzie. This time you'll do what I tell you to do."

Chapter 11

"Dammit, what a mess." Sam Dundee paced back and forth at the foot of the bed in his motel room. "You should turn yourself in, Reece. Tonight."

"I don't know," Reece said. "My gut instincts tell me that now isn't the time, that we aren't any closer to finding the real killer."

"Look, you've got Claire Roberts willing to admit that she lied under oath because Kenny Stanton threatened her, and I persuaded Neil Colburn to tell the police that Tracy Stanton paid him to keep quiet about being with her when your father was murdered. That shoots holes in Kenny's alibi."

"We have no proof that Kenny killed B.K.," Reece said. "If I turn myself in, they'll pack me off to Arrendale, and appeal or no appeal, my chances of ever being set free are slim if we can't prove who really shot B.K."

"The real murderer is going to reveal himself or herself." Elizabeth's gaze softened when she looked at Reece. If only he would allow her to comfort him. No matter how close he let her get, he kept a barrier between them—a barrier of fear and distrust.

"Is that a psychic prediction or just a wild guess?" Reece knew he wasn't being fair to Elizabeth, but, dammit all, he'd had just about enough. He didn't know how much longer he could withstand the temptation to lower his guard completely, to let Elizabeth inside his head and inside his heart. He'd be a fool to keep her with him; she'd be an even bigger fool to stay.

"Neither prediction nor guess." Elizabeth swallowed the tears trapped in her throat. Even knowing where Reece's anger and bitterness came from, she couldn't keep herself from being hurt by his words. "Whoever killed B.K. knows you're innocent, and he or she will soon know that I'm helping you and I've claimed to have a psychic vision of the murder. I don't think they'll wait too long before they make their move."

"She's right," Sam said. "If the real murderer finds you and Elizabeth, he'll do whatever it takes to silence both of you."

"Don't you think I know that." Reece narrowed his eyes, giving Sam a hard look. "I want you to get Elizabeth out of Newell as fast as you can. Tonight, if possible."

"I would agree with you, except for one small problem you've overlooked," Sam said. "The sheriff will be looking for Elizabeth as soon as Kenny Stanton tells them that she's aiding and abetting you. There's no way I can get her out of Newell once that happens."

"What the hell are we going to do?" Reece hated the thought of Elizabeth being in trouble with the law because of him.

"Turn yourself in tonight." Sam nodded toward the telephone. "Call Gary Elkins and tell him to meet you at the sheriff's office. I'll go with you and Elizabeth, and we'll see if we can hoodoo them into believing that Elizabeth isn't involved, that Kenny Stanton is lying."

"I'm not ready to give up my freedom." Reece couldn't bring himself to put his life in anyone else's hands. Not Gary Elkins's or Sam Dundee's. Not even Elizabeth's.

"Wherever you go, whatever you do, I'm going with you." Elizabeth walked over to Reece, clasping his arm in her strong grip.

Reece jerked away from her. "Don't be a fool, Lizzie. You've done everything you can do for me. I don't want you following me around like some lovesick puppy. Just because I'm the first man you ever—"

"Shut the hell up!" Sam bellowed, punching Reece in the chest with his index finger.

Elizabeth placed her hand on Sam's shoulder. "It's all right, Sam. Reece's bark is a lot worse than his bite. He's tried this tactic before and it didn't work. Obviously he doesn't learn from his mistakes."

"Obviously," Sam said.

"How you've been able to put up with her all these years, Dundee, I'll never know." Grinning sheepishly, Reece shook his head. "You can't tell her anything. She knows too damn much. She can look through a guy like he's made of glass. And no matter what you say to her or do to her, she just keeps on caring."

"That's called love and loyalty." Sam placed his arm around Elizabeth's shoulders. "A couple of qualities that were obviously missing in your life, Landry."

"Yeah, so it would seem."

"If you don't intend to turn yourself in tonight, then I suggest that you and Elizabeth go back to Spruce Pine for the time being," Sam said. "If you don't get out of Newell pretty quick, you'll be trapped here."

"You want Elizabeth to go with me?" Reece asked. "I thought you, of all people, would see how dangerous her being with me is."

"I've known since the day she called and told me she was hiding you in her cabin that she was in danger because of you. But she didn't listen to my warnings then. And now it's too late to take her away from you."

"Keep her here. Take her to the police. Make them believe that Kenny's lying, that her only involvement with me is through her visions."

"That won't work," Elizabeth said. "Claire Roberts will tell the sheriff the truth. Besides, Sam is right. I won't leave you. He believes me when I say that somehow, some way, I'm the only person who can save you."

"How?" Reece asked. "By having the real killer come after you?"

"Perhaps. I'm not sure."

"Time's a-wasting," Sam said. "You two go back to Spruce Pine. In the morning Gary Elkins and I will meet y'all at the Burtons' cottage. Be prepared to turn yourself in to the sheriff, Landry, or be a hundred miles away from here."

"I don't like ultimatums."

"And I don't like Elizabeth's life being in danger."

"All right," Reece agreed. "You get in touch with Gary. Give him all the information we've uncovered, and meet us at the cottage first thing in the morning. That will give me all night to sort through things, to decide what to do."

"If you leave, don't take Elizabeth with you."

"She'll be waiting for you at the cottage, whether I'm there or not."

"Hold on just one minute," Elizabeth said. "Nobody's making any decisions for me."

Reece grabbed Elizabeth's arm. "If I run, Lizzie, I'll be running for the rest of my life, and you won't be going with me."

Elizabeth wanted to protest, to tell Reece that she didn't care where he went, she *was* going with him. But she realized that Reece was right. If he didn't trust her enough to accept her help, to believe that Sam and Gary Elkins and Chris Stanton were all on his side, then there was no hope for Reece and her. She couldn't force Reece to trust her or to love her. There was no way she could reach his mind or his heart if he continued denying her entrance.

Elizabeth turned to Sam, pulling free of Reece's hold on her arm. "I'll be waiting for you in the morning. We'll go to the sheriff and tell him everything. The complete truth. And then I'll face the consequences of my actions."

Sam hugged Elizabeth. "Ah, kiddo, why did you have to grow up?"

"He'll do the right thing," Elizabeth whispered to Sam. "I have to believe that he'll decide he can trust us."

"If you're going with me, let's go." Reece swung open the motel-room door.

Elizabeth followed him outside. A slow, steady drizzle fell from the sky. Raindrops pelted her face as she stood gazing out into the dark night.

"Please, dear Lord, please take care of Reece," Elizabeth prayed silently. "Set him free. Give him the peace he's never known."

When Reece prodded her to move, she turned to him, staring into his hard, lone-wolf eyes. He had shut her out. Not one sign of emotion showed on his face.

Elizabeth stepped out of the shower, dried herself off quickly and slipped into clean panties, jeans and a sweater. After towel-drying her long hair, she combed it away from her face. A weariness she had seldom experienced encompassed her, a bone-tired weariness, a heartsick weariness.

In less than a week her whole world had turned upside down, thanks to Reece Landry, thanks to her own obsession with saving him—saving him not only from a wrongful conviction but from a life that had almost destroyed him.

No matter how hard she tried to get through to him, he would allow her only so close and no closer. He had made love to her with a passion she'd never known existed, but he had given only a portion of himself to her, holding in reserve his heart, not trusting anyone enough to share his soul.

Elizabeth felt as if she had lost control of her life, of her thoughts, of her emotions. Reece Landry had become her whole world. She had become so wrapped up in helping him that she'd lost herself.

Elizabeth opened the door to the bedroom she had shared with Reece only last night. It might as well have been a million nights ago. He had been so cold and distant since their return to the cottage. She had no idea where he was. Outside, in the living room or in an upstairs bedroom. Of course, she understood that he, too, had some soul-searching to do. Would he be able to put his trust in others, to accept the advice of his lawyer?

Sitting down at the antique dressing table, Elizabeth ran a comb through her damp hair. She glanced into the mirror, seeing her own image, the wide blue eyes, the mane of dark wet hair, the sad expression she could not banish.

Laying down the comb, she closed her eyes, extinguishing her own image, closing out the world. She hadn't meditated in several days. At home in Sequana Falls, daily meditation was a part of her life, helping her center her energy and focus her abilities. Aunt Margaret had taught her that meditation was the only way she would ever learn to control the great talent with which she had been blessed, the only way her soul could derive true peace.

The day would come when she would be able to shield herself, to protect herself from the psychic energy of others. Aunt Margaret had explained how many years it had taken her to reach a point of self-protection, where she could, at will, block out the bombardment of the energy others emitted.

Elizabeth repeated the word *angel*, using it as her mantra, seeking sanctuary and inner peace in her prayerlike state of meditation.

"An-gel. An-gel. An-gel." As she chanted, her voice became a low whisper, her mind gradually clearing as utter calmness encompassed her.

Reece eased open the bedroom door, stopping dead still when he saw Elizabeth sitting at the dressing table, her eyes shut, her lips moving repeatedly as she whispered a single word. Angel.

What the hell was she doing, his loyal, loving little witch? Casting a spell? Going into a trance? Calling on the heavenly hosts to come to their aid?

The best he could make out, she was praying or something along those lines. He couldn't remember a time since he was a kid that he'd prayed, that he'd asked for someone else's help. He'd begged and pleaded for someone—anyone—to save his mother and him from Harry Gunn. He supposed, in a way, God had answered his prayers, but he had taken his own sweet time doing it. Blanche's death had freed her from Harry; Reece's physical strength had emancipated him from his stepfather's brutality.

Even knowing he was witnessing a private moment in Elizabeth's life, one he had no right to share, he could not turn and walk away. He couldn't stop staring at her, listen-

ing to her, absorbing some of the radiant peace she emanated, like a deep spring bubbling forth pure, clean water.
A warmth spread through his body, accompanied by a
calmness he had never known.

What was happening to him? he wondered. Was Elizabeth delving into his mind? Was she manipulating his emotions?

She looked so serene sitting there at perfect peace with
herself and with the world around her. She was offering that
same peace to him. Did he dare believe in its existence? And
if he did believe, did he have the courage to accept her precious gift?

He wasn't sure how long he stood in the doorway, transfixed by Elizabeth's beauty, both physical and spiritual.
Perhaps it was only minutes. Perhaps longer.

Complete quiet settled over the room. Elizabeth opened
her eyes and turned slowly toward Reece. He saw that she
started to lift her hand to him, but stopped abruptly.

"How long have you been standing there?" she asked.

"Don't you know?"

"Yes, I know, but do you?"

"I don't think I'm ready to accept what you're offering
me." Reece walked into the room, his gaze fixed on Elizabeth. "I want to trust you completely. I want to believe that
my life can be... That I can put the past behind me. All the
anger and pain and hatred. But I can't."

"You don't want to let go of the emotions that have
dominated your life." Elizabeth turned all the way around
on the velvet bench. "You're afraid of the unknown. Of
trust and loyalty and love."

Reece sat on the edge of the bed. Raking his hand down
his face, he wiped his mouth. "You want me to turn myself
in, don't you? You want me to hand myself over to the
sheriff and trust you and Sam and Gary and Chris to save
me."

She smiled at Reece. Tears gathered in her eyes, obscuring her vision. "I know it's difficult for you to accept the
fact that there are people who care about you, but—"

"I didn't ask anybody to care about me." Bent over, his
hands clasped together between his spread knees, Reece

stared at the floor. "I didn't ask you to help me and I didn't ask you to care about me."

Such anger! Elizabeth felt the resurgence of hostile emotions growing inside Reece. He was fighting an inner battle, yearning for something he didn't quite believe in, afraid to relinquish his hold on the old demons that had haunted his life since childhood—the familiarity of their ugly but constant presence the only thing he'd ever been able to count on.

"What if you allowed me to see into your future? If I could promise you that B.K.'s real murderer would be brought to justice and you would be cleared of all charges, would you trust me and the others who want to help you?"

Jerking his head up, Reece stared at her, his amber eyes gleaming with uncertainty. "I thought you said that you couldn't see my future, that our futures were entwined and you would never look into your own future."

"If it's the only way to help you, then I'm willing to try." Elizabeth stood.

Reece glared at her. "No. Don't do it, Lizzie. Don't break one of your sacred rules for me. I've taken enough from you as it is."

Elizabeth walked across the room, knelt in front of Reece and laid her head on his knee. "You're afraid of the future. Even if you're cleared of B.K.'s murder and claim your inheritance, you won't be free. You'll stay in Newell, you'll take over Stanton Industries, you'll avenge yourself against Kenny and Alice and even Chris. But nothing you do will ever change the past. B. K. Stanton is dead. You can't hurt him. Blanche is dead. You can't help her."

Reece stroked Elizabeth's head, threading his fingers through her damp, silky hair. "How the hell can you know me so well? You say that I shield myself from you and yet you seem to see inside my head."

Tears burned in her eyes. A warm, tingling flush of pain spread through her. "It doesn't take a psychic to figure you out." Turning her face just a fraction, she looked up at him. *All it takes is a woman who cares about you,* Elizabeth thought.

Reece's breath caught in his chest, creating an agonized constriction. She was, without a doubt, the most beautiful thing he'd ever seen. Radiant and warm. Tender and caring. He wanted her in a way he'd never thought it possible to want another human being. Not only did he want to possess her body, to make love to her until he was spent, he wanted to cherish all that she was—the goodness that made Elizabeth Mallory unique in a world of lesser women. He wanted to protect her from every harm, to ease her pain, to see her smile, to hear her laugh.

He wanted her to open her arms to him, to call his name, to bring him out of the darkness in which he existed into the warm, pure light of her life.

The truth hit him full force, like a lightning bolt out of the blue. A truth he knew only too well. A truth he had allowed himself to momentarily forget.

Reece placed his hands at Elizabeth's waist, helping her to her feet as he stood, then shoving her gently away from him. Why had he, for one minute, thought he was good enough for Elizabeth? What could he offer her? Nothing. Absolutely nothing she wanted or needed. Right now, as an escaped convict on the run, he offered her danger and uncertainty. If and when he was cleared of B.K.'s murder and could offer her the wealth and power his inheritance would afford him, he could offer her anything money could buy. But Elizabeth would not want material things; she would want his love.

They stared at each other, lone-wolf amber mating briefly with angelic blue innocence. Elizabeth knew he was going to leave her, that no matter how much his soul longed for all she offered him, his inner demons demanded a battle to the death.

He walked away, halting briefly to turn partially toward her as he neared the doorway. "I'll sleep in one of the upstairs bedrooms tonight."

"Yes. I understand."

"Whatever I decide . . . I want you to know how grateful I am for all your help. I probably owe you my life. I'll never forget—"

"It's all right, Reece. You don't have to thank me. I did only what I wanted to do—what I had to do." But I've failed, haven't I? Even if we can save you from prison, will I be able to save you from yourself?

Reece had no idea what time it was, how close to midnight, how close to dawn. All he knew was that he hadn't been able to sleep, that he had spent what seemed like endless hours fighting the demons in his soul. How did a man who had spent his life taking care of himself, never trusting or counting on anyone else, give in to the weakness of putting himself in someone else's care?

Was that his problem? Reece wondered. Did he see trust and caring as weaknesses? Why couldn't he consider them strengths? After all, it would take far more courage for him to willingly turn himself over to the sheriff and put his trust in others than it would to keep on running.

He slipped into his jeans, zipping them but leaving them unsnapped. The chill in the upstairs bedroom cautioned him against walking around bare chested. Lifting his shirt from the foot of the bed, he put it on and walked out into the hall. The cottage was pitch-black, including the stairway, except for the shimmering stream of moonlight flowing through the glass panes of the French door that separated the tiny foyer from the front porch.

Reece made his way down the stairs, his booted feet creating a soft, steady beat against the wooden steps. There was no point in his turning and tossing the rest of the night. What he needed was a shot of whiskey if he could find some in the house, and knowing Tracy's tastes, he figured the liquor cabinet in the living room was stocked.

The living room lay in darkness, the moonlight filtering through the sheer curtains, forming soft, wavy shadows across the floor. Low, golden-crowned orange flames danced atop disintegrating logs in the fireplace. A hushed stillness, the winter peace of nature, the blessed quiet of aloneness permeated the room like a giant sponge that had soaked up a wellspring of tranquillity.

He felt her presence before he saw her. The very idea of sensing Elizabeth without seeing her sent shock waves through Reece. Before he'd met her, he hadn't believed in much of anything, certainly not in anything he couldn't experience with his five senses. But since coming under her spell, he had learned to believe. He had learned to trust. He had learned to care. He didn't know exactly how she'd done it, but Elizabeth Mallory had begun to perform a miracle inside him. A half-formed miracle—incomplete, but the beginning was there.

He stood in the arched opening leading from the foyer to the living room. His heart beat steadily. He heard its thumping rhythm pounding in his ears.

And then he felt Elizabeth's loneliness, the deep sadness that filled her heart. Her quiet, gulping sobs blasted like trumpets when he heard them. She was crying for him. Crying because he could not cry, just as she had done before, the day they had stood on her back porch in Sequana Falls and he had shared a part of his past with her.

He crept into the room with silent steps, wanting to be nearer yet afraid to confront what he knew he would face once he'd touched her. She sat curled up in the white wicker rocker by one of the windows, a flowered afghan draped around her, her legs hugged up against her body, her chin resting on her knees.

She wore her thermal underwear, the ones with the tiny flowers printed on the cotton fabric. Her hair had dried and hung loosely around her shoulders, down her back, the tips almost touching her waist.

The moonlight spread over her, coating her like a sheer, radiant veil. She glowed, lighting the darkness the way stars illuminate the night sky.

Reece wanted to run, but his feet didn't move. If he stayed, he wouldn't be able to resist her. Even now, without touching her, he felt the power of her enticement, calling to him, offering him everything and more, so much more than he'd ever thought possible.

"I'm going to turn myself in to the sheriff in the morning." He heard her gasp softly and swallow her tears.

"I won't desert you," she told him, her voice a tender whisper in the darkness. "I'll stay with you and help you. We'll get through this together."

She eased her legs down, touching her feet to the floor. Draping the afghan across her breasts, she stood. Reece hesitated for one brief second, then he held open his arms. Elizabeth stared at him, her breathing slow and heavy. She walked toward him, each step measured, giving herself time to accept the inevitable.

When she stood less than two feet in front of him, she looked at him, then closed her eyes. Once done, some things can never be undone, she told herself. Be sure you are prepared for this, be certain that, if need be, you can go on without him. Know in your heart that you are willing to raise his child alone—the child he will give you tonight if you make love with him.

The knowledge that she had glimpsed her future shook Elizabeth to the very core of her soul. Never had she allowed herself the freedom to see into her own future. But she had not allowed herself to do so this time. It had simply happened.

She shivered, every nerve ending in her body alive with the knowledge that she was destined to love Reece Landry, that he had been sent to her, in her dreams, in her visions, a gift from the gods.

Reece pulled her into his embrace. The afghan slipped off her shoulders, falling at her feet like a pastel flower bed. She trembled as she slid her arms up around his neck, relaxing her body against his. Accepting. Trusting. Yearning. Loving.

The very nearness of him, the hard, demanding strength of him, the heady, masculine aura surrounding him sucked Elizabeth into a vortex of desire, a whirlpool of passion that demanded she surrender herself.

Reece shuddered with a fierce need to possess the woman in his arms, to lay her down and cover her with his body. He inched his hand up her back, under the fall of silky dark hair, lifting the coffee brown strands, burying his face against her neck, gripping the back of her head with his open palm. She smelled of fresh sweetness, clean and pure.

Elizabeth clung to him, losing herself in the moment, in the feel of him, the hard, lean-muscled feel of a man. Her heart fluttered inside her, like a trapped bird fighting to escape. Her heart longed to escape, to soar, to join with his and become a part of him.

She felt the wild, racing beat of his heart as she laid her face against his chest. She heard the loud, strong pounding. Her whole body throbbed with a need so intense she wanted to scream, to cry out for release, to plead for the exhilarating torment to end.

Reece lifted her head, turning her to face him, lowering his mouth over hers, laying claim to her lips. Elizabeth greeted his kiss with hungry anticipation, relief shooting through her. The tension mounted higher and higher when he thrust his tongue inside, devouring her with his need.

Elizabeth's fingers bit into his shoulders. Reece's free hand roamed down her back, grasping her buttocks, caressing her with a tender fury. He held her head immobile, drinking deeply from her sweetness, wanting—desperately needing—all she had to give.

Their bodies pressed together, her breasts crushed to his chest, his maleness throbbing against her stomach.

Reece tried to speak, tried to tell her how much he wanted her, but words seemed redundant. He raised her thermal top, easing it slowly, inch by inch until it lay in a fat roll under her arms. Her full, round breasts, the nipples jutting into sensitive hardness, beckoned his touch. Reece delved one hand down the back of her thermal bottoms, then reached out with his other hand, covering her breast, kneading softly, then playing with her nipple, pinching it between his thumb and forefinger.

The sheer, agonized delight of his touch spiraled through Elizabeth like fire along a thin trail of kerosene, flames burning higher and higher, quickly out of control. She writhed against him, moaning with a pleasure close to pain.

Shoving back his unbuttoned shirt, she caressed his chest. She loved the feel of his tight muscles, the thick mat of curling chest hair, the tiny male nipples tight with desire.

"I want you," she told him on a breathless sigh. "Make love to me."

She knew what she was asking—all that she was asking. Reece knew only part. He could not know that, tonight, he would give her his child.

She could have turned from him, said no, refused them both the unequaled pleasure of loving each other. She could ask him to use protection, but in her heart of hearts she knew that she did not want to refuse him, she did not want to prevent his seed from creating a new life within her body.

She loved Reece Landry. And she wanted his child.

Reece pulled the thermal top over her head, tossing it to the floor, then lowered the bottoms down her legs and over her feet. She stood before him totally naked, the moonlight creating a halo around her body. Reece shrugged out of his shirt, letting it fall where it would. When he unzipped his jeans, Elizabeth stilled his hands, covering them with hers.

She dropped to her knees, burying her face against him as she clutched the waistband of his jeans and tugged them over his hips. The faded jeans dropped slowly down his legs, landing in a pile of denim at his feet. Reece kicked his pants out of the way.

Elizabeth caressed his stomach, then spread her arms around him, cupping his buttocks, squeezing them.

Reece moaned. She smelled the heady fragrance of his arousal and breathed deeply, savoring the elemental maleness that was uniquely Reece's own. When her lips touched him, he trembled, sighing, almost crying with pleasure.

Her inexperience brought out her insecurities, but the depth of her love overcame her innocent shyness. She made love to Reece, drunk on the power she possessed over him, reveling in the wanton groans she elicited from him. When she took him into her mouth he grasped the back of her head, guiding her, teaching her with his touch.

Unbearable pleasure rocketed through Reece, spilling out of him, saturating the very air he breathed. His chest rose and fell with each labored breath. Slowly withdrawing himself and dropping to his knees, he lifted her face to his, tasting himself on her lips.

Smiling, she shut her eyes, giving herself over to him, allowing him free rein of her body. He deepened the kiss. She clasped his shoulders. He caressed her, his big hands roaming over her back, her waist, inching upward to lift the weight of her throbbing breasts. He kissed her lips, then her chin, gliding his tongue down her throat. Stopping his pilgrimage in the hollow between her breasts, he gazed at her and smiled.

"You certainly know how to bring a man to his knees, Lizzie."

Laughter erupted in her chest, bubbling up and out of her. "Oh, Reece, I—"

He silenced her with his mouth, obliterating her words, keeping her from declaring her love for him. She didn't have to say the words. Her actions spoke for her.

Taking her hands in his, Reece stood and lifted her to her feet. He led her out of the living room and down the hall, pausing every second or two to kiss her. When they entered the bedroom, she lay on the bed and opened her arms, inviting him into the warmth, the passion, the love he could know only with her.

Reece could no more deny her than he could will the sun not to rise or the earth to stop revolving. He came down on top of her, covering her body with his. He made a banquet feast of her, nibbling, tasting, sampling every inch of her, devouring her with his fierce desire.

Elizabeth squirmed beneath the mastery of his hands and mouth, learning exactly how much pleasure a man can give a woman if he chooses to do so. And Reece Landry chose to take her to heaven that night, to give her abundant sensual joy.

Her breasts begged for his attention, then ached with throbbing need when he touched them, kissed them, suckled them. She felt herself drifting in a sea of ever-increasing awareness, finding herself on the brink of drowning in rapture when Reece spread her legs and pleasured her with his mouth. She cried out as her body shook with release.

He lifted himself over her, gazing down at her damp face, her flushed cheeks, her lips moist and open.

"You're an angel, Elizabeth. My angel."

He took her then, before she could respond, before she could proclaim her love. He filled her completely, her body, her heart, her soul. As surely as she knew she loved Reece Landry, she knew this moment was meant to be.

They loved with a wild abandon that neither had ever known or would ever know again, except in each other's arms. It was madness. It was ecstasy.

And when they reached their climaxes, she first and he following quickly, they lay in each other's arms, in the cool, dark stillness of the night, neither of them speaking. He listened to her breathe; she listened to him breathe. Reece pulled the covers up over them. He kissed Elizabeth on the forehead. She snuggled against him.

Smiling, she laid her hand on her stomach. No matter what tomorrow brought, she knew she would never lose Reece. She carried his child in her body. He would be a part of her forever.

Chapter 12

Reece sat straight up in bed, the sheet and quilt falling to his waist. Adrenaline pumped through his body like floodwaters from a broken dam. Something had awakened him. He ran his hand over his face, blinking his eyes. Listening intently, he heard only the sound of his own heartbeat, and Elizabeth's soft, steady breathing as she lay nestled at his side.

He heard a car door slam, and then another. Laughter. Silly, drunken laughter. Tracy Stanton's laughter.

"Dammit!" He muttered the word under his breath as he threw back the covers and got out of bed. What the hell was she doing here in February? He'd had no idea that she used her parents' summer cottage as a trysting place in the winter months. She'd brought him here in May.

The keys to the Jeep and the T-Bird were on the nightstand. If they hurried, they could be out of the house before Tracy and her lover came inside.

Suddenly Reece remembered that his and Elizabeth's clothes were scattered on the living room floor. Damn! Making his way out of the dark bedroom, he eased open the door and dashed down the hallway, bumping into the edge of a small oak table in the foyer. He stifled a vivid curse, damning the table silently.

He could hear Tracy's voice outside, but not yet on the porch. She laughed again, then a deep male voice said something Reece couldn't quite make out.

Thankful that so many windows graced the living room, allowing in the moonlight, Reece scrambled around on the floor, picking up the clothing Elizabeth and he had discarded so carelessly only a few hours ago.

As he made his way back into the foyer, he heard footsteps on the porch, then a loud, heavy thud.

Tracy's laughter echoed in the black stillness. "What's the matter, Jeffie-pooh, are you drunk?"

"Hell, yes," Jeffie-pooh said. "Come on, Trace, give a guy a hand."

"You got down there all by yourself, lover. You can pick yourself up. I'm going inside. It's freezing out here."

Reece heard the key sliding into the lock, and saw two shadows outside the French door. Careful to avoid the foyer table, he rushed back to the bedroom. He pulled on his jeans and shirt, then slipped on his boots, not worrying about his socks. Finding Elizabeth's bag at the foot of the bed, he pulled out a pair of jeans and a sweater, then stuffed her thermal underwear into the bag. Leaning over the bed, he gave Elizabeth a gentle shake.

Elizabeth opened her eyes and smiled at Reece, assuming he had awakened her for more lovemaking. She reached out for him, but instead of encountering his sleek, naked body, she felt her clothes thrust into her arms.

"Get dressed as quickly as you can, Lizzie," Reece whispered. "Tracy Stanton is here. She's brought one of her lovers. They're on the porch, and they're both drunk."

Elizabeth jumped out of bed, pulling on her clothes as quickly as possible. "What's she doing here? Did you know she used this place in the winter?"

"There's no time for questions. We've got to get out of here." Reece pulled Elizabeth into his arms, slipping the keys to the Thunderbird into her hand. "I'll take the Jeep and go straight to the sheriff. You go to Sam's motel and tell him what's happened."

"Oh, God, Reece, they'll hear us when we drive off."

"Probably." He gave her a quick kiss. "No matter what happens, just keep driving. Don't look back. Don't think about me. Don't worry about me."

"What about our bags, our food?" Elizabeth didn't hesitate to follow Reece when he pulled her out of the bedroom and into the hall.

"We'll take our bags." Reece lifted both bags off the floor. "We won't need the food."

"They'll call the sheriff as soon as they hear us. They'll think we're burglars."

"My guess is that Tracy won't call the sheriff. If she did, she'd have to explain what she was doing out here."

"What if we can't get out without their seeing us?"

"Hush. Listen." Reece stopped dead still just before entering the foyer. Keeping Elizabeth behind him, he glanced out into the entrance hall. The front door swung open. The overhead light came on. Tracy Stanton stood in the doorway, her slender body wrapped in a gray fox jacket.

"Come on, Jeffie. Make us a fire in the fireplace so we can warm up."

A tall, lanky young man came up behind Tracy, grabbing her around the waist. "I can warm you up just fine without building a fire."

Pulling out of her lover's embrace, Tracy headed straight for the living room. "You get a fire started, and I'll pour us some drinks."

Elizabeth peered around Reece's side, watching as the other couple went into the living room.

"We'll go out the kitchen door," Reece told her. "We'll have to squat down behind the counter. Be as quiet as you can."

Elizabeth nodded agreement, the roar of her heartbeat drumming inside her head.

"Look, Trace, there's already a fire in the fireplace," Jeffie said.

Elizabeth froze. Reece nudged her. Together they walked out into the foyer and toward the kitchen, Reece carrying their bags, hers in his hand, his over his shoulder.

"So there is," Tracy said. "Isn't that odd. I didn't see a car out front. Wonder who's been here."

"Maybe your parents," Jeffie said.

"They're in Gatlinburg skiing all this week."

Knees bent, Elizabeth squatted beside Reece behind the kitchen counter and they did a quick duck-walk toward the back door. Reaching up in the darkness, Reece grabbed the doorknob, turning it until he heard the lock release.

The lights came on in the living room. Reece jerked open the back door, pulled Elizabeth to her feet and ushered her outside.

"Reece!" Tracy screamed his name.

"Keep running," Reece told Elizabeth. "Get in your car and go straight to Sam."

"She saw you. She knows it's you!"

"Go, Lizzie. Go, now!"

Obeying, Elizabeth made a mad dash through the backyard, but before she could get to Sam's Thunderbird a car pulled up behind her, the headlights blinding her.

"What the hell?" Reece said, turning sharply when he heard the vehicle.

The driver kept the motor running. The bright headlights cut through the darkness, trapping Elizabeth and Reece in their glare.

"Lizzie, come here to me." Reece's gut instincts told him that whoever the driver was, he wasn't the sheriff or any law officer. A shiver of apprehension raced up Reece's spine.

Elizabeth began walking away from the T-Bird and toward Reece. A car door slammed.

"Stay right where you are, witch-woman. Reece's little psychic whore. He can't help you, and you can't help him anymore."

Reece dropped their bags to the ground. Sweat beaded his upper lip and forehead, despite the cold air whipping around him. The sharp, metallic taste of fear coated his tongue. Harry Gunn!

"Let her go, Harry," Reece said. "This is between us. She's got nothing to do with our fight."

Dammit all, why hadn't he remembered Kenny saying that Harry had been following Tracy around? If only he had remembered, he might have been prepared. And Elizabeth. Why hadn't she sensed Tracy's arrival or Harry's? Had she been so consumed by their lovemaking that all else had been obliterated from her mind?

Elizabeth breathed deeply, uncertain what to do. Harry Gunn had come to kill Reece. There was no doubt in her mind about that one fact. But why hadn't she sensed that Tracy Stanton would bring a lover to the cottage, and Harry Gunn would follow her? Only the strongest thoughts and emotions could have blocked out her precognitive powers. Making love to Reece had consumed not only her body, but her mind and her heart. And all her thoughts of the future had centered on the child Reece had given her.

Tracy Stanton ran out the back door, Jeffie following her. "My God, Reece! I had no idea you'd ever come here to the cottage."

"Yeah, pretty good hideout," Harry Gunn said, his voice loud and clear. "I knew if I kept following your brother's wife around, sooner or later she'd lead me to you."

"Are you crazy, old man?" Tracy screamed. "Do you think I'd have helped Reece?"

"When a woman's got the hots for a guy as bad as you do Reece, she'll do anything for him." Harry Gunn stepped around the front of his car, out of the direct glare of the headlights. He held a gun in his hand—an old .38 caliber revolver.

"What are you going to do?" Tracy asked.

"Hey, man you can't—" Jeffie said.

"Hush!" Tracy gave Jeffie a sharp jab in the ribs.

"I'm going to kill Reece," Harry said. "Then I'll call the sheriff and collect that big reward your husband is offering."

"No." The word escaped from Elizabeth's lips like a whisper on the wind.

"Look, Harry, I know you hate me, and if you're determined to kill me, then so be it." Reece took a tentative step toward Harry. "But there's no need to involve anyone else. Let everyone else leave and you and I will settle this between ourselves."

"Stay where you are." Harry pointed the gun directly at Reece. "Nobody's going anywhere. I'm ready to kill the lot of you, if I have to."

"You don't have a quarrel with anyone else," Reece said.

"Maybe I do and maybe I don't." Harry waved the gun in the air, then aimed it at Reece. "He was a smart-mouthed kid." Harry glanced over at Elizabeth. "Always trying to stick up for his mama. His sweet, whore of a mama. How the hell was she supposed to forget about B. K. Stanton when the man's bastard was around all the time?"

Elizabeth sensed an unnatural hatred for Reece emanating from Harry Gunn. She shuddered at the thought of the man's rage. He wanted to see Reece dead. Nothing else would satisfy him.

"Yeah, Blanche never could get over being in love with Stanton," Harry said. "She never loved me. It was always B.K."

Elizabeth knew with certainty that Harry Gunn had hated B. K. Stanton enough to kill him, but she could not sense his guilt or innocence. Harry was too consumed with his hatred for Reece, his determination to kill his stepson.

Harry stood several yards away from Reece, who was only a few steps from the back door where Jeffie held Tracy in his arms. Reece heard Tracy speaking to her lover in a quiet, quick voice.

"Go back inside the house and get to my car. I've got a cellular phone. Call the sheriff's office and tell them what's going on."

Harry jerked his head around, his gaze momentarily leaving Reece to focus on Tracy and Jeffie.

Now, while Harry was momentarily distracted, might be Reece's best chance for jumping him. If Harry was intent on killing him, he might not be able to stop his stepfather, but there was a chance that he could save Elizabeth, as well as Tracy and Jeffie, if he could wrestle the gun away from Harry.

"What are you mumbling about?" Harry asked, staring at Tracy. "You cooking up some scheme to save your old lover? Well, don't try nothing. Harry Gunn ain't no fool."

Tracy glanced over at Reece, then back to Harry. "You're wrong if you think I give a damn whether you shoot Reece full of holes or not. He doesn't mean a thing to me. Hell, if he's dead or rotting in prison, he can't collect his share of B.K.'s fortune, can he?"

"You're lying." Harry turned completely around, grinning at Tracy. "You think I don't know all that boy's talent is between his legs. Women been chasing him all his life. If he was a girl, he'd be a whore just like his mama."

All the anger, the pain, the uncontrollable hatred Reece had felt boiled up inside him. In one, quick calculated move, Reece rushed Harry Gunn, who turned sharply, the gun in his hand gleaming in the glow from his car's headlights.

"Now!" Tracy cried out. "Go now, Jeffie."

Jeffie rushed inside the cottage. Tracy leaned forward, her feet unmoving as she opened her mouth in a silent cry. Just as Reece lunged forward, Harry turned, aiming his gun. Elizabeth ran between Reece and Harry. The gunshot exploded, the sound echoing over and over again in Reece's ears. Somewhere, as if at a great distance, he heard the sound of a woman screaming. Tracy.

Elizabeth felt the impact of the bullet when it entered her side. Searing hot pain gripped her. The world began spinning around and around. Slumping over, clutching her side, she fell to her knees.

Reece slammed into Harry Gunn with deadly force, like the bullet that had wounded Elizabeth. Knocking his stepfather to the ground, Reece grabbed for the gun that Harry held tightly. Reece swung his fist into Harry's face, then lifted the man's head and beat it against the cold, hard earth. Harry's hand opened. The gun fell onto the damp grass.

Mindless, feeling nothing except pure hatred, Reece hammered his fists into Harry Gunn's pale, wrinkled face, then sent several hard blows into Harry's midsection.

Tracy ran out into the yard, kneeling beside Elizabeth. "Jeffie's calling the sheriff. They'll get you to the hospital."

Elizabeth clasped Tracy's arm. "Stop Reece. Please stop him from killing his stepfather."

"Why the hell would you care?" Tracy stared down at the blood covering Elizabeth's side. "The guy shot you."

"I don't care about Harry Gunn," Elizabeth said. "I care about Reece. No matter how much he hates Harry, he would never forgive himself if he killed him. Please, Tracy. Stop Reece."

"All right. I'll try."

Reece drew back his fist to strike again. Tracy grabbed his arm. "Don't hit him anymore, Reece. He's unconscious."

"I'll kill the son of a bitch! I'll kill him."

Tracy circled Reece's arm with both of her hands, tugging on him, trying to pull him away from Harry. "He can't hurt any of us now. He's unconscious. Do you hear me? Elizabeth . . . Elizabeth wants you to stop."

Reece tensed at the mention of her name, suddenly realizing where he was and what he was doing. "Elizabeth."

"She doesn't want you to kill Harry."

Reece glared down at his stepfather, a crumpled heap of flesh and bones, a dirty, stinking, sick old man. Reece stood, his whole body trembling. He saw Elizabeth huddled on the ground, her life's blood seeping out of the bullet wound in her side.

God in heaven, don't let her die. Reece fell to his knees beside her, then sat on the ground, lifting her into his arms. "Elizabeth?"

Gazing up at him, she tried to lift her hand. "Don't worry. I'll be all right."

"Sam knew this would happen. This was what he was afraid of." Reece held her close, tears forming in his eyes. "It's my fault. You shouldn't have been with me. Oh, God, Lizzie, don't die, sweetheart. Please don't die."

"I'm not going to die," she told him. "Not for a long, long time."

"Are you looking into your future?" He kissed her forehead.

"I did that . . . last night." Despite the pain and weakness, Elizabeth felt a great sense of peace. How could she tell Reece that she knew she wasn't going to die because she had to live to give birth to their child?

Jeffie ran out the kitchen door, halting abruptly when he saw Reece sitting on the ground, holding Elizabeth. "What happened? When I heard a gunshot, I thought old Harry had killed Reece."

"Elizabeth ran between Harry and Reece," Tracy said.

"Damn! Is she hurt bad?" Jeffie walked out into the yard and slipped his arm around Tracy.

"I don't know."

"She's going to be all right," Reece said, cradling Elizabeth in his arms, holding her close. Tears streamed down his face.

"I called the sheriff," Jeffie said. "I told him to send an ambulance."

Elizabeth closed her eyes. She felt herself drifting. Reece kept repeating her name, calling her Lizzie. She opened her eyes and lifted her hand to his face. She touched his wet cheek.

"You're crying," she whispered. "Oh, Reece." Then Elizabeth closed her eyes again, drifting into unconsciousness.

Reece had no idea how long he sat on the cold ground, holding Elizabeth in his arms—five minutes, ten minutes. Finally Tracy touched him on the shoulder.

"Let's take her inside where it's warmer."

Reece lifted Elizabeth in his arms and carried her into the cottage. He laid her down on the bed they had shared only hours ago. Reece clenched his teeth at the sight of her bloody sweater. Lifting her sweater, he used it to wipe away the blood. The bullet had entered her upper left side and exited from the front, at her waist.

Tracy stood in the doorway, Jeffie directly behind her, both of them looking into the bedroom.

"Is there anything we can do?" Tracy asked.

"Yeah, go back outside and make sure Harry doesn't come to."

"I'll handle that," Jeffie said.

"I don't know what to do to help her." Reece sat on the side of the bed, holding Elizabeth's hand to his chest. "If it was the other way around and I was lying there, she'd know what to do. She'd go outside and pull up some weeds and grass and perform a miracle."

"You really care about her, don't you?" Tracy walked over, standing by the bed.

"She believes in me." Reece lifted Elizabeth's limp hand to his lips. "She's gone through hell for me because she wants to help me. Me," Reece said with a laugh, the sound an anguished cry, "B. K. Stanton's worthless bastard."

"She loves you, Reece. She risked her life to save you." Tracy laid her hand on Reece's shoulder.

Reece jerked away from her touch. "Where the hell is that ambulance?"

Reece looked up to see the medics carrying a stretcher into the bedroom. Sheriff Bates walked in behind them, two deputies following.

Reece kissed Elizabeth, then moved out of the way. The medics lifted her gently onto the stretcher and carried her outside to the waiting ambulance. He stared at Simon Bates, who aimed his automatic directly at Reece.

"You won't need that." Reece held his hands over his head in a sign of surrender.

The deputies cuffed him, both young men moving quickly to accomplish the task. Reece heard the sheriff speaking, talking to him, barking out orders, but he couldn't distinguish the words. All he could think about was Elizabeth. She filled his mind and heart completely.

Elizabeth opened her eyes to see Sam Dundee looking down at her. She smiled at him. If Sam was with her, then she was safe. Her mind felt fuzzy, her body weightless. What was wrong with her? Why did she feel so strange?

With sudden clarity she remembered the events that had brought her here. She was in a hospital. She glanced around the room, a private room, her bed the only one.

"Hey, kiddo." Sam brushed her hair away from her face with a gentle hand.

"Reece?" Was he in jail? Yes, of course, he had to be. He had promised he'd turn himself in to the sheriff.

"Landry's in jail," Sam said. "They took him there yesterday morning while they were bringing you to the hospital."

"He's all right, then?" Elizabeth tried to lift herself up in the bed.

"Stay calm, honey." Sam laid a restraining hand on her shoulder. "You've got a pretty big hole in your side. The doctors stitched you up, but it'll take a while for you to recover. You'll probably be in here for a few days, maybe a week."

"Is Reece all right? Y'all told the sheriff that he planned to turn himself in, didn't you?"

"Gary Elkins is taking care of everything, so stop fretting."

"What about Harry Gunn?" Elizabeth could see Harry's warped smile, could visualize the gun he'd aimed at Reece, could feel the bullet enter her body. She trembled.

"Are you all right?" Sam took her hand in his.

"Reece didn't kill Harry, did he?" Elizabeth looked up at Sam with pleading eyes. "I can't sense anything. I can't get a handle on... Oh, Sam, please tell me. I... I..."

"Harry Gunn is under guard here at the hospital. He's got a broken nose, a concussion and several fractured ribs, but he'll live."

"Harry hated B. K. Stanton enough to have killed him." Elizabeth held tightly to Sam's hand. "And he is capable of murder. I sensed that about him. And he hated Reece enough to have framed him. That way he could have destroyed the two people he hated most."

"Yeah, you're right, kiddo." Sam stroked the back of Elizabeth's hand, making circles around her knuckles. "The only problem with that theory is that I don't think Harry Gunn was smart enough to have planned the frame-up. Whoever framed Reece was as shrewd as he was devious."

"What about Kenny Stanton? He has no alibi, and we can prove he threatened to kill his father the day of the murder."

"Elizabeth, will you stop upsetting yourself. It's not good for you. You've done all you can to help Reece. Leave the rest up to me and to his lawyer."

"I want to see him."

"Honey, you can't. He's in jail and you're in no shape to go traipsing over there."

Elizabeth read the worry in Sam's mind, picking up on his fear that she would do something irrational when she found out about—

"They're taking Reece to Arrendale today, aren't they? Why? Couldn't they wait a day or two?"

"Reece was arrested yesterday morning. Although the sheriff is willing to reopen the investigation into B. K. Stanton's murder, the fact remains that Reece was convicted of the crime and sentenced to prison."

"Reece will go crazy locked up in a cell." Elizabeth swallowed her tears. "Sam, we've got to find the person who really killed B. K. Stanton."

"We will. I promise. You know you can count on me." Sam released her hand, then sat in a chair beside her bed. "As soon as you're released from the hospital, I'll drive you up to Alto, to Arrendale for a visit with Reece."

"Isn't the sheriff going to arrest me for aiding and abetting a criminal?" Elizabeth asked.

"Looks like the sheriff is going to buy Tracy Stanton's story that she brought you out to her parents' summer house yesterday morning. She said that you were a psychic who'd had a vision about B.K.'s death and you'd come to the family with the news that Reece was innocent. She and Christina decided you should stay on in Newell in case you had any more visions."

"The sheriff didn't actually believe her, did he?"

Sam grinned. "Hell, no, but he's not about to call Mrs. Bradley Kenneth Stanton, Jr., a liar."

"I see. Reece was right about the Stantons' power in Newell, wasn't he?"

"In this case, let's be thankful. You can rest easy now, kiddo. Just get better so I can take you home."

Elizabeth placed her hand on her stomach, reminding herself that she was responsible for the new life inside her. She relaxed against the pillows, breathing softly, suddenly aware of the pain in her bandaged side. She closed her eyes, concentrating on Reece, trying to transmit a message of love and hope to him. As she lay there sending love out into the atmosphere, a dark sense of foreboding surrounded her.

Someone was afraid of her—afraid she knew the truth about B. K. Stanton's murder. He wanted to prevent her from helping Reece, but knew he couldn't risk coming to the hospital.

"Are you in pain?" Sam asked.

"No...not really. Why?"

"You're frowning."

"The person who killed B. K. Stanton is a man." Elizabeth opened her eyes and looked at Sam. "He's afraid I'll be able to identify him."

Sam leaned over the bed, gently grasping her face in his hand. "Turn it off, honey. Shield yourself. You're not strong enough for this right now."

She raised her head, nodding, knowing Sam was right. But without any warning the vision came. She could not stop the flow of color, the formation of images, the whirling, spinning sensation that enveloped her mind.

A huge crowd of people lined the sidewalk. Flanking Reece, two deputies brought him outside the building, hurrying him through the throng of observers.

Someone's thoughts screamed inside Elizabeth's head. *Reece Landry must die. He's caused enough pain. Even if I must sacrifice myself, I won't allow Landry to inherit any of his father's estate. I'll protect...I'll protect...I'll do whatever it takes.*

Bracing her body with her hand, Elizabeth pushed herself into a sitting position, then reached out and grabbed Sam's arm.

"He's going to kill Reece. Today. When they bring Reece out of the jail. He'll be hiding in the crowd."

"Calm down." Sam tried to make Elizabeth lie back down, but she refused.

"Please, Sam, you've got to stop them from taking Reece out of jail today."

"The sheriff isn't going to listen to me, honey."

"You can't let him kill Reece!"

Sam took Elizabeth's shoulders in his strong, gentle grasp, pushing her down on the bed. "I'll go to the jail and see what I can do. If nothing else, I'll keep watch. I'll guard Reece."

Elizabeth took a deep breath. "I wish I could see the man's face, but I can't. He hates Reece. He's willing to sacrifice anything to keep Reece from going free."

"Everything will be all right," Sam said. "Whoever this man is, if he tips his hand today, I'll be there to catch him."

"Are you sure Harry Gunn is well guarded?" Elizabeth asked. "And what about Kenny Stanton?"

"Harry Gunn isn't in any shape to walk out of this hospital, but even if he was, the deputy would stop him. As for Kenny Stanton, I don't have any idea where he is, but I can find out."

"Don't let anything happen to Reece. I love him."

"Yeah, kiddo, I know you do."

Chapter 13

The nurse came in shortly after Sam left and gave Elizabeth an injection. She protested the shot, but the nurse insisted. She had a sneaking suspicion that Sam had suggested they give her something to calm her down a little.

She didn't want to sleep, but the medication overcame her resistance. When she awoke, she rang the nurses' station and asked for the time. It was eleven-fifteen. Surely by now Sam had persuaded the sheriff not to move Reece today. What difference could one day make to the local authorities? Maybe Sam had gone to Gary Elkins and Reece's lawyer had contacted a judge about delaying the transfer.

Elizabeth tried to focus her energy on Reece. Where was he? How was he doing? What was he thinking? With a sudden, sharp clarity, the vision of Reece being led up the sidewalk appeared in Elizabeth's mind. The crowd was pushing closer and closer. Newspaper reporters where shouting questions. Photographers were snapping shots of the prisoner. Sam Dundee and Gary Elkins followed Reece and the deputies. Elizabeth scanned the crowd. Christina Stanton stood beside her brother, Kenny, and his wife, Tracy. Willard Moran stood alone on the opposite side of the walkway. The sun reflected off the muzzle of a gun—a gun aimed directly at Reece. Breaking through the crowd, Elizabeth hurried toward Reece. She saw the startled look on his face, then heard him call her name.

The truth of what would happen hit her with full impact. She and she alone could save Reece. Only she could zero in on the killer. Only she could read a person's mind. She had to go to the jail and stop the killer before he shot Reece.

Elizabeth eased the intravenous needle from her hand. When she tried to sit up, her head spun around and around. Slow and easy, she told herself. You can't pass out. Not now. Taking her time, she slipped out of bed and stood, holding on to the bed rails.

Glancing down at her open-backed hospital gown, she wondered where they'd put her clothes. Damn, they would be covered with blood. Taking tentative steps, gauging her strength as she walked across the room, Elizabeth opened the closet. She sighed with relief when she saw her bag lying on the floor. Bending over, she gasped when the pain in her side sliced through her like a sharp rapier.

She knelt, undid her bag and pulled out a clean pair of jeans and a heavy peach wool sweater. Her shoes lay beside her bag. She dressed as quickly as she could, but each movement came with pain. Pulling her purse out of the bag, she slung it over her shoulder.

Easing open the door, she peered out into the hallway. She didn't see anyone, not even one nurse. She made her way along the corridor to the elevators, punched the Down button and waited. She wondered how close the hospital was to the jail. If necessary, she'd call a cab when she got downstairs.

Once on the ground level, she stopped at the reception desk and inquired about the location of the local jail. She couldn't believe her luck when the young woman told her that the county jail was only two blocks away, directly behind the courthouse.

When she walked outside, the winter wind bit into her heavy sweater, chilling her. The wound in her side ached, and she still felt a little light-headed from the medication. Her pain didn't matter—nothing mattered except saving

Reece. With each step she took, she knew she was one step closer to keeping the man she loved alive.

She could hear the crowd several minutes before she rounded the corner and saw them. Reece Landry's capture and transport to Arrendale had to be the media event of the year in Newell, Georgia. The sidewalk leading to the jail was lined with people, so many people that Elizabeth couldn't even see the sidewalk.

She made her way through the fringe crowd that waited around near the street, dozens of people who were there simply to see the spectacle. Directly in front of her, toward the back of the crowd, stood Kenny Stanton, Tracy at his side. Elizabeth glanced to their right and to their left, searching for Christina. Then she saw her, standing directly in front of Kenny. The whole Stanton family was here to see Reece off. Everyone except Alice.

Kenny was the most likely suspect. No one could hate Reece more than Kenny, unless it was Harry Gunn. Elizabeth tried to connect with Kenny, but found it impossible. The psychic energy coming from the crowd mixed and mingled, making it nearly impossible to pinpoint the exact location of a thought or feeling.

If only she could touch Kenny, she might be able to separate his energy from the energy of those around him. And if he saw her, he would know that she was on to him, and might not make a move against Reece. Regardless of what Kenny might or might not do, she had to approach him.

Breathless from her two-block walk from the hospital, Elizabeth made her way through the crowd, nudging between the curious men and women waiting for a glimpse of Reece Landry. Christina saw her, her eyes widening, her mouth forming a circle. Elizabeth shook her head. Christina nodded.

Elizabeth brushed up against Kenny. Turning quickly, he stared at her. Her knees trembled. She gripped Kenny's arm. Glaring at her, he looked down at her hand clutching his coat sleeve.

She could sense doubts in Kenny's mind—grave doubts. He was no longer certain that his half brother had killed their father.

Kenny looked Elizabeth in the eye, then placed his hand atop hers. "You shouldn't be out of the hospital, Ms. Mallory."

Tracy jerked her head around. "What are you doing here?"

Elizabeth pulled her hand off Kenny's arm, willing herself to find the strength to stand alone. "Please, I have to find him. It isn't you."

"What are you talking about?" Kenny asked.

"You aren't the murderer. You didn't come here to shoot Reece."

The crowd's rumble grew louder. Elizabeth shoved past Kenny and Tracy to see the front doors of the county jail swing open. The sheriff walked out first, followed by two deputies who led Reece down the steps. Sam Dundee and Gary Elkins were only a minute behind the others.

Elizabeth closed her eyes, trying to concentrate, trying desperately to pick up on any kind of signal the killer might be emitting. She couldn't rush in front of Reece this time and take the bullet for him. She had no idea from which direction the bullet would come; the crowd circled Reece.

Hatred. Deep, soul-wrenching hatred. She felt it so strongly that she almost doubled over in pain. And the hatred was directed at Reece—because he was B. K. Stanton's illegitimate son. Because Reece's existence had caused Alice Stanton unbearable shame and heartache. Reece could not be allowed to live, to lay claim to a fortune that didn't belong to him.

"Oh, dear God," Elizabeth said, her voice inaudible in the boisterous racket coming from the crowd. She glanced across the sidewalk. There in the front row stood Willard Moran, dressed in a conservative blue suit, his charcoal gray overcoat unbuttoned, his hand in his pocket.

She looked up the sidewalk. The sheriff was only a few feet away, Reece and the deputies directly behind him.

Reece saw her then, saw her pale face, noted the fear in her eyes. What the hell was Elizabeth doing out of the hospital? When Reece halted, the deputies slowed enough to accommodate him.

Reece called out to Sam. "I thought you said Elizabeth would have to stay in the hospital a few days. What's she doing here?"

Elizabeth's gaze met Sam's, then she looked over at Willard Moran, knowing she and she alone could stop him. He was holding a gun in his pocket, waiting for the moment Reece would pass him, waiting to kill Reece.

Elizabeth nudged her way between two reporters calling out questions to the sheriff and to Reece. Willard Moran stepped onto the sidewalk, between the sheriff and his deputies. Elizabeth ran forward, throwing herself into Willard. The gun in his hand fired, the bullet sailing into the air over their heads. When Willard's body hit the ground, the gun flew out of his hand, falling with a clang onto the edge of the sidewalk.

Reece tried to run to Elizabeth, but the chains around his ankles slowed his gait. Startled by what had just happened, the deputies didn't instantly realize that their prisoner had pulled away from them. They grabbed Reece tightly, jerking him back. He fought them, trying desperately to reach Elizabeth, calling out her name.

Sam Dundee rushed past Reece, shoving everyone in his way aside. The blood surged through Reece's body, his heart pumping wildly as he strained in the confines of his cuffs and chains.

Willard Moran knocked Elizabeth off him. She rolled over onto the sidewalk, blood oozing through her sweater. Before Willard could stand, Sheriff Bates grabbed him, jerking him to his feet. Sam knelt beside Elizabeth, lifting her into his arms.

She felt Sam holding her, heard Reece crying out her name. She wanted to get up, to go to Reece and tell him that she was all right, but she couldn't make her body cooperate. Raising her head, she struggled to sit up.

"Reece...Reece..." She barely recognized her own voice. So raspy. So whispery soft.

"Reece is okay. He's just fine," Sam said. "Take it easy. We've got to get you back to the hospital."

"Elizabeth!" Reece's tortured voice drowned out the crowd's clamor.

Deputies began ordering the bystanders to move away from the scene, to disperse and leave the situation to the authorities. Reporters buzzed around like busy bees; photographers snapped shot after shot—of the crowd, of the sheriff cuffing Willard Moran, of the deputies holding back the crowd, of Reece Landry's tortured face, of Sam Dundee holding Elizabeth in his arms.

"Clear this crowd out of here," the sheriff ordered. He shoved Willard Moran toward a deputy. "Take Mr. Moran inside and detain him until we have things under control out here."

"Reece. I want to see Reece." Elizabeth pleaded with Sam.

The sheriff motioned at the two deputies holding Reece. "Bring Landry over here. Now!"

Reece couldn't get to Elizabeth fast enough to suit him. Kneeling, he cursed the cuffs that bound his hands, that restricted his movements. More than anything he wanted to take Elizabeth out of Sam's arms, to hold her close to him.

"Elizabeth." Tears streamed down Reece's cheeks. He couldn't remember ever crying in front of people, or even crying alone. Not until Elizabeth Mallory had come into his life.

"Willard Moran killed your father," Elizabeth said.

Reece and Sam exchanged knowing looks. "And he was going to kill me, wasn't he?" Reece leaned over, brushing his lips across Elizabeth's forehead. "You risked your life coming here." Reece choked on the tears in his throat. "You've risked your life twice to save me."

"You'll be free now, Reece. Free to live the life you've always wanted." Elizabeth lifted her hand, touching the side of Reece's face with her fingertips.

"God, Lizzie. Dear God!" Reece crumbled, his body shaking with sobs, his head resting on Elizabeth's chest.

She stroked his hair, caressing him with loving fingers. "I won't ever have to cry for you again, will I, Reece? You... you can cry... for yourself now."

Reece jerked his head up. He saw Elizabeth's eyes close and felt her hand drop away from his head.

"Lizzie!"

"Come on, Reece, get up!" Sam ordered. "Get out of the way. I've got to take her back to the hospital."

The deputies lifted Reece to his feet. He watched, helpless to do anything else, as Sam lifted Elizabeth in his arms and carried her down the sidewalk.

"Get Landry back inside," the sheriff told his deputies. "Looks like we're definitely reopening the B. K. Stanton murder case."

Elizabeth sat in the chair beside the hospital bed she had occupied for the past few days. Her bag was packed, and she was dressed in jeans, a blue silk blouse and a brown suede vest. She and Sam were driving home to Sequana Falls today, but before she left, she had to see Reece.

Although Sam had kept her abreast of the events following Willard Moran's arrest, she regretted that she hadn't been at Reece's side to see him through the painful process and to share in the jubilant relief when Gary Elkins had completed the legalities that set Reece free.

Christina had stopped by yesterday to thank Elizabeth for all the help she'd given Reece and to tell her that no one in the family had suspected Willard Moran was capable of murder. The man had been B. K. Stanton's lawyer for over thirty years, a trusted friend. Chris and Kenny had called the man Uncle Willard all their lives.

Willard Moran had loved Alice Stanton with a mindless devotion. By destroying B.K. and eliminating Reece, he had thought to protect Alice from any more hurt and make sure her children's inheritance wasn't squandered on her husband's bastard son. In the end, Willard had been willing to sacrifice himself to achieve his goal.

Elizabeth heard a soft knock at the door. "Come in." She turned to see Sam standing in the doorway, Reece behind him.

"You're all dressed and ready to leave," Sam said.

"The doctor told me to take it easy for a few days, and not to do anything that might reopen my wound again." Elizabeth smiled at Sam, deliberately not looking at Reece.

Sam grabbed Reece by the arm, hauled him to his side, then stepped back into the hallway. "I'll go get a cup of coffee or something while you two visit. I'll be back to get you in a little bit, kiddo.''

Reece stood in the doorway, staring at Elizabeth, his expression grave. ''You look a lot better than the last time I saw you.''

''I feel a lot better.'' Every nerve in her body came to full alert, tingling with excitement and fear. ''Come on in, Reece.''

Reece ambled into her hospital room, his gaze traveling over the walls, the ceiling and the floor. Standing beside Elizabeth's chair, he cleared his throat.

Elizabeth stared at Reece, noting how different he looked from the man who had passed out in her cabin less than two weeks ago. He'd had a haircut, his glossy brown hair neatly styled, and he was freshly shaved. He wore dark brown slacks and a camel tan wool jacket, his tie a conservative beige-and-coral-striped silk.

''You look very handsome,'' she told him. ''Like a successful young businessman.''

Reece knelt beside Elizabeth, resting his big body on his haunches. ''I owe you my life and my freedom, Lizzie. How does a guy repay someone for giving him so much?''

''You'll repay me by making your life count for something, by living well and being happy.''

Reece gripped the metal armrest on her chair. He wanted to touch her, but couldn't bring himself to reach out and take her hand. He wasn't sure how she would accept the news that he planned to stay in Newell and claim his inheritance.

''Sam told me he's going to follow you back to Sequana Falls today.'' If only he could ask her to stay here in Newell with him. If only he could tell her what she wanted to hear. If only he could repay her for everything she'd done for him.

''My life is in Sequana Falls. Aunt Margaret. Mac-Datho. My business.'' She couldn't read his mind, but she knew that despite all he'd gone through and all he'd learned, Reece wasn't prepared to give up his lifelong dreams and start a new life with her.

''I don't suppose you'd consider staying on in Newell.'' He could offer her the world now, the whole world on a silver platter. Wealth, power, social position—all the things he'd been denied because of his illegitimate birth, all the things he'd dreamed of having for as long as he could remember.

Elizabeth willed herself not to cry; she had done too much crying lately. She laid her hand atop his on the armrest. "I wouldn't be happy in Newell. I don't think you will be, either, but you'll have to find that out for yourself."

"Ah, Lizzie, you mean so much to me." Taking her by the hands, he helped her to her feet, then pulled her into his arms. "I've never cared about anyone the way I care about you. You don't know how grateful I am that you came into my life when you did."

She laid her head on his chest. "I don't want your gratitude, Reece. I want your love."

He tensed, every muscle in his body going rigid. "I... uh... I'm not sure I know how to love anybody, especially someone as special as you."

Wrapping her arms around his waist, she hugged him. "There's an old saying, one I've heard Aunt Margaret quote. Something about all the love we come to know in life comes from the love we knew as children."

Reece kissed the top of her head, breathing in that sweet rose scent that would forever remind him of Elizabeth. "Well, that puts it in a nutshell, doesn't it? I don't know how to love because no one ever loved me."

"That's not true." Tilting her face, she gazed up into his amber eyes, those lone-wolf eyes that still proclaimed him an untamed animal. "Despite what you think, your mother loved you. You know she did."

"Yeah, well, maybe she did. In her own way."

"And now you have my love." She ran her fingertips across his jaw. "I love you."

Reece closed his eyes, shutting out Elizabeth's face, protecting himself from the glow of love that surrounded her. Damn, why couldn't he just tell her that he loved her? What made it so impossible?

He couldn't change his past. Not the circumstances of his birth, not B. K. Stanton's denial and rejection, not the years he and his mother had suffered at the hands of his sadistic stepfather. And no matter how much he wanted to be free from all the pain and anger and hatred inside him, he wasn't ready to forgive and forget. He had an inheritance to claim, a company to run, a sister he wanted in his life and a brother with whom he'd have to deal.

If Elizabeth would settle for the man he was, scarred and bitter and hungry for retribution, then he could offer her anything money could buy. He'd give her an engagement ring the size of a dime. He'd build her a mansion as big as the one Alice Stanton lived in.

"Thank you," Elizabeth said.

"For what?"

"For letting down your shield." The tears she had tried to control gathered in the corners of her eyes. "Thank you for sharing your thoughts with me."

He hadn't realized that he had opened himself up to her, allowing her to read his mind. "Stay here with me, Lizzie. Marry me. Teach me how to love."

"You're right, you know, Reece. You can't change the past. But you can let it go. You'll never be happy until you can do that."

Reece clasped her shoulders. "How do I do that? How do I let go of the past when the past has made me who I am? If I let go of the past, I won't have an identity."

"You'll always be Blanche and B.K.'s illegitimate son. You'll always be an outcast in the Stanton family, even if you own controlling interest in Stanton Industries. The only way you can ever let go of the past is to make peace with it, starting with the Stanton family."

"How the hell do you suggest I do that?" Reece ran his hands slowly up and down her arms. "Alice Stanton has every right to despise me. And Kenny hates my guts."

"They don't have to love you or even like you. They'll have to make their own peace with their lives."

"So what should I do, Lizzie?" He held her from him, his big hands shackling her wrists. "Should I walk away and let them have it all? Do you have any idea how much I wanted B.K. to acknowledge me as his son? Do you know how badly I wanted everything that belonged to Kenny?"

"I know, Reece. But are you sure, really sure, that what you once wanted so desperately is what will make you happy now?"

Reece dropped his hands, releasing Elizabeth. "I don't know. I don't know anything anymore. Give me some advice, Lizzie. Look into my future and tell me what you see. Are our futures still entwined?"

Yes, Reece, our futures are still entwined. I'm going to have your child. You'll always be a part of me. "Your future will be what you make it. You should stay here in Newell. Claim your inheritance. Make peace with the Stantons. And if you discover that you don't really want to take over Stanton Industries, then give that job to your sister and come live with me in Sequana Falls."

"Come live with—"

"I love you, Reece. I'll love you as long as I live. I've done all I can to help you, to save you from yourself. The rest is up to you. You have to stay here in Newell and come to terms with your past. When you've done that, and if you decide that you can love me, then come to me. I'll be waiting."

"Elizabeth?"

"You're free, Reece. Free from the past, if only you'll allow yourself to be. You're a man, not a child. You have choices to make. No one else can make those choices for you. You decide what you want from this life, and how much you're willing to give in order to get it."

Several loud, hard knocks sounded at the door, then Sam Dundee walked in, glancing back and forth from Elizabeth to Reece to Elizabeth.

"If we're going to get home in time for supper, we'd better be leaving." Sam picked up Elizabeth's bag. "O'Grady's taking Aunt Margaret and MacDatho up to the cabin, so they'll all be there to meet us."

Elizabeth leaned into Reece, circling his forearm with her hand. She kissed him on the cheek. "You take all the time you need to decide. We . . . I'll be in Sequana Falls."

Chapter 14

"You can't be serious," Kenny Stanton said. "Daddy would be appalled at the very idea of a woman running Stanton Industries."

"Well, Daddy isn't making the decisions." Rearing back in the tufted-leather chair behind B.K.'s desk, Reece placed his hands on his hips and glanced around his father's former office. "Chris and I own two-thirds of the stock in this little family company, and we agree that she's the most qualified person to sit behind the old man's desk and make the decisions that will keep bringing in profits for all of us."

Standing, Reece smiled at his sister, then motioned for her to sit in the chair he had just vacated. Chris, neatly attired in a dark green business suit, took the seat. Grasping the cushioned armrests, she gulped a deep breath of air, then glanced from Kenny's frowning face into Reece's twinkling topaz eyes. Pressing her toe to the floor, she boosted the swivel chair into action, whirling it around and around as she laughed.

"Are you happy, Landry?" Kenny asked, his hound-dog cheeks flushed pink. "You send my mother to a rest home, you persuade my wife to divorce me and now you hand over my company to my sister. You've taken your revenge on me, haven't you? Everything I've had, you've taken away from me.''

"I haven't taken a damn thing away from you, big brother." Reece took a good look at Bradley Kenneth Stanton, Jr., and was amazed that he actually pitied the man whom he'd envied all his life. "Your mother had a nervous breakdown after Willard Moran confessed to killing B.K. I wasn't responsible for Alice's illness. If you're going to blame anyone, blame the man who loved her enough to kill for her."

Kenny glared at Reece. "Well, I can certainly blame you for taking Tracy away from me. You just couldn't leave her alone, could you? What did you do to persuade her to divorce me? Did you promise to marry her?"

"I didn't promise Tracy anything," Reece said. "She knows I'm not interested in her. All I did was drive her to the airport to catch a flight to Reno."

"Humph!" Kenny picked up his briefcase from the edge of B.K.'s desk. "I suppose if I had befriended you the way Chris did, you'd have handed the company over to me, but because I refused to accept you as my brother, you're willing to ruin the company our father spent his life building into a small empire."

Reece chuckled. God, why had he ever thought he wanted to be like Kenny? Why had he ever envied the man his life? Reece realized that he'd been blinded by the glitter of a world forbidden to him. Now that that world lay at his feet, he discovered he didn't want it as much as he'd thought he did.

"If you and I were like this—" Reece wrapped his index and middle fingers together "—I would still want Chris in charge of Stanton Industries. I didn't vote in her favor as an act of revenge against you. I did it because she's the best person for the job."

"I suppose you two think I'll just tuck my tail between my legs and crawl out of here," Kenny said.

"No one would ever think that." Chris whirled around one last time in her chair, then stuck out her foot under the desk to stop her spin. "There's a place at Stanton Industries for you, but it isn't in administration. It's in sales. You're the best salesman I know, Kenny. You inherited that from Mother. My goodness, we both know how persuasive she always was collecting thousands of dollars for her charities. You have that same special way with people."

"What position are you offering me?" Standing in front of his sister's desk, Kenny laid down his briefcase.

"You two work out an agreement suitable to both of you," Reece said. "If you need me for anything, you know where I'll be, Chris. And if you don't need me, then I'll see y'all at the next board meeting."

When he walked out the door, he heard Kenny ask Christina where Reece was going.

"He's going to find happiness," Chris said.

Elizabeth delved her glove-covered hands into the warm clumps of earth, crushing the small clods and sprinkling the soft dirt back to the ground. April showers were long overdue, forecast for tomorrow. She wanted to get the new plants set out so that they could soak up the rainwater that would nourish them.

Margaret McPhearson stood at the edge of the porch, shaking her head as she watched her niece. "Just look at you, Elizabeth Sequana. You're getting dirty, and after I persuaded you to fancy up a bit."

Elizabeth packed the earth around the last plant, then got up and removed her gloves, tossing them onto the steps. "I didn't get dirty. See." She held up her hands, then glanced down at the denim skirt and red silk blouse she wore. "But I can't just sit still waiting for Reece to arrive."

"I don't see why you can't sit down and take it easy. Just because you've been blessed with a total lack of morning sickness doesn't mean you shouldn't take good care of yourself." Margaret walked down the steps and out into the front yard.

"I almost wish you hadn't told me that Reece is coming here today. I've been waiting nearly six weeks. I'd begun to doubt he'd ever—"

"Nonsense. You knew, deep down here—" Margaret thumped her fist over her heart "—that he'd find his way back to you."

"I have to admit that I did try to contact him mentally a couple of times, to let him know that I loved him and I was waiting."

"Maybe you should have used the telephone instead of trying to break through that shield he keeps in place in his mind." Margaret put her arm around Elizabeth's shoulders. "It wasn't easy for me to break through, not at first, but in the last week or so...well, I'd say that, in time, you'll be able to read Reece Landry like a book."

"I wish I had the courage to let you tell me what sort of future you see for Reece and me." Elizabeth turned into her aunt's arms, hugging her.

Margaret patted her niece on the back, then stepped away from her, looking her squarely in the eye. "I wouldn't tell you, even if you asked. You've got the power. If you want to know, look for yourself."

When the front door of the cabin opened, MacDatho bounded outside, O'Grady following at a slower pace. "You 'bout ready to head for home, Margaret?" O'Grady asked.

"Not yet. I want to stay and meet this Landry fellow."

"Are you sure he's coming today?" O'Grady sat down in one of the large wooden rockers that Elizabeth had stationed across her front and back porches. "Seems he'd have called and let Elizabeth know he was coming."

"I'd say he assumes she already knows, which she does because I told her so." Holding on to the side railing, Margaret walked up the steps and sat in a rocker beside O'Grady. "She could've picked up on it herself if she wasn't so all-fired afraid that if she reads his mind, she'll discover he doesn't love her."

"Why don't you two go on home to Dover's Mill?" Elizabeth gazed up at them, the overhead noonday sun almost blinding her. "It may be April and a fairly warm day today, but that wind's chilly and I wouldn't want either of you catching cold."

"We're both healthy as horses," Margaret said. "Besides, we're not going anywhere till we meet your young man."

Elizabeth groaned, knowing when to admit defeat. She wasn't sure she would have gotten through the past six weeks without Aunt Margaret. Leaving Reece had been the most difficult thing she'd ever done, but it had been the right thing to do. If she had made things too easy for Reece, he might never have realized what was important in this life. He might have gone on wrapped up in the past and unable to give or accept love.

"He's coming up the road." Margaret stood, motioning for O'Grady to do the same. "You introduce us, Elizabeth, and then we'll be on our way. Now, you remember what I told you. You take him down to Mama's honeymoon cottage. I've got a surprise waiting there for y'all."

"All right," Elizabeth said. "If he stays, I'll take him to the cottage."

Elizabeth heard the approaching car, then turned to see a new, sleek, dark green Jeep Cherokee pull up and stop in front of the cabin. Reece Landry emerged, big and tall and incredibly handsome in his navy blue cotton slacks and his cream-colored pullover sweater.

"Lizzie." Reece stood at the side of the Jeep, taking in every inch of the woman who'd never been far from his mind these past six weeks. Everything he'd done to put his life together had been for her. And now, free at last from the emotions that had bound him to his past, he had come to her, hat in hand, so to speak, hoping she wouldn't send him away.

"Reece." Elizabeth had to restrain herself from running to him, but she would wait for him to come to her. Only a few feet separated them, but they were his distance to cross, not hers.

"So this is the infamous Reece Landry." Margaret McPhearson, her dimpled chin held high, the sun gleaming through the strands of her white hair, took hold of the railing and began walking down the steps.

"You must be Aunt Margaret." Reece looked at the old woman making her way slowly down the steps. An elderly man followed closely behind her.

MacDatho raced around the corner of the house, pouncing on Reece. Reece scratched his ears. "Hey, Mac, how are you, boy? Have you decided to be friends?"

Elizabeth didn't take her eyes off Reece. She felt her aunt's presence when Margaret walked over and stood beside her, O'Grady taking his place on her other side. "Aunt Margaret, O'Grady, this is Reece Landry."

"We already know that." Margaret waved her hand in dismissal. "What I want to know is why it took you six weeks to get here?"

"I had a lot to settle back in Newell," Reece said.

"Have you got it all settled now?" Margaret asked.

"Yes, ma'am, I do."

"Thought so, but I wanted to make sure." Margaret held out her hand in front of Elizabeth, motioning for O'Grady. The old man stepped forward, took Margaret's hand and led her to the delivery van.

Elizabeth waved goodbye to her aunt and O'Grady as they drove off down the road, then she turned back to Reece. They stood staring at each other, neither moving an inch.

"I've missed you, Lizzie."

"I've missed you, too."

MacDatho sat down beside Elizabeth, always her faithful companion. Why doesn't Reece say something else? she wondered when the silence between them dragged on for endless moments.

"It's a bit chilly out here. Would you like to come in?" She wanted to scream at him, to demand that he tell her why he'd come. Was he here to stay or just for a visit? Had he come to her or had he come for her? Or was he here to say goodbye?

"Elizabeth?" Reece took a tentative step in her direction.

"Yes?"

"Am I too late?"

"Are you ... What are you saying, Reece?"

"I'm saying that I know what I want. I know what will make me happy, and it isn't running Stanton Industries or living in Newell in a mansion or lording it over Kenny that our father left me an equal share of everything he owned."

"What will make you happy?" Elizabeth's heartbeat roared in her ears. This was the moment she'd been waiting for, the moment Reece would come to her, his past behind him.

"Spending the rest of my life with you, Lizzie, that's what would make me happy." He took several giant steps, lifted her off her feet and whirled her around in the air.

She squealed with delight, drowning in the joy of being in Reece's arms. He slid her down his body, depositing her feet on the ground. She lifted her arms around his neck, gazing up at him with all the love in her heart glowing in her blue eyes.

Lowering his head, Reece took her lips in a kiss that took her breath away. She clung to him, responding with equal fervor as he deepened the kiss. He ran his hands over her back, her arms, her waist, her hips. She grasped his shoulder with one hand while she threaded her fingers through his hair at his neckline.

When they had kissed until they were spent, Reece lifted her in his arms and started up the steps, taking two at a time. MacDatho followed them inside the cabin, but stopped outside Elizabeth's bedroom and lay down in the hall.

With Elizabeth still in his arms, Reece eased his knees down onto her bed, the two of them clinging to each other. When she lay beneath him, he started kissing her again as he unbuttoned her blouse. With eager hands they undressed each other. Clothes flew into the air, landing here and there in the room. A shirt on the dresser, a blouse on a rocking chair, slacks on the floor, socks at the foot of the bed, briefs on the nightstand.

"I want you to marry me, Lizzie. I want to spend the rest of my life here in Sequana Falls with you." He kissed the hollow in her throat, his hands inching their way down from her waist to lift her hips. "I'll draw an income from my stocks in Stanton Industries, but I have no desire to be involved in running the company. You can teach me about the nursery business. We'll see if I have a green thumb."

Elizabeth reached up, grasping his shoulders. "You won't be bored living so far away from civilization?"

"I'll never be bored as long as I'm with you, don't you know that?"

"I love you, Reece. I love you so much." She gave herself to him, completely, wholly—her body, her heart and her soul. She was his now and forever.

Reece accepted her offer, thrusting into her with fierce possession, taking her completely, wholly, and giving himself in the same way. At long last he had found a home, a place to truly belong—in the arms of the woman who had been destined to save him from his past and give him a future he'd never dreamed possible.

Their mating was fast and intense, their passion having built to an almost unbearable point by six weeks of abstinence. Their bodies moved in unison, hot and raw and wild, their hands and mouths seeking and finding, giving and taking until fulfillment flung them over the precipice and into total satiation. They clung to each other, their hearts united, their souls forever one.

Elizabeth lay in Reece's arms. He petted her hip. He nuzzled her neck with his nose. She sighed with happiness.

"Elizabeth." Cupping her chin in his hand, he lifted her face. She smiled at him. "I love you. I love everything about you. Your blue eyes, your sweet lips." He kissed her quickly. "I love your body. I love the way it feels when I make love to you. Like nothing I've ever known. And I love your good heart, the way you care about everyone and everything."

A teardrop fell from Elizabeth's eye, ran down her cheek and onto her jaw. One by one other tears followed. "We're going to be so happy."

"Are you looking into our future?" He kissed her on the shoulder.

"No, I... Aunt Margaret did, but she wouldn't tell me what she saw." Elizabeth remembered her aunt telling her to take Reece down to her great-grandmother's cottage today, that she'd planned a surprise for them.

"Well, she'd better have seen a wedding and children and a long, long life for the two of us together." Reece lifted Elizabeth up and over to lie on top of him. He traced a slow, seductive line down her spine.

"Before dark I want to take you to my great-grandmother's honeymoon cottage. I want us to spend our wedding night there."

"We'll go. Before dark." Reece rubbed himself up and down against Elizabeth. "That leaves us all afternoon to make love."

"Let's not waste a minute," Elizabeth said, situating herself to take him into her body.

Elizabeth led Reece through the woods to the small Victorian A-frame cottage standing in the middle of a tiny clearing. A picket fence enclosed the yard where tulips and jonquils bloomed in profusion.

"My great-grandfather built this little cottage as a wedding present for my great-grandmother. They spent their wedding night here and every anniversary for the rest of their lives together."

"I can see why you want us to start our married life here," Reece said, lifting Elizabeth into his arms.

He carried her up the walk, up the steps and onto the porch, MacDatho following. The front door opened to Reece's touch. He carried her inside, then set her on her feet. Mac stretched out across the floor, guarding the door.

Elizabeth glanced around the living room, but saw nothing out of place, nothing unusual. What had Aunt Margaret meant about a surprise for Reece and her?

"What are you looking for?" he asked.

"Aunt Margaret told me to bring you down here today, that she'd prepared a surprise for us." Elizabeth tugged on his hand. "Come on, let's look in the bedrooms."

She led him into the front bedroom, the one that opened out onto the porch. She gasped when she looked at the bed.

There lying on the antique, wrought-iron bed was a wedding dress—her great-grandmother's wedding dress, yellowed with age to a golden cream.

Reece watched Elizabeth as she touched the silk folds of the skirt, as she fingered the lace bodice. He came up behind her, wrapping his arms around her.

"I'd say Aunt Margaret sees a wedding in our future," Reece said.

Elizabeth turned in his arms, burying her face against his chest, breathing in the heady aroma of masculinity that surrounded Reece.

She felt a sudden intrusion into her mind. Smiling, she returned a message to her great-aunt, who had wished her happiness, then told her to take Reece into the back bedroom.

"Come on, I think there's more to our surprise." Elizabeth led him to the small bedroom at the back of the cottage. The last time she'd been in the room it had contained a cot, a cane-bottomed chair and a rickety table that sat by the window.

She opened the door, but stopped dead still when she realized what her aunt had done. The room was now a nursery. The baby bed that had belonged to both Aunt Margaret and her grandmother was the focal point of the room. A crocheted baby shawl lay in a cradle beneath the window. A padded rocking chair rested in the corner, and an open steamer trunk filled with antique toys had been placed against the right wall.

"It looks like a nursery." Reece followed Elizabeth into the room. "I'd say your aunt is trying to tell us that we're going to have children one of these days." He whirled Elizabeth around in his arms. "Would you like that, Lizzie? Would you like a houseful of children?"

"Would you, Reece?"

"Nothing would make me happier than for us to have a child. A little girl who looks just like you."

"Would a little boy do the first time? He won't look just like me, but he'll have my blue eyes."

"Are you saying you've looked into the future and seen our first child?"

"I didn't try to look into the future. It just happened."

Reece lifted Elizabeth off her feet. She wrapped her arms around him when he sat in the rocking chair with her in his lap.

"Wouldn't it be wonderful if our son was conceived on our wedding night here in this cottage." Reece slid his hand up and under Elizabeth's skirt to caress her thigh.

"I'm afraid he couldn't wait," Elizabeth said.

"What do you mean, he couldn't wait?"

"I'm already pregnant, Reece. Six weeks pregnant."

"You're what?" He sat up straight in the rocking chair, almost toppling Elizabeth to the floor. He grabbed her just as she began to slide off his lap.

Tightening her hold around his neck, she looked into Reece's amber eyes—warm, glowing eyes, filled with love. "Come November, I'm going to give you a son."

"When did you find out?" Reece laid his hand across her stomach.

"I've known since the night he was conceived, our last night together. I knew before we made love."

"You wanted my child, even though I had nothing to offer you, even though I couldn't make a commitment?" He hugged her close, his lips covering hers in a tender kiss. "How did I get so lucky?" he whispered against her mouth. "Why me, out of all the men in the world?"

"Because we were meant for each other," Elizabeth said. "You came to me in my dreams, a stranger who entered my heart and never left it."

Reece held her in his arms as they sat in her great-grandmother's rocking chair. Late afternoon turned to evening while they sat in the honeymoon cottage and talked about their future. MacDatho found his way to the bedroom, curling his big body into a ball of black fur beside the rocking chair, occasionally glancing up at his mistress and the alpha male in her life.

Love knows no boundaries and cannot be confined. It transcends time and space. Love is the greatest power on earth and in heaven. Elizabeth and Reece did not question destiny's hand in their happiness; rather, they accepted fate's assistance as a blessing.

* * * * *

Get Ready to be Swept Away by
Silhouette's Spring Collection

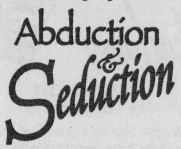

Abduction & Seduction

These passion-filled stories explore both the dangerous
desires of men and the seductive powers of women.
Written by three of our most celebrated authors, they are
sure to capture your hearts.

Diana Palmer
Brings us a spin-off of her Long, Tall Texans series

Joan Johnston
Crafts a beguiling Western romance

Rebecca Brandewyne
New York Times bestselling author
makes a smashing contemporary debut

Available in March at your favorite retail outlet.

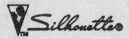

ETERNAL LOVE
by Maggie Shayne

Fans of Maggie Shayne's bestselling Wings in the Night miniseries have heard the whispers about the one known as Damien. And now the most feared and revered of his kind has his own story in TWILIGHT ILLUSIONS (SS #47), the latest in this darkly romantic, sensual series.

As he risks everything for a mortal woman, characters from the previous books risk their very existence to help. For they know the secrets of eternal life—and the hunger for eternal love....

Don't miss TWILIGHT ILLUSIONS by Maggie Shayne, available in January, only from Silhouette Shadows

Now what's going on in

CONARD COUNTY ?

Guilty! That was what everyone thought of
Sandy Keller's client, including Texas Ranger—and
American Hero—Garrett Hancock. But as he worked
with her to determine the truth, loner Garrett found he
was changing his mind about a lot of things—especially
falling in love.

Rachel Lee's Conard County series continues in January
1995 with A QUESTION OF JUSTICE, IM #613.

INTIMATE MOMENTS®
™ *Silhouette*®

And now for something completely different....

SPELLBOUND
R O M A N C E

**In January, look for
SAM'S WORLD (IM #615)
by Ann Williams**

Contemporary Woman: Marina Ross had landed in the strangest of worlds: the future. And her only ally was the man responsible for bringing her there.

Future Man: Sam's world was one without emotion or passion, one he was desperately trying to save—even as he himself felt the first stirrings of desire....

**Don't miss SAM'S WORLD,
by Ann Williams, available this January,
only from**

Maura Seger's
BELLE HAVEN

Four books. Four generations. Four indomitable females.

You met the Belle Haven women who started it all in Harlequin Historicals. Now meet descendant Nora Delaney in the emotional contemporary conclusion to the Belle Haven saga:

THE SURRENDER OF NORA

When Nora's inheritance brings her home to Belle Haven, she finds more than she bargained for. Deadly accidents prove someone wants her out of town—fast. But the real problem is the prime suspect—handsome Hamilton Fletcher. His quiet smile awakens the passion all Belle Haven women are famous for. But does he want her heart...or her life?

Don't miss THE SURRENDER OF NORA
Silhouette Intimate Moments #617
Available in January!

Silhouette

SPECIAL EDITION™

That
SPECIAL
Woman!

HUSBAND: SOME ASSEMBLY REQUIRED
Marie Ferrarella
(SE #931, January)

Murphy Pendleton's act of bravery landed him in the hospital—and right back in Shawna Saunders's life. She'd lost her heart to him before—and now this dashing real-life hero was just too tempting to resist. He could be the Mr. Right Shawna was waiting for....

Don't miss
HUSBAND: SOME ASSEMBLY REQUIRED,
by Marie Ferrarella,
available in January!

She's friend, wife, mother—she's you! And beside each Special Woman stands a wonderfully *special* man. It's a celebration of our heroines— and the men who become part of their lives.

EXTRA! EXTRA! READ ALL ABOUT...
MORE ROMANCE
MORE SUSPENSE
MORE INTIMATE MOMENTS

Join us in February 1995 when Silhouette Intimate Moments introduces the first title in a whole new program: INTIMATE MOMENTS EXTRA. These break-through, innovative novels by your favorite category writers will come out every few months, beginning with Karen Leabo's *Into Thin Air*, IM #619.

Pregnant teenagers had been disappearing without a trace, and Detectives Caroline Triece and Austin Lomax were called in for heavy-duty damage control...because now the missing girls were turning up dead.

In May, Merline Lovelace offers *Night of the Jaguar*, and other INTIMATE MOMENTS EXTRA novels will follow throughout 1995, only in—

INTIMATE MOMENTS®
Silhouette®